Farouk's Fancies

Text copyright 2013 Fiona Deal
All Rights Reserved

This is a work of fiction.
Names, characters, places and incidents
either are the product of the author's imagination
or are used fictitiously.

Chapter 1
Springtime 2013

'Yes!' I exclaimed with a surge of triumph. 'I just *knew* someone famous had sailed on board the *Queen Ahmes*!'

My hand stilled in the motion of reaching out to turn the thick parchment page of the antique visitors book. My fingers hovered over the entry, my gaze coming sharply into focus. I read and re-read the handwritten scrawl just in case I'd made a mistake.

Written in somewhat faded ink, it said, '*I and my party have enjoyed a splendid picnic aboard the Queen Ahmes while sailing among the antiquities of ancient Thebes.*' It was signed, '*Freddy R,*' and there, printed underneath, were the words that arrested my gaze and stilled my reaching hand. '*King Farouk of Egypt and the Sudan; Sovereign of Nubia.*' It was dated 1937.

I sat back under the canvas awning on the sundeck with a small whoop of triumph. My inkling had proved right. And, as luck would have it, King Farouk was someone who could offer not just fame but also a dash of early twentieth century royal glamour to our new venture in offering luxury Nile cruises to the discerning traveller to Egypt.

The *Queen Ahmes* is our dahabeeyah, restored to her former Victorian splendour as a Nile pleasure cruiser by

Khaled, a master craftsman who specialises in renovating antique vessels at his boatyard on the Nile a little way south of Luxor. A dahabeeyah is probably best described as a kind of sailing yacht. They were the original Nile cruise boats, pioneered by Thomas Cook in Victorian times when he introduced wealthy travellers to the delights of tourism in Egypt. He took the basic design from ancient Egyptian prototypes carved onto tomb and temple walls in antiquity. Before the advent of steam ships and the modern diesel-fuelled cruisers, hiring a dahabeeyah was the only way to sail up and down the Nile.

The *Queen Ahmes* is a true vintage sailboat. She sits long and low in the water, perhaps a bit barge-like, with her narrow windows glinting darkly in the fierce sunshine, mostly looking like an ordinary houseboat. Ordinary, that is, until you see her with sails unfurled. She has two. The largest is hoisted at the front of the boat, or the prow as I'm trying to get used to calling it. The slightly smaller one is rigged on a long diagonal pole at the stern. To see the *Queen Ahmes* with both sails unfurled, billowing and snapping in the breeze never fails to raise a lump in my throat. To say Adam and I are proud owners of this beautiful antique vessel would be the understatement of the century.

I felt a slow grin spread across my face. Knowing King Farouk of Egypt sailed the Nile onboard our dahabeeyah gave me not only a deep personal thrill but also a great marketing angle. It was something I could make much of on our new website to attract would-be travellers with the lure of following in glitzy celebrity footsteps. Grinning daftly, I gazed in a kind of entranced wonder at the leather-bound tome lying lengthways across my lap. Then I lifted my gaze and let it travel across the renovated sundeck, imagining Egypt's last reigning king and his party reclining on luxurious loungers in the shade cast by the glorious unfurled sails as the *Queen Ahmes* drifted down the Nile.

Eager to share my find, I jumped up. I left the visitor book in deep shade on deck, protected from the fierce Egyptian sunlight by a cushion, and went in search of Adam. I found him in our newly installed and gleaming stainless steel kitchen. He was brewing fresh coffee and throwing leftover lunch-scraps to the small army of stray cats who patrol the stone causeway where the *Queen Ahmes* is docked.

'What is it?' he asked, pausing mid-throw to level his gaze on my face. A sliver of chicken dangled between his fingers. 'You look like the cat that got the cream.'

'I've made a discovery!'

His lovely blue eyes narrowed on mine, darkly lashed and snapping with humour even as he groaned, 'Don't tell me, Merry. You've located an ancient papyrus that's not seen the light of day for centuries. Or perhaps you've come across a previously unknown royal tomb. No... let me guess again... You've unlocked the deepest, darkest mysteries of the pyramids in the half hour you've been out of my sight since lunchtime.'

'Stop teasing,' I grinned at him, attempting a pout that didn't quite come off. Actually I love it when he teases me, since he always does it with a smile on his face and a soft look in his eyes, and never in the hectoring tones of a certain ex-boyfriend of mine. Adam's always said I have a special talent for uncovering secrets from Egypt's ancient past. And just in case he should be accused of exaggeration, perhaps I should point out I've had all bar one of the experiences he'd just elucidated. And *should* I ever be fortunate enough to unlock the deepest, darkest mysteries of the pyramids, I'll be sure to make a careful note of all the particulars and count myself lucky. 'No, no! Nothing like that,' I said airily, deciding to make him wait. 'I'll tell you all about it upstairs on deck when the others join us.'

I left him to finish brewing the coffee; grinning at the perplexed look he shot me before he turned to throw the chicken scrap through the open window to the mewing cats. I carried a tray loaded with small china cups up the spiral staircase onto the deck. Once I'd deposited them on the low coffee table in the shade, I leaned against the railing on the sundeck, letting the hot sunshine splash all over me.

The view from our licensed berth at a crumbling stone wharf just south of Luxor is truly spectacular. It's possible to glimpse the bronzed rock of the Theban hills in the distance between palm trees that nod conversationally to each other along the riverbank. Donkeys, sheep and goats stray onto the sandbars when their owners are dozing. On the opposite bank, a line of modern hotels stretches down towards the city of Luxor, soft-focused in the heat haze. The dark waters of the Nile in between are often decorated with feluccas zipping past, their triangular sails billowing in the breeze that tends to blow up in the late afternoon to take the edge off the shimmering heat.

The 'others' I'd mentioned were our friends from Cairo: Ted, Walid, Shukura, and her husband Selim. We'd invited them to spend the Easter weekend with us. This wasn't so much to celebrate the religious festival. Walid, Shukura and Selim are Muslim, after all. It was more so we could throw a kind of dahabeeyah-warming party now all the painting and decorating was done.

We'd taken possession of the *Queen Ahmes* from Khaled just before Christmas, and spent the time since lovingly adding all the finishing touches to transform her into a luxury cabin cruiser. We'd set aside a generous budget for décor and furnishings. Adam was more flush with cash than me, having been on the receiving end of bankers' bonuses for a number of years before disenchantment set in. I had my redundancy money to contribute, and knew my savings would see me through a lean year or two if I was careful. So with our budget burning a hole in my pocket I'd indulged in an orgy of shopping, mostly in Cairo, despite the on going troubles there. We knew we couldn't skimp on quality if we wanted to offer genuine luxury Nile cruises for discerning travellers.

My list included muslin drapes, Egyptian cotton bed linen and soft towels, iron bedsteads and antique furniture, all in white to complement the teak flooring and wooden shutters. I'd splashed out on Victorian washstands complete with porcelain pitchers and bowls in delicate designs – this despite the fact that every cabin is equipped with a luxurious modern bathroom, thanks to Khaled's skill in both design and plumbing. Now each of our six cabins (including the one Adam and I had claimed as our own) was an exquisite haven of quality and simple elegance, with a nod to the heyday of Victoriana.

We'd gone to town with no less enthusiasm in the public areas. Our semi-circular lounge-bar-cum-dining room, its shape following the curve of the stern, invited weary travellers to sink onto deeply cushioned sofas upholstered in rich patterned silk, and relax with a drink in hand, perhaps dipping into one of the small library of Egyptian history and picture books we'd lined along one wall. And our pièce de résistance, the upper deck, where I was standing now, was resplendent under its canvas awning with rattan furniture, antique steamer-style recliners furnished with deeply padded cushions, potted palms in deep brass containers, and Turkish rugs scattered hither and thither across the wooden floorboards.

I gazed about me with fierce pride. Alongside all the shopping, Adam had been busy with a paintbrush. Every surface that wasn't varnished wood or polished brass gleamed with the soft calico-white of fresh paint.

It seemed we'd barely blinked and Easter was upon us. We decided it was as good an excuse as any for a launch party. So we'd invited our friends to fly down to Luxor to spend a couple of days with us.

Ahmed, our police chum, had also popped in and out as his duties allowed, although he declined to stay on board overnight saying he preferred 'de solid ground underneath me when I sleep rather dan de fishies of de Nile.'

So, all in all, we'd had something of a boat-full for a couple of days. We'd spent long, lazy hours eating the simple meals Adam and I prepared in the state-of-the-art kitchen Khaled had installed for us – talking, laughing and drinking the rather palatable Egyptian wine.

But all good things must come to an end, as the saying goes. Shukura, Selim and Walid were booked onto a flight back to Cairo this evening, and were right now in their cabins packing their overnight bags for the trip. Ted planned to spend another couple of weeks with us, and was enjoying an early-afternoon nap.

Ted was once Adam's university lecturer; a professor of Egyptology, specialising in philology at the prestigious Oriental Institute, in Oxford. He retired from England to Cairo a few years back, and we have him to thank for helping us out of various scrapes during the time Adam and I have spent in Egypt. Walid and Shukura are our good friends from the Cairo museum. They, too, have played their part in our adventures over recent months. Adam wasn't too wide of the mark when he listed escapades including finding hidden tombs and an ancient papyrus that hadn't seen the light of day for centuries. But for the time being, and for very good reason, we were sharing a pact of silence about the discoveries we'd made. We'd agreed not to speak of them, even among ourselves, on this visit.

I heard Adam call out that coffee was ready, and one by one they climbed the spiral staircase to join me up on deck.

Adam immediately spied the antique visitor book peaking out from underneath the cushion tassels. 'Aha! Is this the tantalising 'discovery' by any chance?' he asked, pulling it out as he sat down and resting it across his knees.

'What is it?' Shukura asked, settling herself into a steamer chair and tucking the colourful folds of her kaftan around her. As ever when she wasn't squeezed into the too-small navy suit she wears to work at the museum, she was swathed in gloriously flamboyant style in bright blues and greens, with a turquoise headscarf covering her hair, and quantities of chunky gold rings adorning her fingers.

I explained my find, pouring steaming coffee into the china cups from a huge silver cafetière, and motioning everyone to help themselves to sugar and milk. 'Khaled discovered it inside an ornate Victorian safe during his restoration of the *Queen Ahmes*. Somehow over the years the iron door-lock corroded and the hinges twisted. I guess the fierce Egyptian heat got to it. Khaled had to resort to a blowtorch in the end to cut through the metal. Inside he found a few old banknotes of various currencies dating to the 1930s, and this crusty-old ledger.'

'Which turns out to be a visitor book,' Ted said, leaning forward to peer at it a bit myopically. Ted is a small, dapper man in his mid-seventies, with a full head of silvery hair and a pair of wire-rimmed glasses that perpetually seem to be about to fall off the end of his nose. 'How fascinating,' he murmured.

'Adam and I glanced through it when Khaled first presented it to us. But it was just after we took possession of the dahabeeyah.' I grinned at Adam. 'We were in the first flush, or more accurately, frenzy, of painting and decorating, remember?'

Adam nodded, smiling, and I let my gaze rest on him for a moment, noting how tanned, lean and fit he looked. Actually, letting my gaze rest on Adam is a little treat I indulge in regularly. I still can't quite believe this is my life now, and how lucky I am. A year ago I was accepting redundancy from a job I'd grown horribly bored with, and plodding along in a relationship that was going nowhere. Sometimes I still have to pinch myself to believe just how much things have changed. Sitting across from me on a rattan armchair, with his dark brown hair glossed by the hot sunshine and his tanned limbs exposed by shorts and a loose t-shirt, he looked relaxed, healthy and very handsome. I gave myself a little shake and watched him turn to the first entry. He frowned over the flowing copperplate script, the ink now faded to a pale yellowy brown. 'It's dated 1897,' he said, glancing up. 'The author signs herself Mrs Florence Merryweather of York, England.'

I grinned at him. 'Yes, I thought it a rather touching coincidence that the first guest to record her passage down the Nile on board the *Queen Ahmes* should have my name – Merry – within hers.'

He smiled into my eyes and I knew we were registering another of those odd little quirks of fate that made our ownership of the *Queen Ahmes* seem predestined. I'm not usually superstitious. But even the name of the dahabeeyah herself, *Queen Ahmes*, seemed prophetic when we first heard it. The original Queen Ahmes, an elusive ancient Egyptian queen, was closely wrapped up in how Adam and I first met, almost a year ago, on the forecourt of Hatshepsut's mortuary temple on the west bank near Luxor.

I enjoyed the little shiver of kismet that snaked down my spine, looking into Adam's blue eyes and watching them darken to violet in that strange way they have when something significant occurs to him.

'So what's the *discovery*, Merry? You were looking incredibly pleased with yourself when you poked your head into the kitchen just now.'

I looked around at them one by one, letting a slow smile spread across my face, and trying to draw out the moment of anticipation for all I was worth as my gaze finally came back to rest on his. 'Flip forwards a few pages. You're looking for an entry dated 1937.'

Adam did as directed and suddenly went very still. I love these little freeze-frame moments of his. In the same way his eyes seem to change colour, a perfect stillness will often settle over him when he's struck by something momentous.

He began to read the entry aloud. Stopped, cleared his throat, and started again. *'"I and my party have enjoyed a splendid picnic aboard the Queen Ahmes while sailing among the antiquities of ancient Thebes."* Signed, *"Freddy R."'* He paused and glanced up into my eyes, finishing almost in a whisper. *'"King Farouk of Egypt and the Sudan; Sovereign of Nubia. 1937"'*

I gave a little whoop, the twin of the one I'd made earlier, and repeated my earlier pronouncement for good measure. 'I just *knew* someone famous had sailed on board the *Queen Ahmes!*'

A slow smile tugged the corners of his mouth upwards, 'I'd never go into bat against your instincts, Merry. They're unswervingly accurate. So, here you are... right again! Wow! King Farouk of Egypt, no less.'

'I'm planning to make a big deal out of it on the website.' I said. 'But I'll need to find out a bit about him first. I can't honestly say I know a whole lot about King Farouk.' I'd devoted the moments not spent shopping and decorating in recent weeks to building our website to manage bookings. I was modestly pleased with the result. It marketed the *Queen Ahmes* as a dahabeeyah offering antique passage in an antique land to those drawn to Egypt by the lure of nostalgia as well as by the wonders of antiquity. This discovery was the icing on the cake.

Adam passed the visitor book around so everyone could exclaim over the hand-written entry.

'I'm with Merry,' Adam admitted. 'I know very little about our royal guest here. I know he was deposed and exiled to Europe when President Nasser came to power, but that's about it. Was he really called Freddy?'

'No,' Walid replied. 'Farouk was his first name. He picked up the nickname "Prince Freddy" when he attended the Royal Military Academy in England in 1935, the year before he became king.'

Walid is the curator of the Egyptian Museum of Antiquities in Cairo. I'd always assumed he knew more about Egypt's ancient past than its more modern history, but he was about to prove me wrong. Between them, he, Shukura and Selim painted a lavish portrait of Egypt's last reigning king.

'Farouk was born into a rather eccentric family,' Walid's wispy hair lifted in the warm breeze blowing across the deck as he studied the faded signature in the visitor book. 'He was the only son born to King Fuad, among a gaggle of girls. A fortune-teller told Fuad that 'F' was his lucky letter. So he gave each of his six children a name starting with 'F'.'

I raised my eyebrows. 'That must have been confusing at bath time.'

Walid smiled at me. 'And Farouk continued the legacy. He insisted his first wife change her name from Safinaz to Farida when they married. And he named his own four children Ferial, Fawzia, Fadia and Fuad.'

'So Freddy was certainly acceptable as a nickname,' Adam murmured.

Shukura leaned back against the cushion on her rattan armchair and gazed across the deck. Her dark brown, kohl-rimmed eyes went a bit unfocused for a moment, then snapped alert again as she sat forward and said excitedly, 'You know Farouk may have been courting his first wife while he was onboard, my dears.' To look at her, Shukura is an Egyptian lady of a certain age through and through. So when she speaks English her Home Counties accent always comes as a bit of a surprise. It's courtesy of the years she spent studying at Oxford. 'The entry in your visitors book is dated 1937, is that right?'

'Yes,' Walid answered, since he was the one still holding it across his lap.

'That was the year after he became king,' Shukura said excitedly. 'He was only seventeen. If I remember rightly, in 1937 Farouk and his family came down the Nile on a tour of Upper Egypt, followed by a grand European tour. Safinaz was the daughter of a lady-in-waiting to his mother. She was invited along to join his sisters. During the tour, Farouk fell in love with the girl, and proposed. They were married early in 1938 and she was renamed "Farida". It's said that during the first months of their marriage, Farouk took her everywhere, and gave her a present every morning. How exciting to think the teenaged king may have been in the early days of his romance when he was on board your lovely dahabeeyah, Merry and Adam. You know, he was very good-looking as a young man, unusual for having blue eyes. It's said he had an almost childlike charm and beautiful manners. To think of him here doing his courting... how romantic!' Shukura is something of a force of nature. This speech was delivered volubly and at high speed.

'So, he was only sixteen when he became king?' I asked.

Selim, Shukura's husband, sat forward and set his empty coffee cup down. Selim is a handsome man in his fifties with lively brown eyes and a thick cap of tightly curled black hair just starting to turn silver at the temples. It makes him look quite distinguished. In contrast to his wife, he speaks English softly and with a pronounced Arabic accent. 'Yes, Farouk was in England at the Royal Military Academy, finishing his education, when his father died. He came to the throne in a blaze of popularity, being the first ruler ever to speak directly to the Egyptian people in a public radio address. He was the only one of his line to speak Arabic. His predecessors in the Mohammed Ali Dynasty all spoke Turkish. So he easily endeared himself to the Egyptian people.'

'But sadly not for long,' Shukura put in with a small shake of her head that made her dangly earrings tinkle. 'He may have been a blue-eyed, charming and well-mannered gentleman, but he'd been thoroughly spoilt as a youngster and now, as king, given ultimate power, huge riches and absolutely no accountability, he set off enthusiastically on the road to ruin.'

Walid nodded. 'It's true. He was a gambler, glutton and kleptomaniac. It was said if there were seven deadly sins, Farouk would find an eighth. He had caviar for breakfast, apparently eating it directly from the can; and the quantities of oysters he ate were legendary. He liked fizzy drinks, and allegedly consumed at least thirty bottles per day! No wonder he became so fat. In later life, someone famously described him as "a stomach with a head".'

Selim sat back and crossed his legs. 'His father gave him his first car, an Austin 7, at the age of eleven; and by the time he'd been on the throne a year he owned several villas, yachts and aeroplanes as well as more than a hundred cars.'

Shukura nodded enthusiastically, setting her earrings tinkling again. 'He had all his cars sprayed red and forbade his subjects to own a red vehicle. That way he could drive recklessly without being stopped by the police. When Farouk raced by in one of his red cars, people ran for their lives. Supposedly, an ambulance followed him to pick up casualties.'

I rather wished I had a notebook with me. Whether the whole being-followed-by-an-ambulance scenario was just urban myth or not didn't matter. It would make for great marketing material on the website.

'He lost fortunes at gaming tables, despite gambling being strictly forbidden by the book of Islam,' Walid warmed to the subject. 'And he became a prodigious womaniser, often boasting of his conquests in front of Farida as their marriage started to disintegrate. He blamed her for providing him with three daughters but no son. Apparently he saw it as a slur on his masculinity. He used to go to nightclubs, and then sleep until lunchtime, and openly took several official mistresses, some of them the wives of other men, until he and Farida finally divorced in 1948. His son Fuad was born to his second wife in the early 'fifties.'

'But the kleptomania was probably the worst of his vices,' Shukura said, her kohl rimmed eyes wide with animation. 'The most famous incident was when he pickpocketed Winston Churchill's pocket watch during a meeting. The watch was an heirloom from the British monarchy.'

I felt my eyes pop.

'Whatever Farouk fancied, he took,' Walid agreed, smiling at my reaction and patting his wispy hair back into place as the breeze continued to riffle through it. 'It may just be rumour, but it's said he took lessons in pick pocketing from a professional thief. At official receptions Farouk stole watches, wallets and cigarette lighters from the other guests. I think the worst incident was when he stole the ceremonial sword, belt and medals from the coffin of the Shah of Persia when it landed in Cairo. It put a strain on relations between Egypt and Persia for years. He was nicknamed "the thief of Cairo". A great reputation for one's king to have, don't you think?'

'But a great story,' I remarked, my fingers still itching for a notepad.

'I'm not sure that was the worst incident of Farouk's thievery,' said a thoughtful voice at my elbow. 'I think we may be about to discover he stole something rather more explosive than that. Something with the potential to shake the very foundations of history.'

All heads turned at this surprising statement, coming as it did from an even more surprising source. Ted had sat quietly throughout our Egyptian friends' telling of King Farouk's biography. He'd been slowly sipping his coffee, staring out across the Nile in a rather dreamy and unfocused way. To be honest, I'd almost forgotten he was there. His pale blue eyes narrowed short-sightedly as his gaze came to meet mine. He pushed his glasses up onto the bridge of his nose. They immediately slipped forward again as they always do, back into their favourite perch right at the tip of his nose. Ted's glasses look permanently as if they're about to fall off.

'Yes,' the professor said sagely. 'There's a suggestion that one of the things he stole back in his heyday as the "thief of Cairo" was one of the famous Dead Sea Scrolls.'

I forgot my fascination with his slip-sliding glasses and stared at him open-mouthed. Judging by the sharp intakes of breath around me, I gathered the others were similarly affected.

Ted peered at us one by one, drawing out the moment as I'd done earlier. 'The suggestion seems to be that the stolen scroll may contain evidence to show some of the key figures in the Old Testament of the Bible were in actual fact ancient Egyptian pharaohs.'

Adam choked. 'Fringe revisionist historians have been spouting that nonsense for years,' he spluttered, looking at his old mentor as if he'd suddenly changed shape. 'I thought serious Egyptologists thoroughly pooh-poohed the whole idea.'

'Yes,' Ted said slowly. 'I think it's fair to say I've always scorned the idea of a direct evidential link between the Old Testament and the pharaohs of ancient Egypt. And I like to think of myself as an Egyptologist with the highest academic credentials.' His pale eyes twinkled, and I thought he might rather be enjoying the shock he'd given his favourite protégé. 'But that was before I heard about the Dead Sea Scroll King Farouk is alleged to have stolen.'

'So, where is this mysterious Dead Sea Scroll now?' Adam managed.

'That, my dear boy, is a very intriguing question, and one I hope we may be able to pursue quite soon, when your first paying guest arrives on board the *Queen Ahmes* next week.'

Chapter 2

Who knows what more he might have said, if only a beaten-up looking taxi hadn't pulled up on the causeway at that moment, honking its horn noisily to announce its arrival and startling a family of herons from the reedy shallows alongside the dahabeeyah. They lifted off into the sky in a flurry of flapping wings. It was a rude reminder that Walid, Shukura and Selim needed to get moving pretty sharpish so as not to miss their early evening flight to Cairo.

I could see they were quite put out at having Ted's tantalising statement dangled before them only to have it snatched away again. While Selim went below deck to collect their bags, Shukura, in particular, beseeched Ted to say more with all the feminine wiles at her disposal. She fluttered her eyelashes and widened her kohl-rimmed eyes at him in a quite theatrical manner. But the professor was not to be shifted.

'No, no; now is not the time,' he said. 'I shouldn't have said anything at all. I just couldn't help but remark on the coincidence of Merry finding an entry by King Farouk in the visitor book just as the suspicion about Farouk and the stolen Dead Sea Scroll has surfaced. I really know very little more than I've said. I'm waiting for the arrival of our guest to learn the full story. I really mustn't say anything more until then.'

Shukura gave in to an excessive bout of tut-tutting, but had no choice but to be left in suspense. 'Yes, well, when you return to Cairo in a couple of weeks time, I expect to be told the whole story.'

Looking at the set determination on her face, I had no doubt Ted would succumb in the end.

* * *

'So, exactly who is this guy who's coming to stay with us?' I asked against Adam's shoulder later that night when we were alone in our cabin. Ted had retired early to his own room, a little further along the corridor on the opposite side of the dahabeeyah from our own. Adam's Indiana Jones-style hat was hanging rather jauntily on the iron bedpost at the foot of the bed, having worked its usual magic. I was feeling sleepily contented from our usual bedtime exertions, but not yet quite ready to drift off into fully-fledged slumber. So instead of snapping out the ornate bedside lamp I'd discovered in an antique shop hidden away in an obscure side street in Luxor, I went on, 'And how does Ted know him?'

'I'm not sure I really know for sure,' Adam murmured against my hair. 'His name's Benedict Hunter, and it seems he's interested in hearing the lecture that guy's giving at The Winter Palace next week, which is why he asked Ted if he could recommend somewhere to stay in Luxor.'

'Well, it's good of Ted to suggest us, considering this Benedict Hunter is willing to pay good money for his board and lodging, but doesn't expect to be cruised up and down the Nile. We really do need to start thinking about advertising for some staff, Adam. Although I'm loath to do so until we've got a few firm bookings lined up. It's all a bit chicken and egg, isn't it?'

'Mm,' Adam murmured drowsily, clearly closer to being fully snatched from consciousness by Morpheus than I was.

'What's the lecture about at The Winter Palace?' I asked, nestling in a little closer alongside him. I was referring, of course, to the fabulous Victorian hotel in central Luxor, famous as the hostelry where Lord Carnarvon stayed during the heady days of his excavations in the Valley of the Kings, and where Howard Carter announced their discovery of Tutankhamun's tomb. It remains a world-class hotel to this day, and holds a special place in my heart as somewhere I'd spent one never-to-be-forgotten night with Adam in the early days of our relationship. I suppressed a small shiver when I remembered we'd actually stayed in the King Farouk suite.

Adam pulled me closer, seemingly willing to postpone sleep for a moment to answer my question. 'It's being given by some Egyptian author called Nabil Zaal. He lives in America these days. He's made a career out of promoting fringe revisionist history with respect to ancient Egypt and the Bible – basically the intersection of the two. He considers himself an independent Egyptologist, and apparently spends a part of every year visiting and studying the sites of antiquity.'

'Ah,' I said on a note of enlightenment. 'Which is exactly what Ted was alluding to this afternoon: claiming some of the key characters from the Old Testament were in fact Egyptian pharaohs.'

Adam grunted. 'Apparently Nabil Zaal has made a lucrative business out of it. He's written loads of books, with sales across the globe. Some people seem to love alternative history more than the real thing.'

'So why should Benedict Hunter be interested?'

I felt his infinitesimal shrug beneath my shoulder. 'I have no idea. All Ted told me was he'd received a letter from Mr Hunter a few weeks ago asking about the lecture, and whether Ted could recommend somewhere to stay. I think Ted once knew Hunter's father, or something like that.'

I gazed up at the calico-painted panelled ceiling. 'So I wonder if he was the one to spill the beans on the whole Dead Sea Scroll scenario.'

'It seems likely,' Adam stifled a yawn.

I turned my face against his chest. 'Intriguing, as Ted says,' I murmured. 'I look forward to meeting this Benedict Hunter.'

'Hmm, not with too much enthusiasm, I hope,' Adam muttered, kissing the top of my ear. 'Now; sleep, Merry. Plenty of time for intrigue later.'

He reached across me to snap out the antique light, and I'd be hard pressed to say whether it was the darkness or sleep that claimed him first.

* * *

Benedict Hunter turned out to be a ruggedly good-looking Englishman of about my age, or perhaps slightly older. I certainly placed him somewhere in his mid-to-late thirties. He had lively hazel eyes with golden flecks in them, framed by gold-tipped lashes, set in a rather craggy face, with firm lips, high cheekbones and a square jaw. I'd bet my redundancy money he was a rugby player, and had once attended an upper crust British boarding school.

Adam welcomed him on board the *Queen Ahmes* with a rather brief handshake and a somewhat narrowed glance.

Benedict, or Ben as he invited us to call him, was charm personified. He spoke in a deep gravelly voice just the right side of gruff. 'Thank you for having me; I appreciate you allowing me to stay with you at such short notice. I know you're not yet fully up and running. Professor Kincaid explained how recently you've taken possession of the dahabeeyah. Please let me assure you I don't expect to be waited on hand on foot. I'm quite capable of pouring my own bowl of cornflakes at breakfast. I can percolate coffee with the best of them. And as for dinner, I'll have whatever you're having, or go out and sample the local restaurants if that's what you prefer.'

I smiled warmly at him. 'Welcome on board the *Queen Ahmes*, Mr Hunter ... I mean, Benedict ... I mean Ben. We should really get you to sign our new visitor's book. You're our first bona fide guest.'

He returned my smile disarmingly. 'I'm sure I'll have no hesitation in giving you a great review if first impressions are anything to go by.'

I shifted rather uncomfortably under Adam's sapphirine gaze.

'This really is a lovely old vessel,' Ben added, including Adam in his smile this time. 'And I can see she's been lovingly restored to her former glory.'

Adam acknowledged the compliment with a brief nod and an even briefer smile. It seemed a good idea to move on, so I invited our new visitor to follow me the few short paces along the corridor to his cabin.

'Please take your time about unpacking and make yourself comfortable. There'll be a glass of whatever your favourite tipple is waiting for you in the lounge-bar before dinner. We'll certainly be happy for you to join us at mealtimes. Just let me know if you want to make your own arrangements.' And I swung the door open and stood back to let him enter ahead of me.

'This is lovely,' he said with a broad smile as he stepped through the door and surveyed his cabin.

Actually it felt rather small with Ben's large frame filling it. I wondered a trifle uncomfortably if some of my little touches of Victoriana were actually a shade too far on the feminine side. Some men seem to get an extra helping of masculinity at birth, and Ben was one of them. I gave a weak smile and found I really didn't know what to say.

'Honestly,' he assured me, apparently taking my silence as doubtfulness that he'd meant it. 'I never dreamed of such opulence. You've certainly captured the Victorian ambience but without concessions on mod-cons that I can see.' He poked his head into the bathroom then turned and gave me a broad smile. 'This is my first visit to Egypt. I'm already enthralled and looking forward to my stay.'

'I'm glad you like it,' I smiled and backed rather hastily out of the cabin, leaving him to unpack his bags.

It felt a bit odd pulling the door closed behind me, leaving this strapping stranger to make himself comfortable in a room I'd lovingly furnished. I hoped I could get used to the idea of my cherished dahabeeyah filled up with total strangers.

I gave myself a small mental shake. I've always prided myself on my practicality. Adam's the romantic one. This was a business, I reminded myself. Not a holiday home for friends and family, despite the enjoyment of the Easter weekend.

Somehow I knew I needed to cut my teeth on Mr Benedict – Ben – Hunter, and go from there.

* * *

Ted was there to welcome our guest for his first pre-dinner drink in the semi-circular lounge-bar.

'My dear fellow, it's a pleasure to meet you,' he said warmly, shaking Ben's hand vigorously and peering at him intently through his glasses.

'Professor Kincaid, I cannot tell you what an honour it is to meet you. Or how much I appreciate you lending some credence to my quest.'

'This would be the search for ancient Egyptian pharaohs among the Old Testament texts,' Adam said, in a spare tone of voice I'm not sure I'd ever heard him use before.

'Ah, I see the professor's told you a bit about the mystery that brings me here,' Ben said, accepting the gin and tonic Adam passed him with a nod of thanks.

'I hope you don't mind,' Ted said quickly. 'Adam and Merry are like family. I trust I haven't broken any confidences.'

'No no, not at all,' Ben assured him. 'I'm hoping you can help me get to the bottom of the puzzle I seem to have inherited. As I'm accepting your hospitality in staying with you, I think the least I can do is share it with you.' He took a small sip from his glass and sank onto one of the deep cushioned sofas, crossing his long legs and looking around him with open appreciation.

'I think we're all intrigued to find out more about this Dead Sea Scroll King Farouk is supposed to have stolen,' Ted said, also accepting the drink Adam poured him, and settling himself onto the re-upholstered Victorian divan, which he found it easier to get up from.

I decided to take some control of the conversation, determined we should start at the beginning. Men, I find, have a habit of starting a story in the middle, and leaving out some of the finer particulars that actually help make sense of things. 'Perhaps you could start by telling us how you know of Ted, and why you wrote to him,' I suggested with a smile at Adam as he handed me my drink. 'I understand Ted may have known your father, is that right?'

'Only in passing,' Ben admitted. 'My father attended the series of lectures Ted gave at the British Museum back in the eighties. He was fascinated by Egyptology.'

'Was your father anyone we'd know?' Adam asked, coming to sit alongside me now he'd poured and dispensed drinks all round. He took a sip of his own gin and tonic and levelled his gaze on our guest.

'No, I doubt you'd have heard of Gregory Hunter.'

The name drew blank looks from us both and we shook our heads, while Ted sat quietly and sipped his martini. I guessed Ben had already furnished him with this part of the story.

'But he did have one very important claim to fame,' Ben went on. My father was a kind of personal secretary to King Farouk – one of the few British people Farouk genuinely liked. They met In Woolwich, when Farouk was finishing his education at the Royal Military Academy. My father was the younger brother of an earl, back in the days when aristocracy counted for something. When Farouk came back to Egypt to be crowned, he asked my father to come with him. They were both only sixteen years old, and I guess it seemed a grand adventure.'

I felt my eyes widen. 'So, without wishing to sound impertinent, your Dad must have had you pretty late in life,' I remarked, no doubt impertinently.

Ben didn't seem in the least offended and answered readily enough. 'Yes, my father was 55 when I was born. It was after Farouk died, and my father returned to England. He met and married my mother in the late sixties, and I came along a couple of years later. I'm an only child. Sadly my mother died of cancer a year ago. My father followed her in late December last year. He was 92.'

'I'm sorry,' I said.

Ben acknowledged this with a small smile, and returned to his story. 'I think it's fair to say my father fell in love with Egypt. He found it hard to leave when King Farouk was deposed. He didn't enjoy living in exile in Monaco or Rome, although his loyalty to Farouk never faltered. After Farouk died, I think he toyed with the idea of coming back here. But the world had changed, and his family was in England, so he ended up back at home. But he remained obsessed by ancient Egyptian history. He read about it constantly, building an extensive library of Egyptological books. And he attended lectures at all the famous museums and universities of the world. He rated Professor Edward Kincaid as one of the finest Egyptologists he had the privilege to hear speak.'

Ted shifted a bit uncomfortably on the divan, and took a hasty sip of his drink, swallowing it in an audible gulp 'I believe I have a vague recollection of him,' he said. 'I seem to recall an impeccably attired, rather military-looking man in his late-sixties coming up to me after one of the lectures at the British Museum. He asked what I thought about the possibility that some of the pharaohs of the 18th Dynasty of ancient Egyptian history were actually key Biblical figures. I might add I was scandalised by the very idea, and told him so. It was precisely the same reaction I gave you, Ben, when you first wrote to me and asked the self-same question. I'm sorry if I was downright rude when I said the whole idea was preposterous.'

Ben waved away his apology with a small flick of his wrist. 'Don't mention it, sir. I know to serious Egyptologists this kind of revisionist history - isn't that what you call it? - is filed away under the heading of mumbo jumbo – along with suggestions that the pyramids were built by aliens and the Sphinx is some kind of tracking device from another world.'

'It's just the lack of archaeological evidence...' Ted started, but stopped since I'd started speaking at the same time, and he was way too well mannered to talk across me.

'Why on earth would your father or you ask a question like that?' I asked, looking at Ben. 'Did it have something to do with the stolen Dead Sea Scroll Ted mentioned?'

'Perhaps indirectly,' Ben said. 'I'm not sure exactly what, if anything, my father knew about the scroll back then. Rumours, perhaps. No, I think it had more to do with an ancient Egyptian scarab King Farouk once gave my father as a birthday gift. Apparently he said to my father something along the lines of, *"As a good Christian man you might want to keep hold of this, my friend; it proves the Biblical Joseph was an Egyptian vizier at the court of the Pharaoh Thutmosis IV".*'

I stared at him bug-eyed, and heard Adam suck in a breath alongside me. 'Wow!' I gulped. 'That's an artefact a lot of Egyptologists would give their eyeteeth for. I'll bet you'd have taken his question more seriously if he'd produced that after one of your lectures, Ted. I wonder why he didn't do so.'

Ben sent me a long, steady glance. 'Because he no longer had it to produce,' he said flatly. 'My father's apartment in Rome was broken into right about the time Farouk died, and the scarab was stolen.'

Adam sat forward. 'So someone knew he had it?'

Ben nodded slowly. 'It's possible; although other items were taken at the same time: a nice watch, a collection of rare stamps and some cash he'd left in a drawer. Although upset by it, I'm not sure my father necessarily saw anything sinister in the theft of the scarab until December last year.'

'What happened in December?' I asked inevitably.

Ben sipped his gin and tonic and looked at me across the rim of his glass. The sinking sun sent fiery rays through the slats of the wooden shutters behind me, and seemed to light golden sparks in his eyes. 'My father received a mysterious letter from Egypt,' he said at last.

He rummaged in his jacket pocket for a moment, and drew out several folded sheets of paper. I could tell by the floppiness of the pages that they had been handled almost to the point of disintegration.

'Here, take a look ...'

He passed them to Adam first, since Adam was nearest, leaning across the coffee table to hand the letter over. Adam unfolded the sheets carefully and frowned at the top one, before passing them on to me. I felt almost as if I was taking hold of a gentleman's cotton handkerchief, such was the fabric-like consistency of the paper as I laid the first page across my skirt so Adam and I could both see it.

'It's written in Arabic,' we said together, our voices overlapping. I stared at the tightly packed writing, the picturesque Arabic script filling both sides of each sheet.

'Yes,' Ben confirmed. 'Professor, are you able to read it, or would you like me to translate?'

I passed the letter across to Ted, who laid the top page across his own knees, and pushed his glasses up onto the bridge of his nose, holding them there with one finger as he leaned forward and frowned over the handwriting.

'Hmm, this is somewhat harder to decipher than the flowing Victorian and Edwardian copperplate in your visitor book,' he said, glancing up at Adam and me. 'But I think I can just about make out what it says.' He squinted over the text for a moment, and then started slowly to translate from the Arabic.

'"*Dear Mr Gregory Hunter. You may not remember me. It was many long years ago that our paths last crossed. You were kind enough once to look after my sisters and me when dear Freddy's new wife started making trouble for us. You and I could both call ourselves young in those days. Today it is a different matter. You must be a man in your nineties, and I am not so many years behind you. The pain of rheumatism plagues my hands and makes it hard for me to write this to you. No longer can I sing and dance as once I did.*

I choose you to write to since you were the man tasked by our dear Freddy each year during your exile with sending me a crate of champagne on my birthday. Perhaps you do not recall it. No doubt it was a small administrative duty for you. But to me receiving the annual gift of champagne was the highlight of my year.

I'm sure you often wondered whether our dear Freddy was perhaps indulging in one of his schoolboy pranks when he claimed to have knowledge that would shake the Christian world to its core.

How he loved to tease. Whilst born to the book of Islam, I doubt he took its teachings seriously. You will no doubt recognise the object in the photograph I include along with this letter.'"

Ted looked up and squinted at Ben. 'Photograph?'

With a rather deliberate air, Ben reached back into his breast pocket. He pulled out a small black and white photograph edged with a white border of the type I'd seen in old family snaps from the sixties. It was a bit creased and the glossy surface was peeling away in one corner. He levered himself forward on the sofa so he could reach across and hand it to Ted.

Ted held his glasses in place with the tip of one finger and peered at it.

'I imagine it's the scarab,' Adam murmured.

Ben acknowledged it with a brief nod, and took the photograph back from Ted so he could pass it across to Adam and me.

36

Adam was just reaching for it when there was a sudden flicker and all the lights went out, plunging us all into darkness. I heard Ben gasp. But the rest of us let out irritated sighs. We were well used to these blackouts by now.

'Don't worry, it's just another power cut,' Adam explained, pushing himself up off the sofa and going in search of the candles and matches we kept handy since these were regular occurrences.

'The Egyptian government is selling electricity to Israel,' I said. 'It's part of a push to kick start the economy – although it's a shame it's at the expense of independent businesses. Outside of the five star hotels, most local restaurants and guesthouses can't afford to run their own generators. So the power cuts are a bit of an inconvenience, to say the least.'

Ben let out a sigh of relief. 'That was a bit creepy. For a moment I thought it was the ancient gods intervening.'

I smiled at him as Adam lit the candles positioned along the windowsill and on the coffee table. It was quite refreshing to meet a man with Ben's aura of masculinity who could also admit to being superstitious.

'Will the dinner be ok?' Ben asked a bit more prosaically.

'Oh yes, the cooker runs off bottled gas, so it's not affected by the electricity supply – although even the gas can be a bit hard to come by these days. I'm not sure we've chosen the most opportune moment to venture into business out here.'

Adam glanced across at him. 'We're learning to cope with all the trials and tribulations of getting a small business up and running in Egypt these days. Now, where were we? He came to sit down again and took the photograph from Ben, holding it forward towards the flame so we could both see it.

It was indeed of a scarab. It looked to be about the size of my palm. It was difficult to tell what it was made from since the picture was taken in black and white - perhaps alabaster, or maybe faience.

'But I don't see any markings on it,' I said with disappointment.

'No, the hieroglyphics would be on the underside,' Adam said, holding one corner of the photograph between his thumb and forefinger and angling it more fully towards the candlelight. 'Was your father sure it was the same one?' he asked doubtfully. 'Scarabs like this can be found all over Egypt, mostly modern tourist souvenirs these days. The genuine ones are pretty much all on display in the museums of the world.'

'Yes, he was certain. See the little chip on the left side there? The scarab Farouk gave my father had exactly the same little flaw in its surface. My father had no doubt it was the same scarab that was stolen from his apartment in Rome.'

Adam handed the photograph back to Ben, who returned it to his jacket pocket. We all looked towards Ted for him to resume his translation of the letter.

'Hang on; let me get you a torch,' Adam said. 'You can't possibly read that by candlelight. It will put an unbearable strain on your eyes.' He jumped up and retrieved the torch we kept behind the bar, handing it across to Ted who focused its beam on the page and started to read.

'"Perhaps you know the claim that this scarab proves the Biblical Joseph to have been an Egyptian vizier to Pharaoh Thutmosis IV, placing him in the middle of ancient Egypt's glorious 18th Dynasty. I believe Freddy acquired the scarab from an antiquities dealer in Cairo – or perhaps he stole it from the poor man; such was his unfortunate habit.

What you may not know is that Farouk was in possession of evidence proving other key figures from the Bible – David, Solomon; perhaps others – were in actual fact Egyptian Pharaohs.'"

Ted broke off and stared up at Adam. He cleared his throat rather noisily, and bent over the letter once more.

'"Do you remember the time the officials from the Jordanian Department of Antiquities visited Cairo? Freddy was fascinated by the discovery of the Dead Sea Scrolls and laid on a glittering reception for the visitors. It was 1950, and the search for more scrolls was still underway in the caves of

Qumran, south of Jericho. Translation of the scrolls had barely begun, but the world's press was agog at the discovery.

The simple fact is Freddy stole one of the scrolls, right from under the noses of the visiting dignitaries from the Jordanian Antiquities Department. I'm not sure whether they realised it at the time, or made the awful discovery later. But what were they to do? Freddy was King of Egypt, and the Arab-Israeli war of 1948 had badly destabilised relations between Arabic nations. Terrified of creating a diplomatic incident, they kept quiet, and Freddy got away with it.

Freddy showed the scroll to my sisters and me one night. He thought it a fantastic joke. He told us he was secretly arranging for someone from the Egyptian Antiquities Museum in Cairo to translate it for him.

That was the last I heard of the scroll for many years.

In the Egyptian Revolution of 1952 poor Freddy was deposed and exiled to Europe where he continued his playboy lifestyle. I don't know why he suddenly started letting it be known that he was in possession of explosive knowledge he was willing to sell to the highest bidder. The rumour is that he was running short on money. I've heard that towards the end, after he was divorced for the second time, he was forced to start selling off his racing cars and yachts. That would have been hard for him. So maybe he saw the scroll as a means to an end - a way of maintaining his luxury lifestyle indefinitely.

As perhaps you already know, he started saying within certain select and private circles that he had a Dead Sea Scroll containing explosive evidence linking the Bible to Pharaonic history. He let it be known he'd hidden it somewhere safe, but was willing to sell it for the right price. But he died before any transaction could be completed.

I tell you this, Gregory Hunter, because I know Freddy truly valued your friendship, and I find there are very few people I can trust. So, let me say this. I know why the scarab was stolen from you, and I know who stole it. More to the point perhaps, I know where the stolen Dead Sea Scroll is hidden.

I will not state here how I have come by this knowledge. I tell you because I feel my own end approaching and I must share what I know with someone. But you are an old man yourself, perhaps ill-equipped to take up this burden. Never mind; there is another. Perhaps if I write to you both, then one of you will find me and I can share my secrets.

I will not approach you directly. Perhaps I am a neurotic and highly strung old woman, but these days I feel myself being watched. Are there others, perhaps, who know what I know… or at least suspect? I do not wish to let it be known that I have contacted you.

So I will not sign myself openly, nor let you know how to reach me directly, just in case this letter should be intercepted. I ask that you come to me. I will send you a clue for how to find me. For now, dear Mr Hunter, I shall sign myself simply… one of Farouk's Fancies."'

Ted cleared his throat, folded the soft sheet of paper, and gazed across at Ben from above the rim of his glasses as, bereft of his finger to hold them in place, they inevitably slid down the length of his nose. 'Goodness me, my boy. What an intriguing letter. So, I have to ask, did any such clue arrive?'

Ben angled himself off the sofa and accepted the letter back from Ted's outstretched hand. He glanced enquiringly at Adam, 'Do you mind if I help myself to a top up?'

Adam jumped up, reminded of his duties as host. 'Of course! Here, let me.' And he took Ben's glass across to the bar and splashed another measure of gin into it.

I'd been so engrossed in the letter I'd barely touched my own drink. After checking nobody else needed a re-fill, Adam subsided back alongside me. As he did so, the lights flickered back on. 'Ah, that's a relief,' I said, blinking as my eyes re-adjusted.

'I thought for a while the old lady must have heard of my father's death,' Ben said, sitting back on the sofa and crossing his legs again as he answered Ted's question. 'He suffered his heart attack just a few days after receiving her letter back in December. He became very agitated after reading it. But he wouldn't tell me what was bothering him. I was in the habit of popping in to see him every day after my mother died, although he remained sprightly and very independent. All that changed when the letter arrived. He read and re-read it about a thousand times a day. He was familiar with Arabic, of course, which I am not – so, at that stage, I didn't know what it said. He stopped eating and sleeping and became feverish. It was at that point I'm afraid I did something rather under-handed. I took the letter from his bedside table one night when he'd fallen into a fitful sleep and scanned it into my computer. Google is a miracle, don't you think? Within a few moments of loading it into the online translator I was reading the same words you've just read aloud for us, professor. I begged my father to tell me what it was that upset him so much. He just kept muttering about Farouk's Fancies.

'A couple of days later he suffered his heart attack. I have to say I was so caught up with the funeral arrangements and, well...' He broke off and cleared his throat, taking a quick sip of his drink. It was plain to see he felt his father's loss keenly. 'I think it's fair to say if I thought about the letter at all it was to curse the old lady who sent it. But then, a few weeks ago, while I was at my father's house clearing out some of his things, this arrived.'

He reached into the side pocket of his jacket this time, and withdrew another folded sheet of paper. I recognised it as a poster, printed on glossy paper. He carried on speaking as he unfolded it:

'There was nothing with it – just this poster on its own. But I recognised the careful hand-written printing of my father's address on the envelope as the same as on the envelope containing the letter. I think this is the clue.'

He held up the poster so we could read it. Printed in English it announced the lecture to be given by the famous American-Egyptian writer Nabil Zaal at The Winter Palace hotel in Luxor. It cited Nabil Zaal as the controversial author of several books linking the Old Testament of the Bible to 18th Dynasty Ancient Egypt.

'The trouble with Nabil Zaal,' Adam said slowly, 'is that he's never been able to come up with a solitary shred of archaeological evidence to support his theories.'

Ben looked back at him steadily. 'Which does not mean such evidence does not exist. It seems to me this little old lady who describes herself as 'one of Farouk's Fancies' might be able to point us towards all the evidence we'll ever need to prove certain Biblical figures were in fact Pharaohs of ancient Egypt.'

I felt a strange shiver snake down my spine as Adam and Ben stared at each other.

Ted sat forward on the divan, speaking into the loaded atmosphere. 'And in sending the poster to your father, it would suggest she might, at this very moment, be right here in Luxor.'

I turned my head to look at Adam. 'I think I might quite like to attend Nabil Zaal's lecture at The Winter Palace,' I said.

Chapter 3

I was sitting up in bed with my laptop open and powered up in front of me when Adam joined me later. He'd volunteered to load the dishwasher after dinner. 'Wow, the story of the discovery of the Dead Sea Scrolls reads like something out of Hollywood,' I exclaimed as he leaned over to drop a kiss onto my forehead. 'Listen to this!' And I read aloud from the website I was looking at, '"*The Dead Sea Scrolls, discovered near the site of Qumran, south of Jericho in the years 1947-1956 were dubbed "the academic scandal of the 20th century" because of the long delay in publication. Over the last 20 years or so, however, they have been fully published, except for occasional scraps that continue to come to light.*"'

He smiled and flopped onto the bed alongside me. 'I can see it's got you hooked, Merry. So, come on then; what have you learnt? We may as well go prepared for this lecture by Nabil Zaal.'

I pulled my knees up so I was sitting cross-legged facing him with the laptop propped open in front of me. 'Believe it or not something like 942 texts were discovered in those caves on the northwest shore of the Dead Sea. Most of them are Biblical manuscripts from what's now known as the

Hebrew Bible. They're the earliest known surviving copies of Biblical documents. They're written in Hebrew, Aramaic and Greek, mostly on parchment but with some on papyrus. Scholars believe some of the manuscripts may date back to almost 500 years BC.'

'A wandering Bedouin tribe found them, if memory serves me correctly,' Adam said, tucking his hands under his head on the pillow, and lying with his elbows poking out and his legs crossed at the ankle.

'That's right. A pair of Bedouin shepherds found the first seven scrolls hidden inside pottery jars in a cave while they were tending their flock. They took them back to their camp and apparently hung them on a tent pole while they decided what to do with them. They took them to some dealer in Bethlehem who told them they were worthless and suggested they might have been stolen from a synagogue. Undeterred, the Bedouin went to see an antiquities dealer at a nearby market who bought the scrolls for some ridiculous pittance of an amount. After that it seems the scrolls kept changing hands until they came to the attention of a scholar from the American Schools of Oriental Research, who compared them to some other ancient texts, realised their significance and announced their discovery in a general press release in 1948.'

I rescanned the text on the website in front of me to remind myself of the core facts. 'The trouble was, no one knew exactly where the caves were located, and the Bedouin tribe had disappeared. The Arab-Israeli war was raging and it wasn't until late in 1949 that the government of Jordan gave archaeologists permission to search the area of Qumran for the caves. That's when the Jordanian Department of Antiquities got involved. It sounds like a bit of a league-of-nations treasure hunt ensued as first one and then another cave was found by different teams of archaeologists, all containing fragments of the ancient texts. The Bedouin arrived back on the scene, and with the monetary value of the scrolls rising as their historical significance was made more public, it became a kind of race to the finish line until, by 1956 a total of twelve caves had been discovered along with several hundred ancient texts.'

'And at some stage after the first frenzy of media coverage, our light-fingered friend King Farouk stole one of the original manuscripts,' Adam mused. 'I suppose you have to admire his audacity. Ah well, there's an old adage that absolute power corrupts absolutely, and Farouk seems to have been the living epitome of it.'

'I wonder why it took so long to publish the scrolls,' I said. 'They're all available here on the Internet these days. But it seems during the latter half of the twentieth century it was claimed they were being suppressed because of the explosive religious knowledge they contained. It allowed authors such as Nabil Zaal to accuse the powers that be of colluding in some great conspiracy.'

'And have they been found to contain any explosive knowledge now they've finally been published?' Adam asked, rolling sideways to face me.

'Nothing in what I've surfed through so far. They're clearly historically significant, but there's no suggestion they contain anything to send shockwaves through history or religion. It seems they were written by some breakaway Jewish sect over the course of something like six hundred years, and then hidden away in early Roman times for reasons no-one's too sure of.'

'So we are left with three possibilities,' Adam said.

I stared at him. I hadn't been aware we were working out theories. Daft of me, since Adam's agile brain is always working out theories, and he loves nothing more than a complex historical conundrum, Egyptological if at all possible.

'First, perhaps there are some Dead Sea Scrolls whose contents have indeed been suppressed, and so what is published online is not the full textual evidence. Second, the kleptomaniacal King Farouk was amazingly lucky to pilfer the one Dead Sea Scroll that contains the explosive evidence claiming that key Biblical figures were in fact Egyptian Pharaohs. Or thirdly the whole thing is a great big hoax and the likes of Nabil Zaal, King Farouk and the Hunters - father and son - have been reeled in hook, line and sinker.'

I tilted my head on one side to look at him, still not sure I was completely seeing the significance of all this. 'Exactly why would it be considered so explosive for key Biblical figures to be proven to be 18th Dynasty Egyptian pharaohs?'

Adam sat up and took both my hands in his. 'Think, Merry. Christian dogma would have us believe the pharaohs of ancient Egypt were pagans – unenlightened worshippers of multiple gods. Most of the Egyptian Pantheon were animal-headed gods, remember. In the Old Testament the pharaohs of Egypt are mostly described as tyrants who enslaved the Hebrews until Moses led them from persecution to the Promised Land and established the state of Israel. If these self-same pharachs were proven to be key Old Testament figures like David and King Solomon – perhaps even Moses himself – it would shake Christianity to the core.'

Put like that I could see where he was coming from. 'So, which of your three possibilities are you leaning towards?' I asked.

'Well, put it this way, I'd love to get my hands on that fabled Dead Sea Scroll.' Then he leaned forward and very gently extracted the laptop from my hands, shutting it into sleep mode and setting it on the bedside cabinet. 'Now, Merry... enough of all this. You were staring at our guest tonight with a rapt fascination I found quite unsettling. I'm feeling a greater than usual need for your undivided attention. And I am not yet at the stage in our relationship where I can sit next to you on the bed and be diverted for long by a historical debate, no matter how Hollywood-like. I can think of several far more interesting things we could be doing right now.'

He pulled me down alongside him and I rolled into his arms with a happy sigh, more than willing to comply with his request for some undivided attention. I offered up a silent but heartfelt word of thanks for Khaled's skill in preserving the original Victorian soundproofing between our newly renovated cabins, and it's fair to say Adam drove all thoughts of Ben Hunter and the stolen Dead Sea Scroll from my mind in moments.

* * *

We shared a taxi to The Winter Palace, since all four of us wanted to attend Nabil Zaal's lecture. Ted, Adam and I squeezed onto the back seat while Ben folded his rangy form onto the front passenger seat alongside our exuberant driver, who regaled us with his life story on the short drive over the bridge and into Luxor. Ben was wearing a tailored linen suit in cream, with a pale blue shirt and patterned tie. Adam, more casually dressed in chinos and a short-sleeved cotton shirt, raised an eloquent eyebrow. 'If he worked for the BBC, they'd introduce him as "our man in Luxor", ready to give his latest report.

I grinned at him, but didn't comment. The truth was, I thought Ben looked rather debonair. Don't get me wrong. Adam is a handsome man. He can still take my breath away with a single glance. But since relocating to Egypt we've both become so used to scruffing about day-to-day in shorts and t-shirts, it made a pleasant change to have a reason to wear something with rather more sartorial elegance. I'd gone so far as to don a pretty summer dress. And, let's face it; sartorial elegance was something Ben seemed to carry off as effortlessly as breathing.

We hadn't spoken further about the mysterious letter from 'one of Farouk's Fancies', or the possibility that the old woman who'd written it might be here in Luxor and hoping to be found.

Our conversation over dinner had been more typical of what you might expect with a house-guest to whom you'd been newly introduced, and who'd come to stay for a week or so. We'd mostly discussed the historical sites in and around Luxor, urging Ben to include as many as possible on his itinerary while he was here. Luxor is often described as an open-air museum, and with good reason. With Karnak and Luxor temples, the Valleys of the Kings and Queens and lots more besides right on our doorstep, there was plenty for him to see and do, should he choose to. I know sightseeing wasn't what brought him to Egypt. But it would seem a shame not to do some now he was here.

To be fair, our destination right now wasn't a bad place to start. The Winter Palace is a magnificent British colonial-era five-star hotel sitting proudly on the Corniche along the banks of the Nile in central Luxor. It looks every inch a palace, painted the colour of soft sand; a graceful design branching out in two long wings from a grand central lobby approached up a sweeping stone staircase complete with a plush red carpet on brass runners running up the centre on both sides. Once upon a time a winter retreat for royalty including both King Fuad and King Farouk, stepping through the Victorian revolving doors into the entrance hall is like stepping back into a more refined and elegant age. The rich colonial design and décor is all lofty ceilings, glittering chandeliers, elaborate cornices and gilt furniture of the type I believe – coincidentally - is known as Louis-Farouk; an imperial French style furniture which was the rage of the Egyptian upper class during Farouk's reign.

Ben stood back to allow me to proceed through the revolving door ahead of him. Nabil Zaal's lecture was being held in the Victorian Lounge. An immaculately attired receptionist greeted us in the lobby and showed us through to an impressively large and grandiose room opening off a huge corridor leading from the entrance hall. Set at the back of the hotel overlooking the stunning gardens, it was opulently decorated in soft shades of ochre and gold, and lavishly furnished, with rich drapes at the windows and a vast oriental rug covering the parquet floor. Adam and I had come here for afternoon tea back during the heady early days of our relationship. We'd been on a mission to survey the hotel's artwork. The room looked slightly different today, set up as it was for a lecture – but no less impressive. Even the rows of chairs where he invited us to sit had seats upholstered in red velvet and backrests painted gold.

We were served tea in fancy bone china cups while the room started to fill up, and invited to help ourselves to the selection of dainty pastries set out on the old Victorian sideboard.

Since we were among the first to arrive, we were sitting towards the front. But I noticed all four of us kept glancing backwards over our shoulders. Although quite what we would say to a little old lady, should we happen to spot her, and surmising she spoke only Arabic, I had no idea.

An expectant hush fell across the room as the hotel's general manager approached the table set out in front of the tall windows. Accompanying him was a wiry man I'd guess to be in his late forties or early fifties, with an angular face, receding hairline and wearing a nicely tailored linen suit that was unfortunately a size or two too large for him. As a small man, it rather gave him the appearance of play-acting at being a grown-up. His eyes were bright and alert, and he surveyed his audience with a smile as the general manager introduced him as 'the famous and controversial Nabil Zaal, who will today share with us his latest theories.'

We all clapped politely, as Nabil Zaal stepped forward and cleared his throat, taking a small sip of water before he started. 'I'm not sure I shall share my *very* latest theories,' he said with a smile. He spoke with an American accent, which perhaps shouldn't be so surprising since Adam said that's where he'd lived for years. 'I am currently setting out to prove that the Giza pyramids are in fact memorial temples to some of the greatest names from the Old Testament of the Bible. It is my belief that the Great Pyramid, built by Khufu in the Old Kingdom of ancient Egypt was in fact built for Noah of the Bible; and that Noah and Khufu are one and the same. It is my contention that the pyramid of Khafre, guarded as it is by the mysterious Sphinx, was actually the memorial temple of Adam. And I believe I shall soon be able to demonstrate that the smaller pyramid of Menkaure was in reality the funerary temple of Abraham.'

His opening announcement was greeted by an audible hush, a tangible stillness and the sound of one or two indrawn breaths. Here was a man who knew how to grab attention.

'But I am in the early stages of my researches,' he continued. 'So I will leave the detail on those particular theories for another day. Instead, let me start by saying this: over the last two thousand years scholars have been searching the annals of history for evidence to prove major

Biblical characters actually existed. As yet, none of these efforts has born fruit. Why? Because most people have accepted the Biblical stories as historical events. So they have been searching for evidence to support their pre-determined conclusions. This has led them to look in incorrect geographical locations and in the wrong historical era. I suggest we should take the exact opposite approach. We should investigate what the historical record says about the Biblical events and not the other way around. In this lecture I will seek to bring to light historical evidence, which I believe has been ignored by many Egyptologists because of the risk of contradicting popular religious beliefs. It is not my intention to offend those among you of any particular religious persuasion. I seek merely to examine the historical facts and arrive at the truth.'

I glanced up from under my lashes at Adam to see how this opening statement was landing with him. Perhaps feeling my gaze on him, he reached across absently and took my hand in his, resting it on his lap. But his gaze remained fixed on the speaker, and I could almost hear the cogs of his brain whirring. I knew it was the evidence he was waiting to hear, not the conjecture or opening gambits.

Nabil Zaal took another small sip of water and let his bright gaze roam across the faces in the room. I felt it skim across mine, and felt a small surge of energy. He was certainly a man who knew how to hold an audience in the palm of his hand. If he wrote the way he spoke, then I could understand why his book sales were so successful.

After this small pause, to allow the significance of what he was saying to sink in, he started once more to speak. 'The Bible, which is notorious for stating names of persons, sites, and even water wells which in many cases have no impact on the story whatsoever, never names a specific pharaoh. The Bible may say, "the pharaoh who raised up Joseph" or "the pharaoh of the oppression" but these pharaohs are never actually named. This seems strange, does it not? It makes me wonder if the names were left out intentionally. But why would this be? Does it perhaps have something to do with the Exodus – which is such a fundamental part of the history of Israel and the Jewish religion? The Exodus is central to Biblical dogma – the story of the oppression of Hebrew slaves in Egypt and their journey to freedom, led by Moses, through the Wilderness of Canaan to the Promised Land.'

As he spoke, the Hollywood image of Charlton Heston's Moses leading the Israelites into the Red Sea pursued by Pharaoh Yul Brynner's army in *The Ten Commandments* played across my inner movie screen, and I felt a jolt of the same excitement I'd felt watching it on TV as a teenager.

'But did the Exodus really occur?' Nabil Zaal asked, interrupting my mental trip to the movies as he gazed around at us all. 'If it did, then it left an invisible trail.' Again, he paused, and let it draw out for a long moment before continuing. 'The purpose of the Exodus story is to tell of the birth of a nation; of people freed from oppression and slavery. But it is a simple fact that excavations at more than fifty sites along the Sinai route have produced no evidence whatever of any mass movement of people. There are no textual records or archaeological artefacts to support the Exodus story. And there is little or no Egyptological evidence of slavery in Pharaonic Egypt. On the contrary, it seems the labour force that excavated the tombs and built the pyramids and temples was well cared for, with ample food and good working conditions. Most archaeologists have abandoned the investigation of Moses and the Exodus as a fruitless pursuit. I believe we should consider the Biblical Exodus as a literary, rather than a historical work And, viewing the Bible in this light, it is my contention that Biblical scholars will never be able to confirm its accounts of Moses, Solomon, David and others. Because I believe these events did not take place in the way the Bible describes them.' He stopped again, took a sip of water, and stared into his glass as he went on, 'But if we look at history and archaeology, I think we are able to identify many of these key Biblical figures ... just not in the place or time the Bible says we should find them.'

He looked up and made sweeping eye contact with every person in the room. 'I shall use this lecture to prove that King David of the Bible was Pharaoh Thutmosis III, that King Solomon was Pharaoh Amenhotep III, and that the Biblical

Joseph was a vizier called Yuya at the court of Pharaoh Thutmosis IV. Yuya was in fact the great-grandfather of the most famous Pharaoh of them all, Tutankhamun. The events all took place during the glorious 18th Dynasty of ancient Egyptian history, when Egypt was the most powerful empire on earth.'

A ripple ran through the audience together with a small buzz of muted conversation as people turned to their companions to exchange whispered comments. I leaned forward to sneak a peak at Ben Hunter, who was sitting further along the row on the other side of both Adam and Ted. His expression told me nothing of his reaction to the lecture, for he was once again craning backwards over his shoulder to scan the faces in the rows behind us. I realised we'd been a bit stupid in allowing ourselves to be seated towards the front. We should have held back so the rest of the audience was ahead of us rather than behind. Ben's roaming gaze stopped suddenly, arrested on a single individual. I couldn't resist a quick glance backwards over my own shoulder to see who he was looking at. Right at the back of the room, sitting perched on the end of a row just in front of the huge folded-back double-doors leading onto the corridor, I spied a small figure. She was swathed from head to foot in the black burka-style robes favoured by Muslim women in Egypt, although with a hijab headscarf that left her wrinkled face uncovered. She was quite clearly an old lady, and an Arabic one at that.

Nabil Zaal coughed, a discreet way of calling his audience back to attention. A trifle reluctantly I turned to face forward again. He gazed around at us earnestly. Introduction over, it was clear he was now moving into the serious business of laying his hypothesis before us.

'While there is no historical evidence to support the Biblical accounts of David, Solomon and Joseph, there is abundant evidence to prove that King David's war accounts match precisely with those of Pharaoh Thutmosis III, and King Solomon's life and peaceable reign mirrors that of Pharaoh Amenhotep III. As for Biblical Joseph, his status and advancement at the Pharaonic court precisely correspond with that of the Egyptian courtier Yuya at the court of Thutmosis IV.'

Adam squeezed my hand, and I knew we were getting to the part he was most interested in. A quick glance around at the audience told me the full attention of everyone I could see was fixed on Nabil Zaal. Who all these people were, I had no idea. I guessed some were Egyptologists or archaeologists, drawn from the various excavation and preservation projects in and around Luxor. No doubt some were simple tourists who just happened to be here on holiday. And, of course, there was our mysterious lady in black sitting at the back. What-or-whoever, one thing was for sure; we were all equally agog to hear how our speaker would support his claims.

60

Nabil Zaal smiled at us. 'Perhaps we should start with Joseph, since his 'rags-to-riches' story is well known thanks to a certain Andrew Lloyd Webber stage musical. Having been sold to traders by his jealous brothers, Joseph was taken to Egypt and became the servant to Potiphar. After being falsely accused of seducing Potiphar's wife he was thrown into prison, where he earned a reputation as a skilful interpreter of dreams. Eventually Joseph was called upon to decipher the dreams of Pharaoh himself. When he correctly predicted a famine and suggested a policy to avert starvation, he was elevated to high office.'

I was quite glad he'd reminded me of the story. It was many years since I'd seen the stage show and though, as a child, I'd known the words to *Joseph and his Amazing Technicolor Dreamcoat* by heart, thanks to my school putting it on as the Christmas play one year; that was a long time ago and I'd grown rusty on the details. Sadly, I'm not able to claim my knowledge of the Bible stories comes from reading the Bible itself. It's fair to say my religious education is woefully lacking. It was never one of the core subjects on the curriculum at my comprehensive school in Kent.

'So, let us look first to the historical record.' Nabil Zaal invited us. 'Do we know of a pharaoh who was given to dreams? Well, it seems to me, the so-called '*Dream Stele*' that lies to this day between the paws of the great Sphinx at Giza, suggests a likely candidate in Pharaoh Thutmosis IV.

Thutmosis was a royal prince, but not the chosen successor to the throne. The story goes that while the young prince was out on a hunting trip, he stopped to rest under the head of the Sphinx which, being already many centuries old, was buried up to the neck in sand. Thutmosis soon fell asleep and had a dream in which the Sphinx told him that if he cleared away the sand from around his body Thutmosis would become the next pharaoh. Thutmosis did as he was bid. His restoration of the Sphinx is on record as one of his great achievements. And he became King. He placed a carved stone tablet, now known as the *Dream Stele*, between the paws of the Sphinx to commemorate his unusual accession to the throne.'

Adam shifted alongside me and murmured into my ear, 'Of course, the *Dream Stele* is silent on the subject of whether Thutmosis ousted an older brother in order to usurp power, and commissioned the Stele in order to justify his unexpected kingship.'

I doubt Nabil Zaal's hearing was acute enough to hear him, but even so he seemed to address his next point to Adam.

'Whatever the truth of Thutmosis' accession to the throne, here we have a pharaoh who clearly saw dreams as predictors of the future. Next, we must look among the high-ranking officials at his court to see if we can identify someone who may be Joseph. Who do we find? None other than Yuya, who had the unusual title "God's Father of the Lord of the Two Lands", i.e. God's Father of Pharaoh. If we turn to Genesis 46:8 we find Joseph, now Vizier of Egypt reassuring his brothers that "it was not you that sent me here, but God, and he has made me a father to Pharaoh."'

Nabil Zaal allowed another long pause to draw out as we absorbed the significance of this, before continuing:

'A simple look at Yuya's mummy, which was discovered in an intact tomb in the Valley of the Kings in 1905, suggests he was not of Egyptian origin. Yuya is the only Egyptian mummy to have his hands placed under his chin rather than across his chest. He has what unmistakeably appear to be Semitic features, and a beard style similar to that of the ancient Hebrews - whereas Egyptian officials were known to shave their facial hair.'

He took a sip of water and went on, 'I would also cite the various different renditions of his name found inside his tomb as highly suggestive. Eleven different spellings were found on his sarcophagus, coffins and other funerary furniture, which suggests to me that the scribes were struggling to record a name for which there was no established spelling. Egyptian names usually indicated the name of the god under whose protection a person was placed: e.g. *Ra*-mos, *Ptah*-hotep, Tutankh-*amun* and so on. It therefore seems possible that Egyptians might have named him after his own God, Yhwh (Yahweh or Jehovah), and that is what the scribes were trying to write.' He turned to a flipchart set up near the window and wrote on it with a marker as he spoke, showing us spellings that included *Ya-a, Yi-ja* and *Yu-i*.

Then he turned back to face us, and asked the question no doubt many of his audience were thinking. 'So, how could a foreigner achieve such prominence at the court of Pharaoh?'

This was clearly rhetorical since he proceeded to answer it without waiting for anyone to respond. 'Egypt was known to take the children of rulers of its vassal states into Egypt, partly as hostages to ensure loyalty, but also to be educated as Egyptians. These young boys were known as "children of the Kap", named after the military school they attended in Memphis. We don't know how Yuya first came to be in Egypt. But the Old Testament tells us that, having been sold into slavery by his jealous brothers, Joseph entered the service of a military man, a captain of the guard called Potiphar. This may well have placed him within the catchment for entry to the Kap'.

He allowed himself a smile. 'So, taken together, there is strong evidence to suggest Yuya was foreign. All of which leads me to the Biblical Joseph.'

'Stuff and nonsense!' said a loud male voice behind me. 'It's all just supposition, with not a single historical or archaeological fact to prop it up.'

Along with everyone else in the front rows, I craned over my shoulder to look at the speaker, a large, red-faced gentleman in a bold printed shirt in livid colours. I wasn't sure whether to put his red face down to apoplexy or a bad case of sunburn. He wagged his forefinger angrily at our speaker and carried on:

'Your theory contradicts the Biblical account regarding Joseph's burial location, which is stated clearly in the Book of Joshua. The Bible states unequivocally that Joseph's mummified body was exhumed and transported to Canaan by the Israelites, while Yuya's – by your own admission – remained undisturbed in the Valley of the Kings.'

We all swivelled back to face Nabil Zaal, as he said calmly, 'Sir, I have already pointed out my belief that the Bible is a literary rather than a strictly historical work.'

'And yet you'll quote quite happily from the Bible when it suits your own purpose!' our companion shot back. 'The title 'God's Father' is not exclusive to Yuya among high-ranking Egyptian viziers. And while I will happily accept that Yuya was Tutankhamun's great grandfather, since recent DNA testing on their mummies has proved it, I cannot make the mental leap necessary to identify Yuya as the Biblical Joseph just on your say-so!'

'Please Harry…' a small female voice, steeped in embarrassment whispered at his side. 'You promised me you'd listen without comment.'

I couldn't help but glance backwards again. Chastened by the meek and mousy woman at his side, the loudly dressed, red-faced gentleman subsided.

Nabil Zaal sipped his water thoughtfully for a moment. He didn't seem too put out by the challenge and I guessed he was pretty used to interruptions of this sort.

I risked another glance quickly over my shoulder. The little old lady, swathed in the black folds of her robe was leaning forward with bright and alert interest. There was no question she spoke English, I decided.

'So, let us leave Joseph for now,' Nabil Zaal said quietly. 'And please let me remind you all, I mean no offence by stating my views. Let us ask ourselves instead if there is any chance that the Egyptian warrior pharaoh, Thutmosis III was actually the Biblical warrior King David.'

'Here we go again,' the man muttered behind me.

'Really, Harry; we shouldn't have come,' his poor tormented wife whispered back.

Nabil Zaal paced backward and forward a bit, then said, 'It is my belief that the Biblical story of David and Goliath is a re-telling of the famous Ancient Egyptian folktale, *The Autobiography of Sinuhe*. I contend that the accounts of the campaigns fought by David, and described in the Second Book of Samuel, are synonymous with the historical wars fought by Thutmosis III and recorded on the walls of Karnak temple, right here in Luxor. The names of a couple of the conquered cities have been changed, and there is a slight discrepancy in chronology. But other than in these small details, the military accounts match exactly. They just happen to be a few centuries apart. My point is this... once again, we have all the historical and archaeological evidence we could possibly want of Thutmosis' military exploits as a warrior king, and none whatsoever of David's. This problem goes away if we accept them as one and the same person.'

Adam leaned towards me and whispered. 'But it's a mental leap, not one backed up by firm facts.'

'And if we take a look at the historical Pharaoh Amenhotep III and compare him to the Biblical Solomon,' Nabil Zaal went on smoothly, 'the similarities to suggest they are one and the same become overwhelming. Both had long, peaceful reigns notable for the lack of military campaigns. Amenhotep was known as a great diplomat and a master of peaceful foreign policy. The name 'Solomon' means safety or peace. Both were noted as great builders. Many of the temples and building projects of Amenhotep survive to this day, including the towering Colonnade at Luxor temple, just a short stroll along the Corniche from this wonderful old hotel.' He gazed earnestly around at us. 'But nothing remains of the apparently extensive building works of Solomon in Jerusalem; despite the fact he was supposedly building later. If we accept Solomon as Amenhotep, we can stop fruitlessly excavating further north, and appreciate his great works right here in Egypt.' He gave a small shrug, as if it was all too obvious for words. But he had yet another similarity up his sleeve, and wasted no time in laying it before us... 'And finally, the Bible tells us Solomon loved women and married only foreign wives. Amenhotep had a harem full of foreign princesses and married Tiye, the daughter of Yuya who, as I have shown, was not native to Egypt.'

'This is too much!' The man behind me bellowed, actually jumping up out of his seat this time. 'You expect us to believe that Yuya is the Biblical Joseph. How then do you explain that, unlike Joseph's sons Ephraim and Manasseh, this daughter – Tiye – is not mentioned in the Bible – not even once, despite her *brilliant* marriage to Pharaoh?!!'

Nabil Zaal's response to this latest challenge was, I thought, actually quite clever. Rather than attempt to answer the question himself he threw it out to the floor and invited other members of the audience to join the debate.

Of course the person who *should* have spoken up, considering his unimpeachable scholarly and Egyptological credentials, was Ted. But glancing at him I could see he rated the entertainment value of the argument that immediately sprung up between different factions in the audience way too highly to have any intention whatsoever of joining in.

I glanced back over my shoulder to see what the little old lady was making of it all. I did a quick double take. She wasn't there. But I thought I spied just a glimpse of a dark burka-like robe whisking out of sight into the corridor.

Excusing myself from the mêlée and glad I'd had the foresight to sit on the end of a row, I whispered to Adam that I'd be back in a minute, and jumped up to follow her.

Chapter 4

I wasn't sure which was worse: the fracas I left behind in the Victorian Lounge or the one I walked into in the lobby. A young man and a young woman were standing in the middle of this gracious and lofty room yelling at each other at the tops of their lungs. It did nothing at all for the rarefied Victorian atmosphere, I can tell you.

'I *told* you it was madness to come! But when do you ever listen to me?' the young man shouted.

'I *had* to come,' the young woman shot back angrily. 'I'd have wondered about it for the rest of my life otherwise!'

He gave a gesture of impatience, exasperation or disgust; I couldn't be sure which. 'You're chasing rainbows!' he accused. 'Honestly Freya! You've got the word *mug* emblazoned right across your forehead!'

She stamped her foot and glared at him. 'Well *somebody* went to the trouble of sending me the scarab! It didn't materialise out of thin air!'

I wasn't the only one brought skidding to a standstill by their altercation. Glancing around I saw quite a few people similarly transfixed. The immaculately attired receptionist from earlier was beside them hopping agitatedly from one foot to the other with a pained expression on his face, looking as if he desperately wanted to intervene but didn't dare. The shoeshine boy in his smart Middle-Eastern uniform of red galabeya and tarboosh was holding his deep-bristled brush up in the air as if he'd been turned to stone. His eyes bulged quite comically as they darted between the arguing pair. Over by the tall marble pillar a pair of smartly dressed young Egyptian men had lowered their Arabic newspapers and were staring open-mouthed. And a family of tourists, bedecked in cameras, rucksacks and baseball caps, delayed their departure through the heavy revolving door for whatever excursion they were setting out on, turning back to gawp quite openly. The only person I expected to see but didn't as I looked around during the momentary freeze-frame pause in the theatrics was the little old Arabic lady I'd set out to follow.

A movement caught my eye and I glanced upwards. The Winter Palace has a fine old wrought iron and marble staircase that curves from one wall in a broad sweep in front of the vast windows that are shuttered and set with heavy Roman blinds to keep the fierce sunshine out, then climbs back on itself to reach the first floor landing. I spied a swish of long black robes disappearing around the final curve out of sight.

'Shame the same somebody who sent you the scarab didn't see fit to honour the hotel reservation they promised you!' the young man rapped out crossly, calling my attention back to the warring couple. 'There's no way I can shell out for us to stay in a place like this!

'If you'd stop yelling at me for a moment, then perhaps I could think straight and see if anything occurs to me,' his companion fired back with a toss of her copper curls.

'What, like conjuring a pair of hotel bookings out of thin air like a magician out of a hat?' he scoffed. 'Good luck with that! We're stony broke Freya, remember? I maxed out my credit card to book my flight and you used the last of the money your grandmother left you to get here!'

'Nobody *asked* you to come along,' she pointed out heatedly. 'I was perfectly happy to come on my own. You just can't resist an opportunity to lord it over me, and to gloat when you think you've proved your point. Well, I'm not prepared to stand here a moment longer listening to you glory in self-righteousness! So I suggest…'

'I came along,' he bit out furiously, cutting her off, 'because I thought you might not be safe! Egypt is in the aftermath of a revolution. There have been skirmishes, political demonstrations and outright riots going on in Cairo pretty much solidly for over a year! And yet you blithely walk in where angels would fear to tread just on the strength of some mysterious scarab and a letter you believe to be from some long-lost relative.'

It's fair to say my ears had already pricked up at the mention of the scarab. Now the suggestion of a letter sent my

72

sixth, seventh and eighth senses zinging. Ben's letter had mentioned there was another…

I glanced up at the sweeping staircase. I had the strongest feeling the old woman was still there, standing back from the bannister, out of my sight – but there nonetheless; watching this little drama unfold along with the rest of us.

The young woman looked as if she was about to explode with temper. 'I have news for you, Josh! Believe it or not, I'm more than capable of looking after myself. I'm sick to death of being told this is madness and standing by mutely while you call me naïve, reckless and irresponsible. I didn't ask you to come. But now I'm asking you to go! I don't want you here! So I suggest you pack up your smug self-satisfaction with your hectoring attitude and your toothbrush and head straight back to the airport to catch the first flight home!'

'I'm not leaving!' he stormed. 'I just want to know what the Hell you think we're supposed to do without somewhere to stay!'

'Then for pity's sake, *shut up* and let me *think*!' she yelled. 'It's possible I misread the letter. Or maybe the person who wrote it made a mistake. It's quite clear they're not used to writing in English. Perhaps there's another hotel with a similar name.'

She broke off to turn to the receptionist who was still bouncing up and down on the spot alongside them, looking as if he had springs welded to the soles of his shoes but couldn't decide in which direction he wanted to jump.

'This is the *Old* Winter Palace hotel, isn't that right?'

'Yes madam,' he said, staring like a bunny caught in headlights. He clearly had no idea how to take control of the situation, poor man; and was clinging onto his customer service training for all he was worth.

'I seem to recall a friend of mine staying in a *New* Winter Palace hotel a few years ago. Is that round here somewhere?'

'No madam. I mean, yes madam. I mean, there *used* to be a hotel by that name. It once adjoined the Old Winter Palace. But it was demolished several years ago as it was considered a modern eyesore that detracted from the Victorian elegance of the original architecture.'

She stared at him with what might have been surprise, confusion or annoyance as he shifted nervously from foot to foot. She clearly hadn't expected to be treated to an insight into the architectural inadequacies of the sister hotel. 'Oh,' she said shortly. 'Are there any other hotels in Luxor with a similar name?'

'No madam. But there is the Pavilion Wing hotel situated in the grounds of this hotel. It shares facilities with The Winter Palace, such as the restaurants and bars, gardens and swimming pool.'

'Perhaps that's what the letter-writer meant,' the young woman said, addressing her companion with a small shrug. 'Where is the check-in desk of the Pavilion Wing?' she asked, glancing back at the receptionist.

'I can show you, madam and sir. It is this way. Please follow me...' He seemed heartily relieved to have hit upon a course of action that gave him something helpful to do, and at the same time removed the troublesome pair from the select and exalted surroundings of the Winter Palace lobby. He led them towards the revolving door with a positive spring in his step.

I watched them go, quite disappointed in a way that the little floorshow was over. I'd have liked to find out a bit more about the letter and the scarab before reporting back to the others. The shoeshine boy and the two smartly dressed Egyptian men also stared after them as they followed the family of tourists outside into the sunshine. One of the Egyptian chaps glanced across at me and raised an eyebrow before disappearing once more behind his newspaper. The other one looked up at the staircase as if a movement had caught his eye.

Reminded of my purpose and guessing the old Arabic woman was proceeding on up the stairs now the theatrics were over, I jolted back into my pursuit of her. As I hit the bottom stair and glanced up around the long, sweeping curve of the staircase, I was just in time to see a swish of black robes disappear onto the first floor corridor.

I took the stairs two at a time and arrived on the landing puffing slightly. I looked left and right along the vast corridor that stretched off both sides of the central staircase along the length of the hotel. It was empty in both directions. But a few paces to my right the staircase swept on upwards again, this time to the second floor landing. Again, I spied that elusive swish of a long black robe at the top as I looked up. She was a sprightly old bird; I'd give her that. And I don't think she was aware I was following her.

I darted up after her again. Puffing a little harder this time, I once again swung my gaze in both directions along the corridor as I arrived on the second floor. I was just in time to see the small be-robed figure disappear into a room at the far end of the right-hand branch of the corridor. There was an audible click as the door closed behind her.

I made my way along the corridor. My feet made no sound on the deep pile carpet and the sensation of stepping back into a bygone age was overwhelming.

I stopped outside the door I'd seen the little old lady disappear through at the end of the corridor. Unlike the others I'd passed, there was no number on the door. The wood panelling was painted a pale coffee colour, like the others, but it didn't have the same modern card-slot that served as a room key and charge card these days. Instead there was a good old-fashioned keyhole. I was tempted to lean forward and see if it was possible to look through it. The thought of being caught in the act deterred me. I had no possible explanation to offer and didn't much fancy the idea of being accused of spying. I dithered a bit, uncertain what to do now I was here. I supposed I could rap on the door and, in all likelihood; the little old lady would answer it. But what would I say to her? Besides, even supposing she was Ben's mysterious letter writer, it was Ben's father she'd written to, not me. I'd followed her on impulse and now realised I'd failed to think it through.

A bit reluctantly I turned away from the door deciding at least I could tell the others her whereabouts so my mission hadn't been completely abortive. I made my way back along the corridor and down the two long sweeping staircases into the lobby. I thanked one of the smartly dressed Egyptian men as he stood back from the bottom of the staircase to let me pass, before he took my place and started to climb the stairs. The other one was still over by the marble pillar reading his newspaper.

There was no sign of the young couple, although the receptionist was back, looking much relieved to have his lobby restored to peace and harmony. Hopefully they were even now checking into the Pavilion Wing finding the mix-up over their hotel booking had been happily resolved.

I re-entered the fray in the Victorian Lounge to find order not yet quite restored.

A man at the back of the room was standing up and wagging his finger at a sanguine-looking Nabil Zaal in a quite aggressive manner. 'I'm sure if I were Steven Spielberg I'd find your claims quite compelling. But how you expect Egyptologists or Biblical scholars to take them seriously I really don't know! To write off the Exodus as a literary device just beggars belief!'

'Come on,' Adam said as I moved to resume my seat. 'Religious squabbles do not float my boat. Let's make a move and leave this lot to fight it out among themselves.'

Ted and Ben followed him out of the row and, acknowledging Nabil Zaal with a gesture of thanks as we left, we made our way back into the corridor and through to the lobby. Other than the shoeshine boy and the receptionist it was empty. The other newspaper-reading Egyptian was no longer lounging by the marble pillar.

'Well, I'm not sure I'd exactly describe that as fun,' Ted said. 'But it definitely had something going for it in terms of entertainment.'

'That chap in the garish shirt was certainly getting a bit hot under the collar,' Ben nodded. 'At one point I thought I might have to step in to avert a punch up.'

'Yup, it's highly emotive stuff,' Adam said. 'People get all stirred up and start taking pot shots at each other.'

'Did you see the little old lady sitting at the back of the room?' Ben asked. 'She was wrapped up from head to toe in a voluminous black robe. She certainly looked to me to be somewhere in her eighties. I wonder if she's my mysterious letter-writer.'

'I not only saw her,' I offered brightly. 'I followed her. She's got a room right here in the hotel. And that's not all. I think I may know the identity of the other person she mentioned she'd written to.'

They all gaped at me.

'She's a young lady by the name of Freya. She's here with a chap I take to be her boyfriend. It seems they were expecting to check in but there was no record of their booking... which hadn't been made by them, by the way. She said something about receiving a mysterious letter together with a scarab...'

'A scarab?' Ben exclaimed, cutting me off.

'Yes.' I nodded. 'That's what first aroused my curiosity. That, and the fact the pair of them were right here in the lobby screaming at each other like alley cats.'

Adam stared at me. 'Merry, I'm not sure I can afford ever to let you out of my sight. As I've had cause to remark before, you really do have the most incredible talent for being on the scene when discoveries are to be made.'

There was no point modestly denying it, since it was true, so I smiled and said nothing. I was starting to enjoy myself. It had been a little while since I'd had that heady feeling of being caught up in something a bit outside of the ordinary. I don't mind admitting I'd missed it. Whether this current rather odd set of circumstances had the potential to reawaken the adventuresome side of me I hadn't known existed a year ago was impossible to know. Let's just say I had high hopes.

'So where's this young couple now?' Ben asked.

'They went to see if their reservation had been made at the Pavilion Wing instead of here. It's built in the gardens of this hotel, rather bizarrely.'

Ben stood looking undecided for a moment. 'I think I should start with the old lady,' he said at last. 'She's the one I came to make contact with.'

'Then I hope you're fit,' I said, a bit ironically, since Ben's rangy frame came closer to sportsman-like than many. 'It's up two huge flights of stairs, each of which is the size of at least three normal staircases put together.' I pointed to the sweeping marble steps that curved round three walls of the vast lobby.

'Isn't there a lift?' Ted asked with a slightly defeated air.

I stared at him. I'd seen Ted make light work of ten flights of stairs not twelve months since so I knew he had it in him. Although, to be fair, he'd been on a mission to rescue his only daughter from kidnap at knifepoint at the time so I daresay fear and emotion had lent flight to his limbs. I decided to appeal to his masculine pride. 'You should have seen the old lady,' I advised him. 'She scampered up the stairs like a teenager. She may well have rheumatism in her hands, but it doesn't seem to have slowed her down too much, even if her singing and dancing days are over. And you're probably ten years younger than she is, Ted.'

Adam took pity on him, shooting me a frowning glance. 'There's a lift over there, look.' He pointed back towards the corridor we'd just walked along from the Victorian Lounge. The lift was as old-fashioned as the rest of the hotel, with a little metal grille across the door. 'It's on the second floor did you say, Merry?'

I wondered if I'd gone too far. 'Yes, at the far end of the right hand corridor,' I said, feeling guilty.

'Shall we meet you up there, Ted?' Adam asked, making for the staircase.

'No, I daresay I can manage the stairs,' Ted said in long-suffering tones, but with a definite glint in his eyes. 'Somehow Merry's got me wanting to prove I'm as fit as a fiddle.'

We all took it for granted we'd accompany Ben on his visit to see the old lady we supposed to be one of Farouk's Fancies. He looked at the three of us a bit askance, but didn't say anything, so we set off up the stairs. I didn't attempt to take them two at a time this time around.

It's fair to say each of us was very slightly out of breath by the time we got to the top of the second flight.

'I really should start running again,' Adam murmured.

Ted wheezed a little, but beamed at me beatifically, delighted to have made it with his masculine pride undented.

I leaned forward and kissed his cheek, delighted by how well he'd risen to my challenge, and that I hadn't been the cause of a heart attack. 'Fit as a fiddle is right!'

Ben glanced up and down the long corridor. 'Right, you said? This way?'

I nodded and we trooped along the corridor until I was able to point out the door the old lady had gone through. 'It's that one.'

'Strange that it doesn't have a number or a card-key swipe,' Adam said, immediately registering what I'd noticed earlier.

'Well, there's nothing for it but to knock,' Ben said. He looked around at us with a meaningful glance.

'Shall we leave you to it?' I said, remembering my manners at long last. My instincts were so aquiver with the sense of intrigue attaching itself to the mystery-woman, I realised I was perhaps over-stepping the mark. A year ago I hadn't known impetuosity was such a driving part of my personality. Now I was wondering if it perhaps wasn't my most endearing characteristic.

'Perhaps just retreat along the corridor a bit,' he suggested, smiling at me. 'I don't want it to appear we've come mob-handed. She'll realise at once I'm not my father, but hopefully she'll be willing to accept me as his substitute.'

The three of us edged backwards out of sight, as Ben reached into his jacket pocket for the letter, then rapped on the door. It opened a moment later and Ben stepped backwards with a look of surprise.

'Yes?'

It was unmistakeably a male voice, and one that had the ring of youth about it.

Ben cleared his throat and stepped forward again. 'Er, hello, yes, I'm sorry to disturb you, but I wondered if perhaps your mother or, as it may be, your grandmother is available? The elderly lady whom I believe is staying here?'

'And you are...?' the male voice spoke English with a distinct Arabic accent.

'I'm Benedict Hunter. I think your, er... I think the lady I seek may have known my father, Mr Gregory Hunter.'

A long silence drew out.

'You know the name of my, er... of the lady you seek?'

'Um no,' Ben admitted, shifting a bit uncomfortably. 'My father received a letter...'

'She wrote to you...?' The note of suspicion and perhaps even hostility in the tone was unmistakeable.

'Well, to my father actually, before he died. Please, may I see the lady? I have a feeling she may be expecting me.'

'I regret,' came the flat response.

'She's not here? I thought perhaps I saw her downstairs, and believed she'd come to this room.'

'Alas, no.'

It was impossible to discern from this bald statement whether the speaker meant she was not there, or whether he was refusing to allow Ben to see her.

I could see Ben was growing annoyed. 'Please will you tell me whether the lady herself is here? I can understand if she may not wish to see me now. But I can perhaps make an appointment…?'

'You say your father received a letter. Perhaps if you tell me what it said…'

I noticed Ben unobtrusively slip the letter back into his pocket. 'I do not feel at liberty to discuss its contents. I believe it to be a private matter between my father and this lady.' He raised his voice, and I knew he was speaking for the benefit of any little old Arabic woman who may be able to hear him from inside the room. 'If you could please just pass on the message that Benedict Hunter called to see her. I am Gregory Hunter's son. I am staying in Luxor for a short while, on a dahabeeyah moored on the Nile. I will leave my contact details downstairs with the receptionist.'

And he turned away from the door with a look of vexation and started striding towards us.

I noticed the door did not click closed behind him. As Ben joined us and we started making our way back along the corridor towards the staircase, I glanced back over my shoulder. It was with a jolt of surprise that I made eye contact with the man leaning forward to peer around the doorjamb. I recognised him instantly as one of the smartly dressed Egyptians who'd earlier been reading his newspaper in the lobby. He was the one who'd stood back to allow me to pass him at the foot of the staircase.

'Well that was an abortive effort,' Ben said in thoroughly aggravated tones. 'What an unhelpful and insolent young man! Who does he think he is, some sort of bodyguard or something?'

I was starting to feel distinctly uneasy about the newspaper-reading pair. I might even go so far as to say suspicious.

'That was definitely the right room, Merry?' Adam queried with a frown. 'You actually saw the old lady go in?'

'I'm certain of it. I watched the black skirts of her robe whisk through the door and vanish.'

'I don't doubt it for a second,' Ben said staunchly. 'There's no question that ungracious individual knew exactly who I was talking about.'

'He certainly didn't put himself out to be accommodating,' Ted said thoughtfully. 'How would you describe his reaction to you Ben, once you told him who you were?'

Ben thought about it for a moment. 'He wasn't openly rude. But when I said who I was it was as if an invisible skin slid down over his face. All his facial muscles seemed to freeze into a watchful mask. I got the feeling more than anything that I'd thoroughly unsettled him and he was covering it up with that veneer of regretful apology.'

'Yes, that was when you mentioned the letter,' Ted remarked. 'I heard the change in his voice at that point.'

'So, what now?' Adam asked.

'Now I think all I can do is leave my details with the chap on reception, like I said, and wait to see if she makes contact. Or perhaps come back and try again tomorrow in the hope our stony-faced friend won't be here.'

Once we were back in the lobby, Ben took out a business card and turned it over. 'This has my mobile number on it,' he said. 'But I'll scribble directions to the dahabeeyah on the back if I may.'

Adam gave him the address of the small causeway where the *Queen Ahmes* was docked and Ben approached the reception desk. I joined him, and favoured the receptionist with what I hoped was my sweetest smile.

'Can you tell us anything about who's staying in the room at the far end of the top corridor?' I asked. 'It's the one without a number and without a key-card swiper. I think one of the guests may be an elderly Egyptian lady. You may have seen her... I believe she attended Nabil Zaal's lecture earlier and you showed her in a little while after we arrived.'

The receptionist gave me a rather strange look, accompanied by a small shrug. 'I regret, madam, I am unable to divulge details of those staying at The Winter Palace.'

'Perhaps if you wave a nice crisp fifty under his nose,' Adam murmured in low tones behind me.

I turned to face him. 'Adam! This is a world-class hotel! It's not the done thing to attempt to bribe the staff!'

He grinned at me, unapologetic, and shrugged. 'Baksheesh is a way of life here. See if you can persuade Ben to try.'

But it seemed Ben was already a step ahead of us. He passed his card across the desk and into the receptionist's hands with an Egyptian banknote wrapped around it. 'I would be grateful if you could place this card inside a sealed envelope and ensure that you deliver it personally to the lady to whom my friend refers... and to nobody else, you understand. Are you able to do that for me?'

The receptionist smiled broadly. 'It will be my pleasure, sir. I will ensure it passes from my hands directly into those of Madam Gadalla as soon as I see her. This will not be difficult since I see Madam Gadalla every day that I am at work here. She has made her home in this hotel for many years; since even before I was born I believe.'

I turned to exchange an incredulous glance with Adam. This was no poor little old lady we were talking about. She must be loaded.

We pushed through the heavy revolving door one by one, emerging into the hot, blinding sunshine on the terrace overlooking the Corniche and the Nile.

No sooner were we about to descend the curving stone staircase, than we were nearly knocked off our feet by the couple careening up it. It was obvious at once that Freya had tears streaming down her face. The young man... Josh, I think she'd called him, was tearing after her shouting, 'For God's sake, Freya! This is madness!'

Strange; I'm pretty sure those were exactly the same words he'd been flinging at her when I stumbled into their earlier altercation. It seemed they were going round and round in verbal circles. And in real ones, too, if seeing them back here was anything to judge by. I guessed it meant there'd been no reservation made for them at the Pavilion Wing.

'Just leave me alone!' she tossed back over her shoulder.

I'm not sure whether Adam realised this was the same young couple I'd mentioned earlier, but he doesn't like to see a damsel in distress, and he has a heart of pure gold. Spinning around as Freya nearly cannoned into him, he reached for her arm,

'Hey, is everything ok? Are you in some sort of trouble?'

Perhaps it was hearing a kind and concerned male voice after all the hectoring the poor girl had been subjected to, but it stopped her in her tracks. She slumped down onto the top step, put her head in her hands and started to cry in earnest, her shoulders shaking as great big sobs wracked her body.

We all stared in consternation.

'For Heaven's sake, Freya! You're making a complete spectacle of yourself!'

'Will you go *away*!' she screamed, flinging out one arm as if she'd like to push him backwards down the stone staircase.

I stepped forward to take control before anyone got hurt. 'Look, if this is about you having nowhere to stay, I think we can help.'

Out of the corner of my eye, I caught Adam looking at me a bit askance. Luckily he has an instinctive ability to tune into my wavelength. I've had cause to wonder in the past of Adam isn't perhaps mildly telepathic where I'm concerned. Whatever, he cottoned on quickly and didn't accompany the look with any sort of comment. I'd rushed into speech without thinking, and yet again Adam was demonstrating his ability to divine where I was going even before I myself was wholly aware of my intentions.

Freya gulped noisily and looked at me through her tears. Josh stumbled slightly as he missed his footing on the steps. He regained his balance and then he looked at me too.

I hurried on while I had the advantage of surprise. 'Listen, we own a dahabeeyah… I mean a houseboat,' I corrected, since it was obvious neither of them had a clue what I was talking about. 'We're turning it into a Nile cruise-boat, but we're not quite up and running yet. Anyway, we're moored not far from here. We have spare rooms, and all mod cons. We'd be happy to put you up for a night or two while you sort yourselves out.'

Adam stepped forward and thrust out his hand. 'I'm Adam Tennyson,' he said warmly, proving me right about him on all counts. I flashed a grateful look into his eyes, thanking my lucky stars for sending me a man so attuned to my subconscious.

'And I'm Meredith Pink,' I smiled. 'But you can call me Merry.'

Of course, I'm quite sure neither one of us was thinking about the scarab.

Josh looked at us suspiciously. He didn't accept Adam's proffered hand and, after a moment, Adam shrugged and dropped it back to his side.

'Why would you do that?' Josh asked, addressing me.

'I was in the lobby earlier when you were having your little – er – discussion. I know there's been some confusion over your hotel reservation. All we're doing is offering to tide you over for a day or two.'

'But we don't know you from – well – from...' he looked uncomfortably at Adam and trailed off.

'It's up to you,' Adam said cheerfully. 'But I doubt you'll get a better offer.'

Freya looked from Adam to me, and back again; then beyond us to where Ben and Ted were standing watching proceedings from the shade of the portico out front of the hotel, also savvy enough to keep from butting in. 'I'm in,' she said squarely, swiping at her tears, then standing up and hoisting her bag onto her shoulder.

'But Freya...'

'Go to Hell!'

'But...'

'Get *out of my way*!'

Josh stepped back as it looked as if she may kick out at him. 'I'm not coming,' he warned.

'Good!' she spat, and marched down the staircase without a backwards glance.

I nodded for Ben and Ted to follow her while I scrabbled about in my bag for a pen and something to write on. I tore a corner off an envelope and scribbled *Queen*

Ahmes onto it. Then I thrust it into Josh's hand. 'That's the name of our houseboat if you change your mind. Most of the taxi drivers will know where it is.'

We left him staring after us as we descended onto the Corniche and stepped into the first taxi to screech to a halt at the kerbside.

I happened to glance up at the hotel's wide cocktail terrace as the taxi pulled off, only to have my glance arrested by the sight of a familiar figure with a newspaper staring after us from behind the balustrade.

So actually there were two young men standing in the shadow of the grand old hotel watching our departure.

Chapter 5

Freya seemed disinclined towards conversation on the way back to the dahabeeyah. There was a defeated slump to her shoulders and a confused little wrinkle between her eyebrows that suggested she felt cast adrift onto a sea of uncertainty since things hadn't worked out as she'd expected today. She seemed both young and vulnerable now Josh wasn't here for her to square up against. I have to say though; it was much easier on the eardrums with only one of them around.

She gazed out of the taxi window, taking in the sights and sounds of Luxor as the taxi drove us through the dusty streets. I wondered what she was making of it. Luxor is a green city, although one perpetually coated in a fine layer of wind-blown sand. The streets are tree-lined and the central reservations, painted with black and white chevrons at kerb level, are planted with an abundance of shrubs and bushes. Bougainvillea grows wild and free, not just the ubiquitous bright pink but a riotous mix of colours including yellow, orange, lilac and white, sometimes all in bloom at once on the same tree. Hibiscus flowers nod pinkly at passers by from the hedgerows, and mimosa trees laden with yellow blooms droop over the pavements spreading shade and shedding their petals in equal measure.

It's also noisy, dirty and bursting with life in both human and animal form. Stray dogs, mangy-looking cats, donkeys laden with sugar cane, and random chickens and goats roam the streets. Men, dressed in long galabeya robes with turbans wound around their heads, sit about in doorways and on carpet mats along the kerbside, smoking cigarettes or the local water pipes and sometimes playing dominoes. The women in their voluminous black robes resemble nothing so much as great big bats with their wings folded in walking along the streets. And the traffic noise is incessant. Drivers live by their horns as much as their wits. Mopeds and scooters are the favourite mode of transport, although no one bothers with crash helmets. Moped riders weave in and out between the blue and white taxis, donkey carts, horse drawn carriages and tourist coaches, honking merrily. Somehow, miraculously, they manage to avoid colliding with anything. This has always been a matter of some wonder and incredulity to me; but I've seen so many near misses that these days I forget to hold my breath and squeeze my eyes tight shut. I guess that means I have graduated to the status of a local.

If it's possible for a place to be decrepit and falling apart on the one hand and bursting to life on the other – Luxor is that place. It's jaded, shabby, and has a perpetual look of a building site about it. Unfinished red brick buildings abound, with their copper construction poles sticking up in the air, and random chunks of concrete and masonry lie scattered hither and thither along the pot-holed streets. In fact, it's unusual in Luxor to see a domestic building that's actually complete. But leaving the city behind, the landscape becomes one of verdant agriculture; big square fields of sugar cane, wheat and okra line both sides of the road, ready for harvesting at this time of year, giving way to banana plantations and the thick grasses and palm trees that line the banks of the Nile and the canal that runs a little way inland from it on the west bank.

I've grown so used to the clashing colours, sights and sounds of this city I now call home, I've stopped seeing them through the eyes of a visitor. But looking at Freya's pale little face pressed against the window taking it all in, I was reminded how strange, foreign and exotic it all seemed when I first visited. To be fair, I'm not sure I'd have been brave enough to stay here permanently if I didn't have Adam to join me in the venture. I took his hand alongside me on the taxi seat and gave it a gentle squeeze. He squeezed it back and, not for the first time, I wondered if his thoughts were running along similar lines. He has an uncanny ability to tune into my wavelength.

Back onboard the *Queen Ahmes* I gave Freya the cabin between the one Adam and I share, and the one I'd allocated to Ben. I looked at her forlorn and tearstained face and her travel-crumpled clothes and felt a surge of real sympathy for the predicament she found herself in.

'I'm sure your boyfriend will come round,' I said warmly. 'You'll see, he'll probably turn up at the foot of the gangplank with a bunch of flowers and a pretty apology before suppertime. You've both had a long and stressful day. It's understandable to take it out on each other, but I'm sure things will seem a bit brighter in the morning.'

She gazed at me, then around at the cabin, then back at my face again. 'He's not my boyfriend,' she said in a thin, flat voice, pushing a coppery curl behind her ear.

'Oh! I – well, I –'

'He's my cousin,' she went on after a small pause while I got to grips with my discomfiture. 'He thinks of himself as some kind of self-appointed guardian angel. He recruited himself to the role when my parents died. They were in a plane crash when I was quite small. His dad and mine were brothers. We share a small flat together in Lewisham. It belonged to my grandmother before she died.'

'Oh,' I said again. 'I see.' But I wasn't sure I did completely. 'I'm sorry.'

She sighed and slumped on the bed. 'I didn't want him to come, but he went on and on about Egypt being unsafe since the revolution. In the end I said he could camp out on the floor of my hotel room – that was when I believed one had been booked for me – so long as he bought his own ticket.

But I wish I'd stuck to my guns. He's done nothing but lecture me since – well – since the letter from Egypt first arrived.'

'This would be the letter inviting you to come to the Winter Palace Hotel, where a reservation supposedly had been made for you?' I hazarded.

'Yes,' she said, with a small, defeated kind of shrug. 'I hate that he's been proved right. I really have been horribly naïve, haven't I?' A fresh sheen of tears glittered in her eyes.

'Well I don't know the full story. Who was the letter from?' I figured I might as well keep fishing since she seemed inclined to talk.

'That's just it, you see. I don't know. That's why Josh has been so sceptical and downright suspicious about the whole thing. It was signed with the initials FF. It came in a package containing this...' She took the scarab out of her pocket and set it on the bedside table, staring at it for a long moment as if she half expected it to disappear before her eyes. 'It's an Egyptian scarab,' she explained, as if I may never have seen one before.

Of course my fingers were itching to reach out and pick it up. I suppressed the urge. I hoped if I could win Freya's trust there'd be plenty of time to study the scarab later. It looked to be made of blue faience, small enough to rest comfortably in the palm of my hand. It was hard to tell, but I thought there might be a small chip along the left hand side.

'I believed the letter-writer sent it to me as a token of trust and good will. Apparently it's supposed to be lucky. I have no idea who FF is. But I have the strongest impression it might be someone related to my grandmother.' A big, fat tear squeezed out of the corner of her eye and rolled slowly down her cheek. She made no attempt to brush it away. 'She died last year. I miss her terribly. She took me in and brought me up after my parents were killed.' She stared at the scarab again. ' I have to say so far I don't feel very lucky.'

I looked at her sad little face, big eyes and the dejected droop of her narrow shoulders, and tried unsuccessfully to pinpoint who she reminded me of. Much as I wanted to wring every last detail out of her, I decided it probably wasn't fair to take advantage of her current overwrought state. Besides, she'd said enough to confirm she was exactly who I thought she was.

'Freya, listen. I'm going to bring you a big pot of tea. I suggest you take a long, hot shower then climb into bed and have a good, long sleep. You can join us for dinner up on deck later, if you wish. Or I can send you something to eat on a tray, whatever you prefer. For now, just get some rest. You're welcome to stay for a few days. Once you're feeling a bit brighter perhaps we can help you to investigate what went wrong with the hotel reservation. There must be some explanation.'

She looked at me a bit blearily through her tears, 'You're very kind.'

'Yes – well – just relax,' I said briskly, suppressing the little stab of conscience reminding me I was guilty of having an ulterior motive for inviting her to stay. 'There's a bathrobe and slippers in the wardrobe if you don't feel like getting dressed again later. The air-conditioning control is on the wall here.' I made for the door, and then turned back with my hand resting on the doorknob. 'Oh, if Josh should happen to put in an appearance; what would you like me to do?'

She gazed at me across the cabin, ' I really couldn't care less about Josh,' she said tonelessly.

* * *

'Well, Merry; I'm not sure quite how you managed it, but it was neatly done. You made the whole thing look remarkably easy.'

Adam and I were mixing cocktails in our gleaming stainless steel kitchen, ready to carry them up on deck for a sundowner with Ben and Ted.

'What do you mean?'

'Simply that within twenty-four hours of learning the mysterious old lady who signs herself 'one of Farouk's Fancies' wrote not just one letter but two, you've managed not only to identify the other recipient, but to somehow sweep her under your wing and invite her to stay. I hope the old lady is grateful to you, since you now have both the objects of her search together under one roof, and we've left a message telling her exactly where to find them.'

'I was just lucky to be in the right place at the right time.'

'Yes, and not for the first time,' he said, shooting me an arch look from under his eyebrows. 'It's a talent I stand more and more in awe of each time it happens.'

I grinned at him and splashed Bacardi on top of the ice and muddled mint leaves in the frosted glasses on the counter. 'Odd about Freya's hotel reservation though, isn't it? And there's something deeply suspicious about that pair of young Egyptians. At first I thought they just happened to be in the lobby when the theatrics kicked off between Freya and Josh, in the same way I was. But now, when I look back on it, I can't help thinking they were somehow casing the joint, almost as if they were watching and waiting for something to happen.'

'*Casing the joint?*' Adam teased. 'Merry, you've been reading too many far-fetched crime novels.'

'You know what I mean! It just strikes me as beyond the realms of coincidence that one of them should answer the door to Ben when he went in search of the old lady, and the other one should be out on the terrace, apparently keeping an eye out for Freya.'

'You may be right, but for now it's all supposition and conjecture.' He passed me the soda syphon from the enormous refrigerator, and I topped up the glasses. 'We'll just have to see if the old lady makes contact or if we can somehow get to see her when they're not about.'

* * *

Despite the sinking sun, heat still shimmered across the deck. The great sun god Re was making his daily descent beyond the burnished bronze Theban cliffs to spend the twelve hours of night sailing through the underworld on his solar barque. He would rise again in the east at daybreak. It was a journey he'd been making since the dawn of time. The sun sets at six in the evening and rises again at six in the morning in Luxor in April, a nice neat package of night and day that lends itself to mysticism. It's not hard to see why the ancient Egyptians deified the solar disc. The sun in Egypt demands awe, respect and submission. It scorches down from hard, hot skies during the day and sets each evening in a fiery blaze of hothouse colours, giving way to the intense velveteen blackness of the night.

While I was sure Ben was itching for a proper conversation with Freya as much as I was, he took her temporary absence with equanimity. For a while we sipped our cocktails in silence and let the great fireball in the sky cast its spell, content to sit back and enjoy the grand spectacle of an Egyptian sunset. The black silhouettes of the palm trees and dainty minarets were etched charcoal-like against a livid orange sky. The chanting of the muezzin in a distant mosque – tuneless and droning though it was – added something exotic and a bit mystical. A flock of birds flapped noiselessly across the glowing embers in the sky. Whatever other changes in the landscape, the sunset was somehow timeless. We shared it with the pharaohs and common folk of ancient Egypt, whose faces once glowed radiant and golden in the fiery rays of the setting sun in just the same way ours did now.

Slowly, the sun slid beyond the horizon, leaving the soft purple haze of dusk, then darkness gathered her warm cloak around us. Adam and I popped back below deck so he could refresh our drinks while I checked on the lamb and date tagine I was preparing for dinner. Middle Eastern cuisine is a joy since once it's all chopped into the tagine with its strange conical lid, mixed with exotic herbs and spices and topped up with water it pretty much cooks itself. Adding a spoonful of dark honey and giving it a quick stir, I reassured myself it could look after itself for another half-hour or so, and followed Adam back up the spiral staircase to rejoin Ted and Ben on deck.

Adam lit a couple of hurricane lamps and we settled back to the sound of the Nile lapping against the side of the dahabeeyah, and the chirruping of the crickets along the riverbank. The Theban Mountain is lit at night, the creases and crevices in the rock picked out in silvery graphite tones against the inky night sky. It provided a timeless and mystical backdrop as our discussion turned inevitably to Nabil Zaal's lecture.

'So, what did you make of him?' I asked my question of no one in particular, not really minding which of my three companions should answer since I was interested to hear each of their opinions.

'A good speaker,' Ben said consideringly. 'I found myself hanging on his every word. Starting off with his theories on the pyramids was something of an attention-grabber. I can see a few Biblical scholars getting het up over that book when he publishes it. Perhaps being controversial is part of his sales pitch.'

'He certainly seems to enjoy letting off a few fireworks.' Adam said, settling back and sipping his drink. 'I think he positively relished the challenge he got from that bloke sitting behind us today.'

'Yes, I have to say I thought our Mr Zaal a surprisingly engaging sort of fellow,' Ted said. ' I found myself unexpectedly warming to him and rather hoping he might turn out to be right in some of what we might call his "leaps of faith". But I have to conclude that if he'd submitted the content of his lecture as an undergraduate term paper back at Oxford, I would have felt compelled to fail him.'

'There wasn't a shred of real evidence,' Adam agreed. 'Entertaining though it was, I don't think I heard anything today to persuade me to take him seriously. One thing's for sure, though. If the stolen Dead Sea Scroll turns out to be for real I'll bet Nabil Zaal would sell his soul for it. The trouble is, because it took such a long time for the contents of the Scrolls to be published – remember, Merry, it was referred to as "the academic scandal of the twentieth century" – it allowed revisionist historians like Nabil Zaal to come up with all sorts of preposterous theories and claim they were being suppressed because they contained the evidence to turn religious history on its head. But those scrolls that have now been published haven't exactly set the cat among the pigeons. So it all seems to be resting on the single scroll stolen by our sticky-fingered friend, King Farouk.'

'You think it's a hoax?' Ben asked with narrowed eyes.

'I'm not sure what I think,' Adam admitted candidly. 'But it sounds about the best chance of concrete evidence Nabil Zaal's ever going to get a shot at.'

'Oh I don't know,' I piped up. 'I've been treated to two quick glances at Freya's scarab and I'd be willing to hazard a guess it's the same one stolen from your father, Ben. It may not reveal too much about King David or King Solomon, but didn't you say King Farouk was convinced it was carved with texts proving the vizier Yuya at the court of Pharaoh Thutmosis IV was the Biblical Joseph?'

'You've seen it?' Ben sat forward in his seat.

'Only fleetingly,' I admitted. 'She waved it under Josh's nose to prove a point when they were trading insults at The Winter Palace. And she took it out of her pocket and put it on the bedside table in her cabin when we got back here earlier. I won't swear to it, but it looked to me to have a little chip in the same place as the one you showed us in the photograph you were sent.'

'So we might have some concrete evidence sitting right here with us on board the *Queen Ahmes,*' Ted said.

'I'd give my eye teeth to take a look at that scarab,' Ben breathed. 'Especially in the company of an Egyptologist who'll be able to translate its inscriptions and say whether it's genuine or not.' He nodded respectfully at Ted.

'Why are you so sure it's likely to have any inscriptions at all?' I asked.

Adam sipped his drink. 'Because that was the whole point of them. You could think of ancient Egyptian scarabs as a bit like modern-day Twitter,' he said with a smile. 'Excavators have found hundreds of scarabs issued by Pharaoh Amenhotep III with inscriptions announcing his marriage to Queen Tiye, along with some of the other major events of his reign. So it seems scarabs were used as a way of getting messages passed to the populace. Amenhotep III was Thutmosis IV's son, and Tiye has been proven through DNA testing to be the daughter of the vizier Yuya. These so-called 'marriage' scarabs issued by Amenhotep III were big news. They announced Pharaoh was marrying a commoner, and Tiye went on to become one of the most powerful Great Royal Wives in all of ancient Egyptian history. It's certainly possible some of these so-called 'marriage' scarabs had something to say about the father of the bride. And if he were a foreigner, meaning the new Great Royal Wife was not Egyptian, perhaps Amenhotep felt unusually constrained to announce his intentions to his people.'

'This is most intriguing,' Ted interjected. 'Especially since, to my knowledge, Amenhotep III's 'marriage' scarabs did indeed name both the father, Yuya, and the mother, Thuya, of the bride. It's almost as if the Pharaoh wanted to draw attention to Tiye's non-royal status. But, to my certain knowledge, none of the scarabs so far found has gone further by actually telling us any more about Yuya's descendency. All we know for sure is that Yuya and Thuya were given the unprecedented privilege of a burial in the Valley of the Kings. It was a mark of the most incredible royal favour.'

I couldn't resist interjecting, 'So it does rather make you wonder if Yuya had done something particular to distinguish himself, beyond being a royal vizier and the pharaoh's father-in-law. If he happened also to be the man who averted seven years of famine in Egypt by correctly interpreting the previous pharaoh's dreams, you can see why his son-in-law might want to grant him special honours.'

Adam grinned at me. 'Nobody loves a highly fictionalised account of ancient Egyptian history quite so much as you, Merry. You know what, you've even got *me* hoping that scarab turns out to be the proof we're all longing for! I don't think I could bear your disappointment otherwise.'

I was about to take an indignant swipe at him for teasing me again, when a small voice speaking from the spiral staircase interrupted me. 'Am I too late for dinner?'

We all turned to stare at the small figure bundled up in a bathrobe, standing a bit uncertainly about half way up the staircase. I couldn't help but wonder how much she may have overheard.

I sent her a bright smile. 'Of course not, Freya. We haven't eaten yet. How are you feeling?'

'Well, I couldn't sleep,' she admitted. 'But I feel better for the shower and some time to rest.'

A brisk breeze blew across the deck, rattling the hurricane lamps and causing their flames to flicker wildly, sending an eerie glow leaping through the shadows.

'Let's eat downstairs in the lounge-bar,' I suggested. 'The breeze quite often gets up in the evenings at this time of year. We'll be more comfortable below deck tonight, I think. With luck we'll be spared another power cut.'

Adam extinguished the hurricane lamps and Ted helped me gather the glasses, and we trooped in single file down the spiral staircase, following Freya inside the dahabeeyah into our semi-circular lounge-bar in the stern of the boat. Ted and Ben went to their cabins for a quick brush up before dinner, and Adam went into the kitchen to prepare the couscous.

'This is lovely,' Freya said, looking about her as I set the glasses behind the bar, and started making up the table for dinner. 'You really have recaptured the sense of the olden days. I feel a bit as if I've stepped back in time. Do you mind me wearing a bathrobe for dinner? I can easily go and get changed.'

'You're fine as you are,' I reassured her. 'We're pretty informal and, as I said earlier, we're not quite up and running. We don't have any staff yet. It's just us. So there's no need to stand on ceremony. Just relax and make yourself at home.'

She wandered across to the bookshelves and spent a few moments in a silent study of the various Egyptological reference, history and picture books we'd lined along one wall.

'Adam's dream is to be an Egyptologist,' I told her, lighting a couple of candles on the table to add to the ambient glow cast by the lamps. 'And Ted *is* one; well, at least he was before he retired. But I'm not sure you ever actually stop being an Egyptologist once you're qualified as one. He was a professor in ancient languages at the Oriental Institute, Oxford.'

She turned a rather luminous gaze on me. 'Do you think he'd be able to read the markings on my scarab?'

I could have kissed her. She seemed determined to make things easy for us. I'd been wondering how we might go about asking if we could all take a look at it. 'I think it's a pretty safe bet he'd be able to do so, yes. He's made a career of translating papyrus and deciphering hieroglyphics.'

'Not that it's likely to give me a clue about who sent it,' she said with a small downward curve of her mouth. 'But it would be good to know what all those funny carvings on the underside actually say.'

'Then I'm sure the professor is your man,' I smiled encouragingly. 'I'll tell you what. Let's have dinner, and then maybe afterwards you can show him the scarab. I'm sure we're all interested to see it.'

Of course, what I should have done was to get her to go and retrieve the scarab from her cabin right away.

By silent mutual consent the conversation remained general over dinner. I was silently congratulating myself that, with no effort of my part, Freya was so willing to show us the scarab. I should have remembered pride comes before a fall. And the others seemed a little uncomfortable at having a young woman in her dressing gown at the dinner table. For Freya's part, I was quite amused to see the way her gaze kept swinging between Ben and Adam. Perhaps she wasn't used to having two such good-looking men across the table from her at dinner. But, all things considered, conversation was light and superficial. My tagine was a big hit, and Adam's couscous complemented it perfectly; blended with chopped herbs and a few flaked almonds.

'I shall have no hesitation whatever in recommending the *Queen Ahmes*,' Ben said, looking into my eyes and smiling. 'You've set a very high standard. And last night I had one of the best night's sleep I've had for ages.'

I smiled back, delighted with the compliment, and saw Adam shift a bit in his seat. I couldn't help but wish Ben might direct one of his charming comments at Adam once in a while. I sipped my wine and changed the subject, suggesting Ben might like to take a look at Luxor or Karnak temples tomorrow.

I don't know what sixth sense it was that made me feel suddenly that something was wrong. Perhaps I heard something; a noise that wasn't the usual creaking of the old timbers in the dahabeeyah or a log being washed against the side of the boat or the stray cats fighting on the stone causeway.

'What was that?' I cocked my head to listen.

Everyone stopped.

'I don't hear anything,' Adam said.

I listened a moment longer, reassured by the silence. But still the little prickling feeling wouldn't go away. I shrugged it off and accepted the refill of wine Adam offered me. I was just raising the glass to my lips when another little sound made me stop with it raised half way.

'I think there might be someone outside on the gangplank.'

'I'll bet it's Josh!' Freya cried, jumping up. 'Honestly! He can't leave me alone for a minute!'

'Well, we can hardly turn the poor kid away if he doesn't have anywhere to stay tonight,' Adam said, pushing his chair back from the table.

I cast a quick glance at Freya's mutinous expression. No need to stand back and light the blue touch paper. If Josh was standing out on the gangplank it seemed to me it was already well and truly lit. I had no doubt we were about to be treated to another firework display.

'Let's at least go and see what he has to say for himself,' I urged her. 'Come on; there's enough tagine left over for him if he's hungry. And we've still got a couple of cabins going spare. You don't have to see him if you don't want to Freya – at least, not until the morning. I can give him a cabin and take him some dinner on a tray.'

'Oh alright then,' she said with a toss of her copper curls. While I'd guess Freya to be into her twenties, in that moment she didn't look very far into them. Josh seemed to bring out the worst in her.

We all trooped across the lounge-bar and through the door into the narrow corridor where our cabins were located.

I think the first thing that alerted us that everything was not as it should be was the sight of Freya's cabin door standing wide open.

'I'm sure I shut that behind me earlier,' she said, pulling it closed as we passed. But even then it didn't really register.

It was only when we reached the little reception area at the front of the dahabeeyah where the gangplank is lowered against the crumbling stone wharf until we pull it up at bedtime that the first inkling of what had happened hit me.

There was no sign of Josh on the gangplank or anywhere along the narrow causeway, although a couple of stray cats sloped out of the shadows no doubt hoping for scraps. I distinctly heard the sound of a scooter or moped firing up on the riverbank behind the little cluster of palm trees.

'That's strange,' Ben said from behind me. 'There's no one here.'

Adam turned to look into my eyes, and I knew we were sharing a single thought. We turned together, bumping into each other in our haste to check if our awful suspicion was correct.

'Freya, I just want to take a quick look inside your cabin,' I told her, almost pulling her along from the reception area, while Adam paused to pull up the gangplank.

'Why? What's the matter?' she asked with wide eyes.

'Can we open the door?' I was turning the handle as I asked the question. We hadn't had locks fitted on the doors yet, since we hadn't quite completed all the tasks needed to get the *Queen Ahmes* ready for fee paying guests.

I saw at once that the scarab wasn't where I'd last seen it, resting on the bedside table where she'd put it when she retrieved it from her pocket earlier.

'Did you put the scarab away anywhere?' I asked urgently.

'No, I –' she trailed off as her gaze fell on the empty bedside table. 'My scarab!' she squealed. 'It's gone!'

Chapter 6

'I'm afraid we haven't been entirely straight with you, Freya,' I admitted, deciding it was time to come clean.

'What do you mean?' she sent me a look a bit like a cornered rabbit, pulling the white flannel bathrobe closer around her.

We were back in the lounge-bar. I'd poured out steaming mugs of hot coffee all round. 'It's just, you see, your scarab provided something of an ulterior motive for inviting you to come and stay.'

'What do you know about my scarab?' She was curled into one corner of the soft-cushioned sofa, and looked as if she'd burrow even further back if she could.

'Sadly not as much as we'd like,' Adam interjected. 'We were rather hoping for the chance to study it. I guess now it's been stolen we've lost the opportunity.'

'But I don't understand,' the poor girl said with a perplexed frown. 'How did you know I had the scarab before you asked me to stay?'

'You were waving it around in the lobby of The Winter Palace during your – er – discussion with Josh,' I reminded her.

'Well, yes – but why should that mean anything to you?'

Ben reached into his jacket pocket. I rather liked the fact he insisted on wearing a jacket for dinner. He was a bit old school, like Ted who always donned a tie before sitting down for his evening meal. I guessed it said much for a public school upbringing. Although Adam, who'd also had a public school education, was in his shirtsleeves (it was a very nice shirt, patterned in deep shades of blue, and matched his eyes), teamed with his favourite pair of chinos. 'Does this look familiar?' Ben handed the black and white photograph across to Freya.

She stared at it with bulging eyes for a moment. 'Well, it's not in colour, so I can't be sure. My scarab is kind of a turquoise blue. But yes, this little chip on the side – it certainly looks like the one I was sent.' She looked up and sent a confused look into Ben's eyes. 'Where did you get this photograph?' It was a reasonable enough question I thought.

'I have a feeling the same person sent me the picture of the scarab as sent you the real thing,' Ben took the photograph back from her outstretched hand and secured it back in his pocket, where he rummaged for a second, then pulled out the letter and handed it to her.

She unfolded the floppy paper and stared at it in consternation. 'But it's written in Arabic.'

'Yes, the person who wrote it knew the person she sent it to both read and spoke the language.'

'That person wasn't you?'

'My father.'

I decided it was time to take control of the conversation, since Ben seemed to be starting in the middle again, which wasn't helpful to anyone.

'Ben's father was invited to come to Luxor every bit as cryptically as it seems you were. Although no one suggested they'd booked a hotel room for him. It seems Ben's father may once have known our mysterious letter writer – albeit many years ago. Sadly he died before he was able to respond to the invitation. So Ben is here in his place. We think the person who signs herself with the initials FF on your letter…' – I decided I'd leave her appellation as 'one of Farouk's Fancies for later – '…may be an elderly Egyptian lady called Madam Gadalla who has a suite at The Winter Palace Hotel. What her reasons are for inviting you and Ben's father here are a bit unclear. But they seem to have something to do with the scarab she sent you, and a missing Dead Sea Scroll.'

Taking in the bewildered look on Freya's freckled face I could see I hadn't succeeded in making things any clearer. 'But how did you link me and my scarab to the letter Ben received?'

In a few short sentences it was told. 'So, you see, we knew she'd sent another letter and when you showed up at The Winter Palace yell – I mean talking – about being sent a mysterious letter and a scarab, we simply put two and two together.'

'But now unfortunately the scarab has been stolen,' Ted said, bringing us back to the point. 'It's a great shame. I would very much have liked to study it. I wonder who took it, and why?'

'Oh, that will just be Josh,' Freya said with another of her rather juvenile shrugs. She pushed her copper curls back from her face in an impatient gesture that made me wonder why she didn't get it cut if it bothered her so much, constantly flopping in front of her eyes. 'He'll have taken it to teach me a lesson, to try to put the wind up me. He'll be furious that I came away with you, and this is exactly the type of thing he'd do to get back at me.'

They really did carry on like a pair of teenagers. I decided if I ever had them in the same room together I'd bang their silly heads together. Having Freya around certainly made me feel exceedingly grown up, which made quite a nice change to be honest. I thought about the sound of the moped engine I'd heard firing up on the riverbank. 'I very much doubt it was Josh,' I said.

I noticed Adam looking at Ben with a narrowed gaze. I guessed he was wondering if Freya's door had been open when Ben returned to his cabin to don a jacket for dinner. Adam didn't seem to have warmed to Ben one hundred percent. But casting a quick glance at Ben's face as he leaned forward to top up his coffee from the pot, I couldn't believe he was our mysterious thief. While he hadn't been in the room when Freya was saying how much she'd like Ted to have a go at translating the scarab's inscriptions for her, he needed Ted to make sense of the ancient texts – if indeed ancient they were – as much as she did.

'Freya, I know this might be an awful cheek,' I said. 'But would you mind sharing the contents of your letter with us? It's just, it seems to me there's something rather strange going on. I don't understand why you'd be told a room had been booked for you, only to turn up and find it isn't so. And I think there's something rather sinister about your scarab being stolen out from under our noses. There may be something in your letter that will give us a clue about what's going on.'

I watched her re-fold the fabric-like paper of Ben's letter. There was something about the content of that letter that had been niggling away at the back of my mind since Ted had translated it out loud for us. But I was at a loss to put my finger on it. It was just a vague impression of something out of place and a bit incongruous. I hoped hearing the contents of Freya's letter might help me pinpoint it.

She handed Ben's letter back to him then stared across at me. 'If you don't think Josh stole the scarab, who do you suspect?'

'That's just it, I don't know. But in Ben's letter the old lady told us she felt she was being watched. And I don't think

I was the only one to see the scarab when you waved it about in the lobby of The Winter Palace today.' I thought about the two newspaper-reading young Egyptians, one of whom had opened the door to Madam Gadalla's suite, while the other seemed to be keeping watch on the terrace. Almost all Egyptian men seemed to own a scooter or moped these days. 'I have a feeling more people than just us are aware of the possible importance of that scarab and perhaps also the mysterious Dead Sea Scroll.'

'It's in my cabin.' Freya said, getting up. She moved across to the doorway and stood there a bit uncertainly, looking nervous.

'It's ok,' Adam said. 'I've pulled up the gangplank. No one can get on board now unless they want a dunking in the Nile.' He got up. 'But I'll wait here with the door open while you go and get it, if you like.'

She was back in moments, looking relieved to find the letter hadn't been stolen, too. Hers had obviously suffered less handing than Ben's. It still resembled the piece of paper it was, rather than a gentleman's handkerchief.

She sat back on the sofa, tucking her legs up underneath her, and pulling the bathrobe closed at her throat. 'Shall I read it to you?'

'If you don't mind.'

Freya took a small sip of coffee. 'It doesn't have a 'Dear Freya', or anything. It just kind of starts.' And she started to read.

'"It was once said that the letter F was lucky. Your name is Freya and your mother was Florence. But these are not Egyptian names. Your grandmother's name was Sofia – not so Egyptian a name – but she was Egyptian nonetheless. This, no doubt, you know; although she left her homeland before your mother was born, and never returned.

It is a sad thing to leave Egypt, never to return. This, tragically, was the fate of our last king; although he was allowed back in death for his burial. His name was Farouk, supposedly another lucky name. I hope yours has proved luckier than his.

I knew him once, and so did your grandmother. We were girls together, Sofia and I; and there was one other, Rosa – although I struggle to speak of her. We called him Freddy. Perhaps this surprises you; to be on such intimate terms with a crowned monarch. Yes, we were intimate. We sang and danced for the King, and provided the entertainment for his guests at the lavish parties he loved to host.

Sadly these good times came to an end all too soon. Freddy was sent from his palace in Alexandria across the sea to Europe for his years of exile.

It spelled the end, too, for our little troupe of three. Sofia left for England. There were people there who could care for her in her condition. Rosa went to Europe. But I will speak of her no more. I remained here in Egypt, where I live to this day.

My child, I would like you to visit me here. I have stories of your grandmother and our girlhood together. These are stories you should hear now she has passed on. You should know of your roots I think, as your parents no longer live. Ah, life. It flows like the waters of the Nile. I watch these waters flow by my window, and I remember.

I have led a comfortable life, but it draws towards its close. Alas, we cannot live forever. We must pass on what we know, or it must die with us.

Freddy looked after me, you know. Yes, even from exile. He never forgot my birthday. He loved us all three, I think. But perhaps I was his special fancy. Come, and I will tell you my stories; and give to you that which should now be yours since I have no children. I send you a gift with this letter. It is a gift with a special meaning, but only to those who are willing to open their minds. Bring it back to me, and I will explain. But, for now, accept it as a token of my good will. The scarab beetle is supposed to be lucky. I hope it brings you good fortune.

I have reserved a room for you at The Winter Palace hotel in Luxor. Come during the first week of April. I will be waiting.

Yours with the affection of one who once called your grandmother sister, FF'"

Freya stopped reading, carefully folded the letter and slipped it into the pocket of her bathrobe. She looked around at us with wide, luminous eyes and I realised who she reminded me of. It had been tugging at me all day. It was Bambi, from the Disney cartoon. Her hair was the same colour as Bambi's coat, and with her wide eyes, young, coltish appearance and rather naïve innocence she was a dead spit for the little deer. Bambi lost his mother too, I remembered. I felt another surge of sympathy for her.

'Does it help?' she asked.

'What an intriguing letter,' Ted said, clearing his throat. Funny, I was sure they were exactly the words he uttered after translating Ben's missive.

I didn't respond to Freya's question or Ted's comment immediately. I was lost in thought but it wasn't getting me anywhere. Something in Freya's letter snagged on the niggly little feeling Ben's letter had given me, but frustratingly I was no closer to pinning it down.

'Well it doesn't give us any clues about who may have stolen the scarab,' Adam said. 'But it certainly makes you wonder about those stories of hers, and who else might like to hear them.'

'We should have approached her straight away during the lecture,' Ben's frustration was clear. 'The trouble is we couldn't be sure it was her.'

'I think we can be pretty sure the Madam Gadalla who has a permanent suite at The Winter Palace is our letter writer,' I said. 'What I sincerely hope is that she's ok. We saw the strength of feeling Nabil Zaal's beliefs sparked amongst some members of his audience. If anyone else suspects Madam Gadalla has information, or knows the whereabouts of ancient artefacts linking key Biblical figures to the pharaohs of the 18th Dynasty of ancient Egypt, she could be in danger.'

* * *

We decided there was only one thing for it. We needed to head back to The Winter Palace first thing in the morning. Both Ben and Freya needed to attempt to make contact with the old lady who'd written to them. It seemed like a good idea to investigate what had gone wrong with Freya's hotel reservation. And I was keen to see what I might be able to find out about the two young Egyptian men who'd been hanging about in the lobby.

We spent the rest of the evening giving Freya a summary of the contents of Ben's letter, and filling her in on the contents of Nabil Zaal's controversial lecture. Her eyes were wider than ever when we finished. 'So you think this

Madam Gadalla might have invited Ben and me here to Egypt to tell us about the Dead Sea Scroll King Farouk stole – perhaps even to give it to us?'

'It would seem to be a possibility since she claims to know where it's hidden – although what she expects you both to do with it is anyone's guess. It's a mysterious old web she's weaving. You're sure your grandmother never mentioned anything about King Farouk?'

'No, never,' she assured us earnestly. 'I knew my grandmother was Egyptian of course. She always spoke with an accent. But she never spoke to me about Egypt or her past. The first I ever heard about King Farouk, or even her sister, was when the letter arrived. I wonder why Madam Gadalla didn't sign herself with her real name. You say FF stands for 'Farouk's Fancies'. So, are we supposed to deduce that's what King Farouk called all three of them – my grandmother Sofia, Rosa and Madam Gadalla herself?'

'That's certainly the way I'm interpreting it,' I said. 'As a kind of collective nickname. It sounds like they were a little troupe of singers and dancers.'

'My grandmother loved to sing,' Freya volunteered. 'She had a beautiful voice.' A sheen of fresh tears sparkled in her eyes, and I decided it was time to draw the evening to a close.

'Bed time,' I announced. 'Freya, you've had a long and trying day. You need a good night's sleep.'

Personally, I didn't sleep well at all. I didn't like the thought of some mysterious stranger setting foot onboard the *Queen Ahmes* with nefarious intent while we were at dinner. I'd always felt completely safe living on the dahabeeyah moored at the riverbank. But now I wasn't so sure. Even though I knew Adam had pulled up the gangplank, my inner alarm system was on heightened alert and super-sensitive; my ears attuned to every small sound as the current brought the usual driftwood and other river detritus to nudge against the wooden hull.

I made a mental note to remind Adam we needed to get on with the task of hiring some staff. To be fair to Adam he'd made quite a study of the local employment rules and regulations during breaks from expertly wielding a paintbrush over the last few weeks.

We'd need a captain to sail the boat, a chef to prepare the delicious meals our guests would expect (my tagines were fine for the time being, but they wouldn't pass muster in the long term), and a housekeeper-chambermaid-cum-serving assistant to help with the front-of-house service. Our crew, once we hired them, would live aboard during our cruises in their own quarters below deck. Khaled had done a fine job turning these tiny spaces into cabins with private facilities, little portholes and even air-conditioning; so I felt quite proud of the working conditions we were able to offer our new employees.

I'd furnished the staff quarters without quite the same concern for luxury as elsewhere aboard the *Queen Ahmes*, but with no compromises on quality.

I wondered if perhaps we ought also to hire a security guard. Even without the advent of our uninvited visitor tonight, these remained troubled times in Egypt. Post-revolutionary clashes continued in Cairo, sometimes political but also increasingly motivated by religion. The latest violence to erupt was between Moslems and Coptic Christians outside Cairo's main Coptic cathedral. I could only feel sorry hearing the News. It was sad for the people of Egypt and it certainly didn't bode well for the return of a thriving tourist industry any time soon. Visitors to Egypt needed to feel safe, and I was suddenly very aware of the responsibility Adam and I had taken on inviting Ben and now Freya to stay with us.

I curled myself against Adam's warm chest. As his arm came around me I finally fell asleep wondering if perhaps we could entice our pal Ahmed away from his job in the tourist and antiquities police in Luxor. He'd make a great security guard. But Ahmed is not a great lover of the water. He likes the feel of solid ground beneath his feet. Still... he might be able to recommend someone...

We woke to one of the white-skied days Luxor is sometimes known for. The Theban hills were lost in haze and a misty sheen of heat hung heavy over the landscape making everything look just slightly out of focus. It's caused by occasional strong breezes, I think, blowing dust high into the atmosphere. The Nile glittered with wind-tipped waves, causing the dahabeeyah to rock gently in her mooring. It betokened a hot day in store.

Breakfast was dispensed with quickly. We kept it simple; just fruit juice, cereal, toast and coffee. I noticed Freya fiddling with her mobile phone.

'What's wrong? Aren't you able to get a signal? It is sometimes a bit hit and miss around here.'

'No, it's not that.' She pressed a couple of buttons and gave up. 'It's just I thought I might have heard from Josh by now. But he hasn't left a message. I've tried texting him and I've left a voicemail message saying you're all really nice and I don't mind if he wants to come and stay here too. But he hasn't come back to me. I guess I must have really annoyed him yesterday, running off and leaving him like that.'

With a supreme effort of willpower I managed to prevent myself from reminding her that she'd said she couldn't care less about Josh and told him to go to Hell. 'You're worried about him?'

She gave one of her maddening shrugs, and I wondered suddenly whether for Freya there was perhaps only one thing worse than having Josh dogging her footsteps, and that was *not* having him dogging her footsteps.

'I expect you'll find him camping out on the steps of The Winter Palace waiting for you,' I said brightly. 'He must know we're bound to take you back there to try to figure out what happened to your hotel reservation.'

We called on one of our regular taxi drivers to take us back into town. Generally Adam and I join in with the locals, zipping around Luxor on our scooters. But with guests to transport, a taxi is really the only option. And it's an inexpensive way to get around. Most of the taxi drivers recognise us now, so we thankfully don't have to bother with the usual haggling battle to fix a price.

After a short ride, we found ourselves once again climbing the sweeping stone staircase leading from the Corniche up to the entrance foyer of this grand dame of Victorian hostelry, The Winter Palace Hotel.

Freya looked along the wide terrace in both directions, but Josh was nowhere to be seen, so we approached the revolving door. Stepping into the lobby never fails to impress me. It really is a throwback to a long-gone age of opulence and refinement. A quick glance around was enough to tell us that Josh was not in the lobby either. As a matter of fact, the whole place was pretty much deserted.

The same immaculately attired receptionist who'd greeted us yesterday was on duty. We removed our sunglasses as we moved from the white glare outside into the cool interior of the hotel, and approached him.

According to his polished name badge, he was called Mohamed. Unsurprising, really. It seems fifty percent of all Egyptian men are named in honour of the Prophet. He looked up as we approached and a smile of recognition warmed his features.

Ben was the first to speak. 'Good morning, you may remember us from yesterday. I left my card for Madam Gadalla, and I wanted to check whether you've passed it on to the lady.'

'Sir, you required that I should give it directly from my hands into hers,' Mohamed said with a small nod to show he'd understood his task.

'That's right. And have you?'

'Alas, it has not yet been possible for me to carry out your instruction, sir. It is unusual, but I have not had the pleasure to see Madam Gadalla since you have departed from here yesterday. Mostly I see her every day. But...' He gave a small shrug to account for his inability to explain the change in routine. 'You see, sir; I still have the envelope here...' He turned and reached towards the row of cubbyholes behind him where keys and messages were left for residential guests. His reaching hand stilled. 'Ah... How strange...'

It was immediately apparent the envelope with Ben's card inside it was no longer there.

My suspicious mind flew directly to the newspaper-reading Egyptian who'd answered Ben's knock on Madam

Gadalla's door yesterday, and a hard knot of certainty formed about how our uninvited visitor had known how to find us last night.

Freya pulled at my sleeve, much more interested in her own predicament. 'Can we ask him about my hotel reservation?'

We'd agreed Ted would do this, since he speaks fluent Arabic. Mohamed's English was good, but probably not of a sufficient standard to understand our questions about the mysterious reservation-that-wasn't.

Ted stepped forward and pushed his glasses up onto the bridge of his nose. Whilst I couldn't follow his words, I knew he was asking Mohamed if he could tell us anything about a booking we believed to have been made by Madam Gadalla a month or so ago for a guest by the name of Freya Paige. Mohamed looked at Freya and nodded his understanding. It was clear he remembered her from yesterday, and the absence of her reservation at the point of check-in.

He ceased his tut-tutting over the missing envelope and turned his attention to his computer. We waited while he punched a few keys on his keyboard and clicked away on his mouse with a small frown on his face.

'Ah yes,' he said at last and his expression cleared. 'It returns now to my memory. Yes, Madam Gadalla did come to this desk and make a booking. But only a few hours afterwards her nephew came back and gave instructions for it to be cancelled.'

'Her nephew?' I queried, looking first at Adam, then at Freya. 'Freya, did your grandmother have any other children besides your mother?'

'No, she was an only child.'

'So, we seem to be left with a son of Rosa...' I deduced, '...the one Madam Gadalla mentions in her letter, but tells you she doesn't wish to speak of.' I turned back to Mohamed. 'Does Madam Gadalla's nephew live here at The Winter Palace too?'

'Oh, no ma'am. But sometimes he comes to visit his aunt. I recognise him and his brother.'

Two Egyptian men, I thought, once again reminded forcibly of the pair from yesterday; although they were much younger than I might reasonably expect nephews of such an elderly lady to be. 'Were they here yesterday?' I asked quickly. 'Over by that pillar, reading newspapers?'

Mohamed gave me a rather confused look. 'Oh, no ma'am. Only one of Madam Gadalla's nephews was here yesterday. He's the famous one - the writer who yesterday gave the lecture. This lecture you all attended, yes? His name is Nabil Zaal.'

I could feel myself growing more intrigued and bewildered by the moment. 'Was Nabil Zaal the one to cancel the reservation that Madam Gadalla made for Freya Paige?'

'Oh, no ma'am. That was the other nephew, the brother of the famous one. His name is Ashraf Zaal. He is more often here in Luxor to visit his aunt. The famous nephew lives today in America.' He looked incredibly proud to know so much.

'And is Nabil Zaal still here? Is he perhaps staying at The Winter Palace?'

'Oh, no ma'am. He left yesterday for Cairo at the end of his lecture. He was only with us here in Luxor for a very brief visit on this occasion. I believe he plans to give a similar lecture at the Mena House Hotel near the pyramids.'

We all stared at each other in consternation. Ben stepped forward, 'Mohamed, thank you; you've been most helpful. We're here this morning to visit Madam Gadalla, at her invitation I might add. Would you be so kind as to telephone to let her know we're here, or should we go straight up and knock on her door?'

For the first time Mohamed looked at the five of us a bit dubiously. Perhaps the magical effect of the sweetener Ben had given him yesterday was starting to wear off. 'It is quiet now,' he said with a quick glance around the empty lobby. 'I can accompany you to see if Madam Gadalla is available to see visitors.'

With a gracious inclination of his head, he stepped out from behind the reception desk and led us across the vast entrance hall towards the staircase. We trooped up in a parody of our climb yesterday.

Ben and Freya had both brought their letters with them, by way of introduction or calling cards. They led our approach along the wide corridor to the familiar door, each holding their letter in hand ready to show.

The sense of anti-climax when Mohamed's rap went unanswered was perhaps unsurprising. Somehow I think I'd already guessed Madam Gadalla wasn't there. I'm not sure whether I was relieved or disappointed to find the young Egyptian man from yesterday was equally absent.

'Mohamed, there was a young man here yesterday. He answered the door but refused to let us in. Do you know who he was? I'm guessing he was too young to be Madam Gadalla's nephew Ashraf Zaal.'

He shook his head. 'No ma'am. This person I do not know.'

We all looked at the closed door, at a bit of a loss for what to do next.

I could feel a strange sense of foreboding creeping over me. I didn't feel at all happy about Madam Gadalla's safety. 'Mohamed, I know this may be a strange request, but are you able to check inside the room? We can wait outside here in the corridor. It's just I'm a bit concerned that you haven't seen Madam Gadalla since yesterday.'

Perhaps he shared my sense of unease, because he raised no objection. 'I will find the housekeeping manager,' he offered. 'This person will have a key. We clean and service Madam Gadalla's suite every day.'

We hung around a bit uncertainly in the corridor while the housekeeping manager was duly summoned. Every now and then one of us approached the door and pressed an ear against it, hopeful for any sound from within. But all was silent.

Eventually the housekeeping manager arrived with the key. He looked a bit askance at the five of us loitering in the corridor and generally making the place look untidy, but at a few murmured words from Mohamed he did as he was bid and opened the door.

I would have given anything to follow him into the room for a good old nosey round. But this was clearly inappropriate. All I managed was a sneak peak as the door opened then closed behind him as he entered. I glimpsed an elegant room, stuffed with rather heavy old-fashioned looking furniture, and an ornate mantelpiece lined with black and white photographs and what looked like glass bottles.

It only took a few moments before the door re-opened and the housekeeping manager re-joined us in the corridor. I was reassured at once by the normal look of him that he hadn't come across anything untoward inside. I'd had horrible visions of the old lady lying dead in her bed. But all he could do was shrug and confirm what we already knew. Madam Gadalla wasn't there, and neither was anyone else.

But then he looked at Mohamed and added something in Arabic. We all looked at Mohamed for a translation.

'It seems Madam Gadalla may have been gone for some time,' he said. 'Her bed was not slept in last night and the fresh towels brought yesterday have not been used.'

I watched the housekeeping manager turning the key in the lock to secure the door feeling distinctly uneasy. 'Is it possible Madam Gadalla travelled to Cairo with her nephew Nabil Zaal for his lecture there?'

'Oh, no ma'am,' Mohamed assured me. 'I made the taxi reservation personally to take Mr Nabil Zaal to the airport. And I instructed the porter to assist him with his luggage. I can be quite sure he travelled alone.'

We all stared at each other. There really was only one conclusion we could draw. Madam Gadalla had disappeared.

Chapter 7

'Merry, why are you so determined to see something sinister in all of this?' Adam asked, and I could see he was frowning slightly behind his sunglasses.

We'd come into the grounds of The Winter Palace for a drink at the outside bar overlooking the swimming pool. Despite the abortive main purpose of our visit, Freya seemed reluctant to leave, as if Josh might put in an appearance at any moment and she didn't want to take the risk of missing him. Adam and I had come to the terrace bar to give our order for sweetened lemon juice all round (it's wonderfully refreshing on a hot day) while Freya, Ben and Ted took a stroll around the botanical gardens that constitute the grounds of the old hotel. The gardens are full of rare plants and almost-century-old-trees; a welcome respite of lush and tranquil greenery full of birdsong in the noisy dust-pot that is Luxor. I think Freya was secretly hoping to find Josh camping out el fresco in the shrubberies. In this wish, I felt sure she was destined to be disappointed. For one thing, had Josh taken it into his head to make temporary camp in the Winter Palace gardens, I was pretty certain one of the gardeners would have discovered him by now. The hotel employs a veritable army of them. But, perhaps more to the point, I couldn't help but think that if I were a young twenty-something man in Josh's situation, having suffered the trials and tribulations of yesterday, I would most likely have spent last night drowning my sorrows in a local bar and would right now be sleeping off a hangover in one of Luxor's cheaper hostelries.

I looked at Adam's frowning face and answered his question with one of my own. 'Don't you think it's odd that Madam Gadalla should disappear at the precise moment Ben and Freya both arrive in Luxor?'

'Perhaps she doesn't know they're here.'

'Oh yes, I'm sure she does,' I countered. 'For a start, she invited Freya to come at the beginning of April, which is now. And Nabil Zaal's lecture was on a fixed date. Always presuming it was in fact Madam Gadalla who mailed the poster to Ben's father's address, then she would have known exactly when to expect him. Add to that the fact that Ben announced himself and where he was staying in stentorian tones loud enough to wake the dead when he knocked on her door yesterday – and I'd swear she was inside – then I'd say she knows for sure he's here. Oh, and I'd put money on her being on the staircase yesterday, watching the little firework display Freya and Josh treated everyone to.'

His frown deepened. 'So why didn't Madam Gadalla make herself known to them? It seems very strange to me.'

I matched his frown with one of my own. 'I wonder if that whole thing about Freya's lack of a reservation might have put the wind up her. Maybe Freya being turned away at the point of check-in was the first Madam Gadalla knew about the booking she'd made being cancelled. She must have realised someone had intervened. If she really did feel she was being watched, I can imagine that putting the frighteners on her. And, of course, when Ben knocked on the door, that young Egyptian man was in her room; so perhaps she felt it might be unsafe to acknowledge him.'

'You're still determined to see those two Egyptians as suspicious?'

'Well, yes. The more I think about it, the more I think there was a watchfulness about them that was a bit unnatural. They saw Freya's scarab, too. And if Josh wasn't the one to steal it, then my money's on one of them. Somehow I can't quite imagine little old Madam Gadalla hitching up the skirts of her niqab to pay a trip to the riverbank on a moped to steal back something she gave away freely.'

'Ah, you heard the moped too, did you?'

'Yes, it was no casual thief. Whoever it was knew exactly what they were looking for, and precisely where to look for it. Ben not only announced where he could be found for Madam Gadalla's benefit; he told that young Egyptian too. And the Egyptian's chum saw us whisk Freya off with us in the taxi. As I said to Josh, most of the taxi drivers in Luxor know how to find the *Queen Ahmes*. I don't imagine it would have been too difficult for one of them to slip behind the reception desk in a quiet moment and pilfer the envelope Ben left with Mohamed.'

'It all seems a bit surreal to me,' Adam said. 'I mean, why should Madam Gadalla go to the trouble of writing to two almost complete strangers in England about King Farouk, the scarab and – in Ben's father's case - the Dead Sea Scroll, when she has a nephew in Nabil Zaal who's made a career out of linking the Bible to Pharaonic Egypt and who would probably give his right arm for the evidence she's alluding to? She could surely take him into her confidence without the need for all the cloak and dagger stuff. It doesn't make any sense.'

'I agree. And I think that's part of the mystery. There's obviously more to this whole thing than meets the eye. I'm sure there's a clue in those letters she sent to Ben and Freya. I just haven't been able to put my finger on it yet. But there's something in what she wrote that struck me as not quite right. It's been niggling away at me, but always just out of reach. It's driving me nuts.'

He took off his sunglasses, folding them up and putting them on the blue and white checked tablecloth. Then gazed across at me with a soft and, to my way of seeing it, rather sad-edged smile. '*Mystery*, Merry? *A clue*...? Are we back on another quest to solve a puzzle and see where it leads us?'

I looked back at him a bit uncertainly, not sure how to interpret his expression. 'Does it bother you?'

He let out a small sigh. 'No, it's not that. If there's a Dead Sea Scroll hidden away somewhere that links Biblical figures to the pharaohs of the 18th Dynasty, then I'd muscle my way to the front of any queue to see it. And I can see the whole thing's got you transfixed. It's quite clear you thrive on this sort of thing.'

'And you don't?' I was thinking of the Boy's Own spirit of adventure he'd shown on some of our previous exploits.

'Well, yes; I won't deny it's got my interest piqued,' he admitted. 'But I'm not sure I'm ready to dive back into detectival waters quite so soon. It's hard to explain it, Merry, especially with you looking at me like that, but these last few months while we've been getting the *Queen Ahmes* kitted out have felt like an idyll. Don't get me wrong; I knew it couldn't last forever. But there's been something rather wonderful about it – just you and me together, and our dream of sailing up and down the Nile. I always knew we'd have to have other people along; I mean, we're hardly going to turn it into a thriving business enterprise with just the two of us on board. But I'm not sure I expected our very first fee paying guest to be a sharply-dressed and silver-tongued Englishman who'd turn up and offer you the chance at another tantalising mystery to solve in return for his board and lodging.'

I stared at him. 'Is that why you've been a bit cool with Ben? Are you jealous?'

Adam grinned at me a bit goofily. 'Damn! Have I let it show? I'd hoped I was a bit less obvious than that. I don't like to think I'm submitting to the clutches of the green-eyed monster, but I have to admit I've not found it easy sharing you over these last few days since Ben turned up with his letter. I wish I could promise you a fresh mystery to solve every few months as we sail up and down the Nile, but the truth is, it's just going to be me, and the tourist sites. I hope it can be enough for you, Merry.'

If this weren't Egypt, where public displays of affection are frowned on, I'd have launched myself at him and demonstrated just how passionately I believed he and the *Queen Ahmes* were everything, and more, I could ever want. But this being Egypt and, mindful of the tender and conservative sensibilities of the watching waiters and the pool attendant sitting under an umbrella at the top of his ladder-chair, I restricted myself to some less effusive reassurance, reaching across the table to squeeze his hand, but putting as much feeling into it as I was capable of. I made a mental note to leave him in no doubt of how much he meant to me when we returned to the privacy of our cabin on board the dahabeeyah later.

The truth is, I found his admission of insecurity incredibly attractive, and loved him all the more for it, if that's possible. I've never been one for the type of man who's forever flaunting his machismo. Adam's sensitive and rather poetic soul is far more my cup of tea. Added to the daring and downright bravery I'd seen him display on more than one occasion – performing daredevil rescues on jagged clifftops and, on one never-to-be forgotten occasion, saving a hapless maiden from the jaws of a deadly crocodile – I'd say it's a pretty intoxicating mix. He has me heart, body and soul; but a little bit of vulnerability is never a bad thing in a man. And this proof that he didn't take me for granted just served to increase my sense of how incredibly fortunate I am to have found my soul-mate.

Suffice it to say by the time the others re-joined us and our lemon juice was served, my wicker armchair was butted up as tight as it would go against Adam's and we were grinning foolishly at each other, once more completely at one.

'No sign of Josh?' I managed to make a question out of this statement of the staringly obvious.

Freya wrinkled her brow worriedly, and I felt a pang of guilt for my own personal happiness in the face of her patent anxiety. 'No. He's still not answering his phone or responding to any of the messages I've sent him.'

Ben smiled at her 'I'm surprised your fingers aren't worn to the bone with all the texting you've been doing.'

'Maybe our paths crossed on the way here,' I suggested, trying to look on the bright side and keep Freya's spirits up. 'We'll probably get back to the *Queen Ahmes* to find him loitering on the causeway keeping company with the stray cats. I'm sure it's a simple misunderstanding, Freya. Maybe he forgot to charge his mobile, and it's run out of battery life. There's sure to be a straightforward explanation.'

She sipped her lemon juice looking hopeful, as if she desperately wanted to believe me. 'I should never have flounced off and left him like that,' she murmured. 'I'll never forgive myself if something's happened to him.'

So much for cursing him to Hell, I thought archly (and not for the first time).

'Nothing's likely to have happened to him,' I assured her. 'Egyptians are some of the friendliest people in the world – a bit 'in-your-face' with tourists, I'll grant you; but, honestly, they have hearts of pure gold. Josh will be fine, as I'm quite sure we'll see for ourselves later.'

'In the meantime, there's the mystery of the missing Madam Gadalla to ponder,' Ted said.

'Yes, Merry and I have been doing exactly that,' Adam nodded, putting his sunglasses back on again.

'I can't help but wonder what, if anything, Nabil Zaal might know about the story of the Dead Sea Scroll and the scarab,' Ted went on. 'Considering it's his aunt who claims to know the whereabouts of one, and was in a position to package up the other and send it to England, I'd say it raises all sorts of questions about where he got the inspiration for the career in alternative history he's made for himself.'

'His mother must be the mysterious Rosa referred to in Freya's letter,' Ben added. 'And mine makes it clear King Farouk showed the stolen Dead Sea Scroll to all three of his 'fancies', which must surely mean the three sisters – so it's always possible Nabil Zaal's mother said something to him that got him started.'

Freya wrinkled her nose and said, 'Yes, but she didn't have the evidence; and she may not have known about Madam Gadalla's claim to know where the scroll is hidden. So all she had to go on was what King Farouk showed them all those years ago.' She tilted her head to one side as she concentrated on trying to slot together the pieces of the puzzle we had so far.

'Nabil Zaal must have got wind of his aunt's claims,' Ben added.

'But surely he saw her sitting at the back of the room for his lecture the other day,' Ted frowned. 'I find it hard to believe he could have carried on as he did in the face of all that ridicule if he had even the smallest suspicion that his aunt might possibly have access to evidence that would silence his doubters once and for all.'

'It's a right old mystery, that's for sure,' Ben said, draining his glass and returning it to the table top with a bit of a thunk.

I looked across at our companions. The truth was it was Ben and Freya's mystery, not ours. Adam, Ted and I couldn't lay any sort of claim to it except by association – which made this rather different from our previous adventures. So I suppose I could kind of see where Adam was coming from in what he'd said earlier. It made me wonder a bit about our two houseboat guests, and what had drawn them to Egypt beyond the obvious invitation extended in Madam Gadalla's letters. Freya, I felt, might be on a search for family. It was obvious she missed her grandmother with a pure and heart-touching grief and, having lost her parents so young, I felt she might be looking for a sense of somewhere to belong, somewhere she had roots. Ben was somewhat more complex to work out. Sure, the letter his father received was intriguing, particularly to anyone with more than a passing interest in Egyptology or the Bible. But I sensed Ben was here more to find out about a chapter in his father's life as a younger man caught up in a slice of modern history than out of any specific desire to prove Joseph of the Bible and Yuya of the mid 18th Dynasty Pharaonic court were one and the same, or that any of the other key Biblical patriarchs were in fact ancient Egyptian pharaohs. I agreed with Ted, the one with that particular passion was Nabil Zaal, but I really couldn't begin to guess how, if at all, he fitted into the picture.

'It seems to me we've struck a bit of a dead end,' Adam said. 'Madam Gadalla seems to have vanished into thin air. Beyond waiting for Mohamed to contact us if she reappears, I don't really see what more we can do.'

'I still wonder if perhaps you're right in what you suggested earlier, Merry,' Ted said, 'Perhaps she's gone to Cairo to see Nabil Zaal's lecture at the Mena House.'

'Then I don't think much of her manners,' I muttered. 'It's very rude to disappear off somewhere else just as her invited guests arrive in Luxor. No, I'm not sure she's done that. It seems highly illogical – unless she was genuinely fearful for her safety and thought getting away from here was the only way she could protect herself. It makes me wonder if we shouldn't perhaps ask Walid or Shukura to attend the lecture in Cairo, just to see if she shows up. They're friends of ours who live in Cairo,' I explained for Ben and Freya's benefit.

'You know, that's not a bad idea,' Ted nodded.

'But, for now, I see nothing for it but to head back to the dahabeeyah.' I caught Freya's little look of panicked concern and hastened to reassure her. 'If Josh comes looking for you here, Mohamed knows to redirect him to the *Queen Ahmes*. Give him time, Freya. He'll turn up. You'll see. I really don't think we can sit about here all day on the off-chance that either Josh or Madam Gadalla will suddenly re-appear.'

So we paid for our drinks, strolled back through the beautiful gardens and made our way through the hotel lobby and out onto the Corniche, where the taxi driver was obligingly waiting, enabling us to politely but firmly fend off the caleche drivers and pedlars of dubious goods who immediately made a beeline for us as we descended the red carpeted stairway.

The taxi driver deposited us on the riverbank above the jetty where the *Queen Ahmes* was moored. It was immediately apparent as we made our way carefully down the crumbling stone steps onto the causeway towards the dahabeeyah that something was pinned to the door, which Adam had carefully locked behind us earlier when we left for our trip into Luxor. I spotted it first, since Adam was preoccupied helping Ted to negotiate the potentially lethal steps. I made a mental note to fix a railing before our offer of Nile cruises for discerning travellers got underway for real. Egypt is not the most health-and-safety-conscious of countries. It's fair to say access onto cruise boats up and down the length of the Nile is usually via ridiculously steep and often crumbling stone steps. It would be all too easy for an unwary guest to miss their footing and have a nasty fall. I was determined to offer something less hazardous. Inflicting broken bones on our guests would not be an auspicious start to our business venture – or to their vacation for that matter. And I should imagine the companies stumping up for a claim on their holiday insurance policies might take a pretty dim view of it too.

Freya spied the note almost at the same moment I did and jumped eagerly down the last few steps. No need to concern myself about the prospect of *her* turning an ankle, I noted ruefully.

'It must be from Josh,' she cried, skipping along the causeway and down the gangplank, which Adam had left lowered for our return.

It was a single sheet of paper, secured to the door with a brass drawing pin. Her face fell as she removed it from the door and unfolded it. 'Oh! It's not from Josh,' she declared, and handed it to me.

I squinted at it in the sunlight as the others joined us on the gangplank.

'Let's get inside,' I suggested. 'We can read it in the cool.'

The air-conditioned interior of the *Queen Ahmes* was a welcome respite from the bright white heat outside. I made myself comfortable on one of the sofas and started to read aloud.

'"It is good that you have come. I am impatient to see you. But it is not good for us to speak openly. I ask that you meet me where we can talk unobserved. Come this afternoon at three o'clock. I will be waiting with the monkeys at the doorway of the mighty bull in Wadi-al-Gurud. Watch that you are not followed."' I looked up and met Adam's eyes. 'That's strange; it's signed with the initials 'WV'.'

'WV?' he repeated. 'Not FF?'

I shook my head, frowning.

'And yet, surely it must be from our mysterious correspondent Madam Gadalla,' Ben said, scratching his temple. 'She must have helped herself to the envelope I left for her after all, just without that receptionist chappie Mohamed noticing. Where's she suggesting we should meet her? In Luxor zoo?'

I looked at Adam. 'I wasn't aware Luxor had a zoo.'

'It doesn't,' he confirmed, tilting his head to one side and frowning. 'No, I think the initials 'WV' stand for the Western Valley, near the Valley of the Kings.'

'That seems a rather odd choice for a clandestine meeting,' I remarked. 'Very remote, and not very comfortable.'

'Perhaps remote is exactly what she's hoping for. I would think a tomb might fit the bill perfectly. Although I'll grant you there's unlikely to be anyone on hand to serve tea and cake, as would have been the case at The Winter Palace.'

'You've lost me,' I said. 'Who said anything about a tomb?'

Adam gazed at me. 'It's where the references to monkeys and a mighty bull are pointing. The Western Valley, which branches off in a different direction from the main canyon that contains the Valley of the Kings, is known in Arabic as *Wadi-al-Gurud*, which translates as "Valley of the Monkeys". It got the nickname on account of the numerous representations of baboons in several tomb paintings found within the wadi – or valley. One of them is that of Amenhotep

III. My guess is it's the entrance to his tomb that she proposes for this meeting.'

'There's a certain sort of logic to it,' Ted offered. 'Amenhotep III was the one who issued the marriage scarabs, announcing his betrothal to Yuya's daughter, Tiye – probably very similar to the scarab stolen from Freya last night. He's the pharaoh Nabil Zaal would have us believe is one and the same as King Solomon. But I was under the impression the tomb of Amenhotep III was closed to the public. I'm pretty sure a Japanese expedition has been undertaking cleaning and conservation work there for many years.'

I stared down at the sheet of paper in my hand, feeling a prickle of unease. 'So if we take this note at face value, we're supposed to believe Madam Gadalla will be waiting at the entrance to his tomb at three o'clock this afternoon, are we?' I frowned. 'It sounds decidedly dodgy to me.'

'You don't think it's from Madam Gadalla?' Adam's eyes narrowed on my face.

'I'm not sure I know what to think. It has the distinct feel of a trap about it, that's all. I mean, don't you think it's a damned odd place for a little old lady who suffers with rheumatism to choose for a meeting, no matter how cloak and dagger she might be trying to be?'

Ben frowned at me. 'So if not Madam Gadalla, then who?'

I turned my head to look at him. 'Well, I'm guessing it wasn't our mysterious disappearing letter writer who stole Freya's scarab last night. It strikes me there are others with an interest in your being here. And, let's face it; those two young Egyptians could equally well have helped themselves to that envelope from behind the reception desk. We obviously weren't explicit enough in instructing Mohamed to keep it on his person.' I looked up at him and shrugged. 'Whether this note is intended for you or Freya, or maybe both of you, is impossible to say.'

'Why don't we compare the handwriting?' Freya chipped in. 'Surely all we need to do is check the note against Ben's letter and mine to know if it's from the same person.'

We all agreed this was a good suggestion and moments later had all three pieces of correspondence lined up on the bar. I lifted my head after studying them. 'Allowing for the fact that Ben's letter is written in Arabic, If the two English versions are not by the same person then somebody's gone to a lot of trouble to make the writing look alike.'

'The trouble is when an Arabic person writes in English there's a similarity in the way they form the letters,' Ben said in frustrated tones. 'I've noticed it when the French and Germans write in English, too. There's a certain distinctiveness about the lettering that marks it out as a foreign hand writing English, but it's hard to tell one from another. It was a great idea, Freya; but I'm not sure we're any further forward.'

'So it seems if we want to know for sure who sent this note and what the hell is going on we have no choice but to keep the assignation,' I said bluntly. 'Either way, we'd better get a move on if we want to have some lunch before we go.'

Chapter 8

I took it for granted that we'd all make the trip, since Ben and Freya felt like our responsibility as they were staying under our roof. We certainly couldn't allow them to go marching off into a possible trap without a protective escort. Besides, they didn't know the way to the Western Valley. Ted declined the opportunity to accompany us. He said his days of hiking over the treacherous terrain of the Theban Hills in temperatures approaching forty degrees were behind him, particularly in view of the uncertain welcome that awaited us. He proposed instead to stay behind and put a call through to Shukura suggesting that she and/or Walid might like to attend Nabil Zaal's lecture at the Mena House Hotel. I had no doubt whatsoever if he spoke to Shukura that she'd winkle the whole story out of him. I remembered the determined set of her jaw when Ted dropped his first hint about the stolen Dead Sea Scroll. Besides, I was perfectly happy for Ted to stay behind, a), for his personal safety – just in case – and b), because it meant we could contact him if we ran into any problems and he could raise the alarm if necessary.

Neither Ben nor Freya seemed to mind my assumption that we should accompany them. It was Adam who looked at me a bit askance as I packed water bottles from the fridge into a rucksack, then bent down to tie up the laces on my trainers.

'Merry, it's not our mystery,' he reminded me gently, and I glanced up to see him leaning against the kitchen counter looking distinctly uncomfortable. 'Just suppose that note really is from the enigmatic Madam Gadalla. I'll grant you it's damned odd to think of a little old lady with rheumatism hiking through the Theban hills in the hottest part of the day. But if I've learned anything at all in the year I've known you it's that all things are possible. So if we run with that scenario, she may not be best pleased if we're tagging along to make up the numbers. Surely she wants the opportunity to talk to Ben and Freya, or perhaps Ben *or* Freya, as it may be, in private, without us being there with our big ears flapping in the wind.'

'You may be right,' I acknowledged with a shrug. 'But I'm much more inclined to be deeply suspicious of the whole set up. In fact, I've been wondering if we shouldn't perhaps get Ahmed to come along. I think I'd feel a whole lot more comfortable about Ben and Freya's safety with a police escort.'

Adam's frown of unease deepened. 'And what about *our* safety? Merry, if you're right, and let's be honest, you usually are; then I can't allow us to go marching out into that wilderness of rock and sand. What if we really are walking headlong into some sort of trap? And I don't think we can ask poor old Ahmed to go putting his job in jeopardy yet again.

He's not long been back at work after his sick leave from the last episode we involved him in.'

'He got *himself* tangled up in that,' I reminded him with some heat. '*We* didn't invite him to tag along. Besides, since when did you become so risk averse? What happened to the devil-may-care man who fantasised about being Indiana Jones? I'd have thought if there were any chance of getting a step closer to discovering the truth about the fabled Dead Sea Scroll you'd be willing to take a gamble on the possibility of a trap. We're alert and ready for it and we can leg it at the first sign of trouble, even without Ahmed acting as bodyguard.'

He stared at me, and I realised I'd raised my voice at him for the first time ever. 'Oh God, I'm sorry Adam.' I flung myself at him and hugged him hard.

He extricated himself gently, pulled back and grinned at me a bit lopsidedly. 'You're right though. I don't know what's come over me. I just have this overwhelming urge to wrap you in cotton wool, Merry; and myself along with you. Shake me hard, and hopefully it'll jolt me out of it.' I hugged him instead but he set me gently away from him, shaking his head as if clearing it of cobwebs. 'You're right to remind me about the scroll, too. To Hell with it! We've been in some crazy scrapes before and we've faced them together and emerged unscathed. If this turns out to be a trap at least we're going in with our eyes wide open and our antennae up. And it does seem to be our only chance of finding out what the Hell is going on. But, even so, I don't think we should just take it as read that Ben and Freya are happy to have us tag along. Don't you think it might be courteous to at least ask them?'

It was a fair point and I conceded it, kissing him for good measure to seal our return to unity. Moments later I preceded him into the lounge-bar, where Freya was applying sunscreen to her forearms, which were exposed by the form-fitting T-shirt she was wearing tucked into pale blue denim jeans. Ben was lacing his feet into a pair of scuffed walking boots.

I looked at Ben's footwear in surprise; impressed he'd had the foresight to pack such sensible shoes for his trip.

He caught my glance and smiled up at me. 'My father always said the terrain could be a bit uneven underfoot around the temples and tombs. I always intended to do a little sightseeing while I'm here. So I thought I'd better come prepared.'

I nodded. 'And a good thing, too. If my memory serves me correctly, the Western Valley is accessed by a dirt and stone track that winds its way between towering rock cliffs, and it's littered with massive boulders and covered with loose scree.'

'The tomb of Amenhotep III is probably a walk of at least a mile from the car park,' Adam added.

'Freya, have you got some sturdy shoes?' I asked. 'Oh, and you'll both need hats. The sun is ferocious once you get out among the desert rocks. Now, we can come with you and show you the way, or Adam can draw you a little map – which would you prefer?'

I caught the sideways glance Adam shot me, eyebrows raised. I'm not sure my way of putting it was quite the courteous question he'd envisaged. He knew as well as I did that phrased like that, they really had little choice but to let us come along.

'You are a manipulative imp, Merry,' he murmured in my ear a few minutes later as, hats in hand and water-bottle-filled rucksacks on our backs, we followed Freya and Ben down the gangplank and into the waiting taxi, which would deposit us at the Valley car park.

I squeezed his hand, unrepentant. 'Sometimes the ends justify the means,' I demurred. 'I, for one, am very keen to find out who pinned that note to our door. Because I don't for one minute believe it was Madam Gadalla.'

* * *

The tombs in the Western Valley have been catalogued under WV numbers. WV indicates Western Valley, mirroring the KV (King's Valley) system in the main Valley of the Kings. The tomb of Amenhotep III is recorded as WV22. Adam was right; it was a walk of at least a mile from the car park near the ticket office – the starting point for visitors to both Valleys.

Tourists very rarely venture into the Western Valley, as it's located somewhat off the beaten track. There's just a small signpost, reading 'Tomb of Ay' which points the way among the barren and inhospitable rocks of the deep ravine that leads to it. Since most tourists seem never to have heard of Ay, the penultimate pharaoh of the glorious 18th Dynasty, who succeeded Tutankhamun to the throne of ancient Egypt, few bother with the special trip necessary to visit his final resting place. They prefer to follow their tour guides into the ubiquitous tombs on every sightseeing itinerary, such as those of Tutankhamun himself (which is, frankly, disappointing, being small and mostly undecorated) and of the Ramesside period, which are large and whose colours and wall reliefs are stunning and remarkably well preserved. Perhaps for this reason, we encountered not a soul as we struck out along the rocky dirt track that branched off at right angles from the tarmacked roadway leading from the car park to the Valley of the Kings. We told the taxi driver not to wait, since we had no idea how long we'd be. As he drove off in a cloud of dust and loose chippings, I was quite relieved to turn my back on the line of souvenir shops, teeming with trinket sellers waiting to pounce on unwary tourists, and enter the sun-baked canyon of mellow gold rock. But soon the desolate isolation of the place started to press down on me.

The Western Valley tomb guard was nowhere in evidence in his little hut near the entrance to the canyon between the towering cliffs. I recalled Adam and I had paid him a king's ransom in baksheesh on our previous trip, when he'd been prevailed upon to unlock the Tomb of Ay for us. But, on that occasion, the person on duty in the ticket office had let him know we were on our way. We'd come as simple sightseers on that occasion, eager to visit the tomb of the elderly pharaoh who'd played such a significant part in our recent adventures. Today the guard was nowhere to be seen.

'It really is a silent and haunting sort of a place, isn't it?' I said after a while spent listening to nothing but the sound of our four pairs of feet crunching over the scree-covered terrain.

'I imagine this is what the Valley of the Kings was like back in the days of the early explorers,' Adam remarked. 'Before it was overrun by tourists jabbering away to each other at the tops of their voices in countless different languages. Remember the ancient Egyptians believed the Valley to have been watched over by the protective goddess Meretseger, whose name translates as "she who loves silence".'

Despite the intense heat, I gave a small shiver. I found the stark isolation forbidding. There wasn't so much as a solitary blade of grass to relieve the glare of the sun off the bleached rock. Heat beat down from above and rose from below. My sunglasses and the broad brim of my straw hat were unequal to the task of shielding my eyes from the fierce glare, forcing me to squint as I tried to watch where I was going. Soon rivulets of perspiration trickled down my face and my hair stuck damply to the nape of my neck. I plodded on like a donkey, putting one foot in front of the other and trying to think cold thoughts. I wondered if the others were feeling the dizzying effects of the heat as much as I was. The torrid Egyptian summer was not even upon us yet, but out here in the rocky terrain bordering the vast Sahara, you could be forgiven for thinking it had arrived early. The merciless sun beat down from an endless white sky, turning our trek through the canyon into a test of endurance.

I wondered if Madam Gadalla, if indeed Madam Gadalla it was, had had the sense to hire a donkey to bring her into the Valley. It was hard to imagine the old lady tramping through the rocky terrain in her long black robes and hijab, no matter how acclimatised to the heat she may be. With every tortuous step I became more and more convinced it was someone other than our mysterious letter-writing friend who was waiting to make our acquaintance out here in the wilderness, despite Ben's hopes to the contrary.

Ben started out on our hike with his camera in hand. It was a proper photographer's camera, not the small pocket-sized digital variety that Adam and I used. He was taking photographs of the rock formations in the cliffs that rose up sheer and almost vertical from the valley floor. But I noticed as we penetrated further into the canyon a water bottle soon replaced the camera, which he now wore slung around his neck instead.

Freya seemed lost in some reverie of her own. She tramped forward with her head down, her face obscured by the peak of her baseball cap, not taking any apparent interest in her surroundings. She was walking behind Adam, pretty much following in his footsteps as he led the way further into the ravine. I guessed she must still be worried about Josh. I have to admit I was surprised he hadn't put in an appearance by now. When I'd first spied the note pinned to the door of our dahabeeyah, I'd also immediately leapt to Freya's mistaken conclusion that it must be from him. I was starting to find his prolonged absence a bit unsettling, especially if he truly saw himself in the guardian angel role Freya had described. Still, it was only twenty-four hours since we'd whisked Freya away from the steps of The Winter Palace and into a taxi, I reassured myself. Assuming he'd gone off in a huff after her precipitous behaviour, I guessed maybe he'd decided to let her stew for a while. Presumably he knew she was safe with us, and he knew where to find her, so I could only assume he wanted her to sweat it out a bit. Although I'm not sure even Josh could have imagined how literally she'd be doing so, with her T-shirt clinging damply to her slender frame and the tracks of perspiration visible on her dusty cheeks as she raised her water bottle to her mouth.

After we'd trudged about half a mile into the valley, Adam called a halt for a short break. We took the weight off our feet by perching on scattered boulders, drinking thirstily from our water bottles. I passed round the packet of digestive biscuits I'd brought with me.

'I wouldn't want to be caught out here in a flash flood,' Adam commented conversationally.

'Flash floods?' Freya said, looking sharply along the rock-strewn canyon as if she half expected to see a tidal wave rushing towards us.

'It rains here?' Ben said in a disbelieving tone of voice, shading his eyes, tipping his hat back and craning back to peer up at the endless empty sky.

'Not often, but on the rare occasions when it does it can be quite heavy,' Adam nodded. 'The ground's so dry it can't absorb the water, so it rushes through the valleys between the rock in great rivers of mucky, debris-filled water. Some of the tombs in the Valley of the Kings have been badly damaged by floodwater. You know, there are warnings in some of the guidebooks not to come here if a rainstorm is forecast. They tell tourists in no uncertain terms they're unlikely to survive if a flash flood races through the valley.'

'What a cheery thought,' I said, observing the pale cloudless sky and thankful for a fine outlook.

Ben glanced at his watch. 'We should get moving,' he said. 'Is it much further?'

'About the same distance again as we've already walked,' Adam advised him.

'Damned odd place for a rendezvous,' Ben muttered. 'If the note was from Madam Gadalla, I don't know why she couldn't just have hung around the dahabeeyah until we got back. This seems unnecessarily arduous. It strikes me a man could expire out here in this wilderness and be a dried out husk before anyone discovered him.'

I had some sympathy with his point of view. The sun raked at my shoulders through my long-sleeved cotton top, and as I slid off the rock I'd chosen to rest on and trudged forward again sharp stones prodded my feet, even through the soles of my trainers. I wondered how Freya was faring in her little lace-up plimsolls, the most sensible footwear she'd brought with her. In fairness, she'd been expecting to make Madam Gadalla's acquaintance in the refined luxury of a five-star hotel, not this rubble-strewn furnace of a place. I was forced once again to agree with Ben's muttered assessment and to wonder at the sense of our willingness to walk recklessly into a possible trap, despite my earlier bravado. But sitting about on the *Queen Ahmes* on the off-chance of something happening to shed light on things held even less appeal. At least this way we stood some chance of discovering what this was all about, and perhaps an opportunity to steal a march on things.

We trudged on through a bright white heat that really didn't lend itself to conversation. I observed Ben glancing frequently at his watch and lifting his eyes to scour the rocky terrain ahead of us.

'The tomb is just along here on the left,' Adam said at last.

We followed the natural curve in the rock, with the cliff towering above us. Adam took my hand, scanning the rocks with an avid, alert gaze. The tomb of Amenhotep III was carved into the lower part of the cliff face downwards from the valley floor. Wooden steps with a fixed wooden handrail on either side led down to a metal grille, which barred entry to the tomb itself. A cursory inspection was all that was necessary to reveal the big padlock securing the grille tightly closed. I let out a little puff of disappointment. It didn't seem likely we'd be visiting Amenhotep's tomb today. An even more cursory inspection revealed there was no little old lady waiting patiently for us in the shade of the entranceway. Nobody else was in evidence either. Ben glanced once more at his watch, and then walked backwards away from the tomb, his gaze raking the cliffs on either side. There was nothing to see except tumbled rock and the sheer, craggy face of the cliffs rising steeply from the valley floor.

'Nobody's here yet,' Freya stated the obvious. In this stark, rocky wilderness an approaching figure would have been easy to spot.

'We're late,' Ben said shortly, with a hard stare at Adam.

'Maybe our host is watching from the shade of a convenient boulder,' Adam suggested, with an equally hard stare at me. 'If that note was from Madam Gadalla, she was expecting one or two people, not four. Perhaps she observed us approaching and it spooked her to see we'd come mob-handed.'

'Shall we give her a shout?' Freya suggested.

'You and Ben can announce yourselves and Adam and I can retreat out of earshot, if you like, ' I nodded, even while I glanced around at the massive rocks that littered the valley floor and the foothills all around us with a growing sense of unease. The feeling of being watched was overwhelming.

'We'll wait,' Ben decided in a tone that brooked no argument. 'Perhaps she's just been delayed.' His determination to cling to the belief it really was Madam Gadalla who'd set up this rendezvous was quite touching, however far-fetched it might yet prove to be.

Adam and I retreated a little distance to perch side by side on a wide rock, conveniently set in the deepest part of the shade. We availed ourselves of our water bottles once more, and I munched my way through another couple of biscuits, telling myself perhaps I was wrong to have sensed eyes observing us. We had a pretty clear view along the track in both directions and were bound to see someone approaching. I reminded myself firmly that keeping this assignation was surely our best if not our only chance of finding out what was going on.

We waited; five minutes, then ten.

I looked uncertainly at Adam. 'Could we have mistaken the meaning of that note? Is there anywhere else in Luxor where monkeys and mighty bulls might have any relevance?'

'None that I can think of,' he shook his head. No, I'm certain this is the place. Why else the initials VV?'

I shrugged and gave up the speculation. I watched Ben sitting tensely on his own rock near the tomb entrance. He looked about as relaxed as a coiled spring and his frequent glances at his watch betrayed his growing impatience. Freya sat on a smaller rock a little way away from him with her legs crossed at the knee, fidgeting and picking at her fingernails, one foot jerking up and down. I glanced back at Ben, sensing his growing agitation and suspecting he was on the verge of losing his temper and suggesting we'd come on a wild goose chase and should head back to the dahabeeyah. Looking at him, I caught the movement when his straight, muscled body went suddenly rigid and his head snapped upwards, his gaze focused on something. I followed the line of his sight, and I saw it: the flash of sunlight catching on metal among the rocks on the slope behind the tomb. Adam must have seen it at the same moment. Suddenly I wasn't sitting perched comfortably on top of the rock anymore. I was being dragged urgently behind it and flung down onto the sand, spilling biscuit crumbs as I went. Adam's taut body landed on top of mine. The breath left my body in a great whoop as I felt myself pinned down beneath him.

Just in time. I heard the inarticulate shout of a male voice. And then what could only be a gunshot, although I'd never heard the sound in real life before. It shattered the limpid heat of mid-afternoon and ricocheted off the towering valley cliffs in a seemingly unending echo that finally died away into silence only to be replaced by an even more horrific sound. Freya was screaming at the top of her lungs.

'What the...!' Adam scrambled off me and jack-knifed up so he could peer across the top of the rock. 'My God! Ben's hurt!'

I pushed myself up alongside him and gingerly raised my head from behind the rock so I could see. There was no point congratulating myself on the accuracy of my sixth sense. I'd anticipated some sort of trap, but not danger exactly; and certainly not an armed ambush. Freya was crouched alongside the small boulder she'd previously been sitting on. She was holding the sides of her head, with her hands over her ears, almost as if she wanted to drown out the sound of her own screams. They echoed down the canyon in the way the gunshot had just done. Her staring eyes were fixed on Ben's inert frame lying on the ground a few feet in front of her.

A wave of sickness washed over me as I saw the spreading pool of blood seeping into the gravelly sand alongside him. It was my fault. Sensing some sort of subterfuge, I should never have allowed any of us to come.

Adam started scrambling round the side of the rock.

'Adam! No!' I reached out to drag him back. 'There's a crazy person with a gun out there!' But he was already beyond my reach, crouching low as he left the protective safety of our boulder, then straightening but keeping his head down as he ran towards where Ben was lying sprawled in front of the tomb.

Heart-in-mouth, I desperately scanned the foothills and rocky slope behind the tomb entrance where I'd seen that stomach-lurching flash of gunmetal; dreading to see it again.

Adam dropped down onto the stony ground alongside Ben. I could see Ben was trying to lever himself up onto his elbows, grunting with pain and exertion. Thank Heaven! He wasn't mortally wounded then, or even unconscious. As he moved, it was clear the injury was to his left leg, a gash just above his knee. It was bleeding copiously. Adam half lifted, half dragged him backwards, trailing blood, until they both collapsed into the shady protection of another fallen rock close to where Freya was crouched.

She stopped screaming. The sudden cessation of noise left a rather eerie silence in its wake as the far-off echo of her screams faded away into the far recesses of the canyon.

I kept on frantically scanning the cliff side, looking for any sign of movement and trying to get my bewildered brain to make some sense of what had just happened. I tried to form a mental image of a little old Egyptian lady wielding a firearm, but it wouldn't come. Of course not! I'd never for a moment believed she'd left the note pinned to our door. Somebody else knew about the scroll; that was for sure. And, whoever they were – and, let's face it, I'd had my suspicions from the start – they were clearly prepared to resort to violence to meet their own ends.

Long minutes drew out tensely while we all held to our protective positions behind our various rocks. No sound stirred the silence now the echo of Freya's screams had faded away. The only movement was a hawk riding the airwaves high above us. I watched it, squinting against the white brightness until my eyes were narrow slits. High up in the vast, empty sky it hovered and dipped on wide, motionless wings. I wondered about the view it had from up there; what it could see that I couldn't; what hidden danger lurked among the boulders strewn across the cliff side.

I glanced at my watch. It was half-past three. I wondered how long we were supposed to maintain this tense stand off, but the simple fact was none of us dared move. And our assailant – or maybe assailants – appeared in no hurry to make himself – or perhaps themselves – known to us, and start dictating terms. All I could imagine was he / they thought

Ben's knowledge about the Dead Sea Scroll was greater than in actual fact it was. Perhaps our hidden sniper believed Madam Gadalla had been a little more explicit when she'd written to Ben's father than was actually the case. Whatever; the only person I was aware of who knew for sure about the letter was one half of the newspaper-reading pair, the one who'd answered her door when Ben knocked on it. I could only assume it was this same individual, or his sidekick, who'd relieved Freya of her scarab yesterday evening. But why they should want to shoot Ben was beyond my imagining. And they didn't seem in any great hurry to relieve my curiosity.

I felt physically sick with guilt. One thought kept drilling woodpecker holes in my brain. This was my fault. If I hadn't insisted on the hare-brained scheme to walk headlong into what I fully suspected to be a trap, just on the off-chance that it might enlighten us to what was going on, Ben wouldn't be hurt. Of all my reckless acts – and there had been a few – this was by far the worst. And when I considered how much worse it could be, if only our hidden assailant had aimed a little higher, I came out in a cold sweat all over.

More minutes dragged by. I watched Adam remove his shirt and tear a long rip in the back, which he matched with another until he held a strip of cotton in his hands, discarding the remains of his torn shirt. He tied a tourniquet of sorts around Ben's thigh and gradually the bleeding slowed. The puddle of blood where Ben had first been struck and had fallen was drying to a dull brown stain on the rocky ground and the trail of blood leading backwards from there to where he was now lying resembled streaks of brown paint brushed across the pebbly terrain. Freya was hunched against her rock with her knees drawn up to her chest. She was a picture of misery and fear. Thankfully our water supply was plentiful, and we were out of the full sun in the shadows cast by the cliffs and the boulders behind which we crouched.

As the hour crept past four in the afternoon the shadows began to stretch and lengthen. We still had a good couple of hours of daylight before the sun started to set, sinking out of sight behind the cliff top. The thought of nightfall made me bold enough to call across to Adam as loudly as I dared. 'Surely we're not going to stay here all night?' I knew the temperature out here on the edge of the desert would drop sharply after dark, and all sorts of night-time creatures would commence their nocturnal wanderings. Frankly, I doubted we'd last a night in the valley. I wondered how long it would take Ted to grow concerned at our failure to return, and to act upon it. I comforted myself with the thought that at least he knew where to look for us.

'You're not to move, Merry!' Adam commanded, although I'd given no indication that I intended to. 'I have no idea what's going on here, but I don't like it. We can't leave until we know it's safe. And Ben's in no fit state to hike back in any case.' He shifted up onto his knees and cupped his mouth with his hands. 'Hey! You out there with the gun! Why don't you show yourself and let us know what you want!'

There was no response, just a stretching silence. He scoured the cliffs with his gaze and shouted again, this time in a rather halting Arabic. Once again, silence engulfed the echo of his voice.

'Perhaps they've scarpered,' I called after a while. It was true the horrible feeling of being watched had gone. It seemed the four of us were alone out here. I wondered why I hadn't thought of my mobile phone before. Of course! We needed to telephone for help – always assuming my phone could pick up a signal out here in the valley.

Cursing my stupidity for not thinking of it earlier, I was reaching into my rucksack to retrieve it when an unexpected sound stopped me. My hand stilled in the motion of untying the drawstring. I darted a glance back across the top of my rock at Adam, whose head had jerked up, listening. 'What was that?'

The silence drew out as we strained our ears for any repeat of the sound we'd heard. 'I could've sworn someone said, "Help!"' I called softly.

'Me too.'

I was just starting to think we must have been mistaken, when the sound came again. It was unquestionably a faint cry for help echoing up from the place on the hillside where the gun had flashed earlier.

Adam started to scramble to his feet.

'No, Adam! It might be another trap!' I shouted urgently.

But Adam wasn't the only one to leave the sanctuary of his rock. I watched in amazement as Freya jumped up. 'Josh?' she called out frantically. 'Is that you?'

It was unquestionably a male voice, speaking English, my poor brain told me, but beyond that my comprehension failed.

'Freya?' the same male voice called back, in a somewhat sepulchral tone, from the cliffs.

'My God! Adam! It has to be Josh! But what the Hell's he doing out here with a gun?'

'Stay exactly where you are, Freya,' Adam ordered. He didn't use that tone often, but when he did I'd noticed it had the effect of eliciting immediate respect and a corresponding willingness to obey him. Freya's feet didn't move but she ripped off her sunglasses and raked the cliff side with her gaze as if she'd developed x-ray vision and could see through the fallen rocks to pinpoint her cousin's position. 'And you, Merry,' Adam issued the same instruction in the same tone to me. It stopped me in my tracks as I was about to step out from behind my boulder to join him. 'Josh?' he lifted his head towards the hills, cupped his hands around his mouth again and shouted a repeat of Freya's question. 'Is that you?'

'Help me,' came the faint cry of response.

'Are you hurt?'

'My head…'

Adam tuned to look at me and we exchanged a glance loaded with questions. 'Are you alone?' Adam yelled back.

'Yes. Please help me.'

Adam didn't move immediately. 'Have you got the gun?'

There was a short pause. 'Yes, it's here.' The voice sounded weak, as if it were taking some great effort to speak.

'Ok. Now I want you to throw it as far away from you as you can. Do you hear me? Nobody is going to come anywhere near you until you've tossed the gun out of harm's way. Can you do that?'

There was another pause. I narrowed my gaze on the part of the rock-strewn hillside where I'd seen the flash of gunmetal earlier. The sun had moved and long violet shadows now stretched across the terrain. As I watched, a black smallish object arced into the air and clattered down among the rocks, coming to rest on the stony scree close to the tomb entrance. I could see it quite clearly from where I was crouching – a hand gun then.

Freya darted forward while the gun was still in mid-air. She scrambled up into the boulder-strewn foothills with Adam hard on her heels.

As she reached the spot where the gun had been flung from, she let out a distressed cry and dropped down onto her knees.

It was enough to have me jumping to my feet. I stumbled across the uneven terrain, ignoring the protests of muscles grown cramped and stiff crouched behind my rock. It took me only a few moments to reach them. Adam, bare-chested, was on one knee, bending over the inert form sprawled on the ground between the rocks. 'He needs a doctor,' he grunted, holding his palm against Josh's perspiring forehead. 'I can't tell how badly he's hurt.'

Freya was crouched on the other side of Josh stroking his hair back from his brow and making small wordless sounds of comfort.

A single glance was enough to tell me he had a nasty gash in the back of his head. His hair was matted with blood. The smear of blood on the rock just above where he was lying suggested that's where he'd struck himself on falling. The young man himself appeared barely conscious. His eyes kept drifting closed and he seemed to have a hard time focusing them when they fluttered open again.

'What happened?' I asked stupidly, trying, and failing, to make sense of things. 'Josh can't have been the one to lure us here. He can't possibly know the Arabic name for "the Valley of the Monkeys".'

'You're right, Merry.' Adam looked up. 'But nevertheless, I'd lay odds on him being the one to fire the gun. Look at the marks on his hand. My guess would be it's his first experience with a firearm. The gun clearly recoiled in his hand and knocked him backwards off his feet. I think he struck his head on this rock as he fell.'

'You're joking!' I gaped with disbelief. 'A gun can do that sort of damage to the person firing it?'

Adam nodded grimly. 'At least to mere mortals outside of Hollywood action films. Most of the guns used in the movies have a recoil that would instantly kill the person firing them in real life. The kick back from handguns can be quite vicious – like a kick from a mule – as you can see.'

Freya looked up with a little whimper. 'But why would Josh want to shoot at Ben? He doesn't even know him!'

'And, more to the point, how would Josh get his hands on a gun?' I said darkly, taking a hold of myself and looking at the tell-tale marks in the shale and sand that suggested he hadn't been alone. There were clear signs that someone else had climbed upwards through the rocks to scale the cliff, perhaps more than one person. They would have been out of sight to those of us down among the rocks near the tomb entrance, hidden by a slight overhang in the cliff as they made good their escape. It was actually a very good spot for an ambush, with a readymade getaway route. I wondered how long they'd been in position and waiting before we turned up.

'You'd better get your mobile phone, Merry, and pray for a signal,' Adam said. 'With two wounded men to take care of, I think we need Ahmed out here.'

Chapter 9

It is, as I've had reason to note on a previous occasion, quite handy to bear wounded men into a hospital in the company of a police officer. It discourages the medical staff from asking awkward questions. This is a distinct advantage when these questions are of a nature one would distinctly prefer not to answer, as was the case right now.

Our friend Ahmed, of the Luxor tourist and antiquities police, definitely has his uses. Aside from the uniform, his sheer physical stature and girth provided a further deterrent to anyone who might have thought to probe too deeply into what actually happened.

I think it's fair to say that Ahmed was in his element from the moment he arrived in the Western Valley, sending up a cloud of dust as his police car tore along the sand-and-scree covered valley floor flanked by an ambulance. Both vehicles screeched to a stop not far from the tomb entrance, sending up an impressive spray of loose chippings; and it suddenly – and belatedly – dawned on me that we probably could have asked our taxi driver to bring us into the valley, and avoided the need for the sweaty, dusty trek through the rocky terrain during the hottest part of the afternoon. There was a roadway of sorts, for all that it was sand-blown, littered with pebbles and strewn with chunks of fallen rock.

I'd told Ahmed there'd been a shooting in the rather garbled call I'd put through to him (the garbled nature was accounted for just as much by the intermittent mobile signal, which kept breaking up, as by my inability to put clearly into words what had happened). It was quite comical to watch the way he flung his door open and used it as a cover to emerge, ducking, from his car with his own police issue sub machine gun poised and at the ready. It rather put me in mind of old Starsky and Hutch re-runs, and I was quite sure Ahmed was aware of the comparison and was playing the part of 'TV cop' for all he was worth; even if only in his own imagination. Nobody loves a drama quite so much as Ahmed, particularly if he has an opportunity to cast himself in the starring role. Police officers in Egypt routinely carry firearms. It's a sad fact (for Ahmed) that he's never had the chance to use his. There have been one or two occasions during our acquaintance with him when I'm sure he's been itching to. It's a pity he wasn't with us when Adam had his close encounter with a crocodile. A gun saved the day on that occasion but sadly (for Ahmed) he wasn't the one firing it.

Adam went forward to meet him with the handgun hanging upside down from his hand with the trigger casing looped onto his middle finger.

I'm sure Ahmed was longing to tell someone to stick their hands up, but he could hardly demand it of Adam, shirtless and so obviously ready – eager, in fact – to hand over the weapon. And since both Ben and Josh were injured and sprawled helplessly on the ground, with me tending the former and Freya the latter, it was an altogether disappointing (for Ahmed) rescue attempt.

It was actually the ambulance we were more in need of in the first instance.

While the ambulance crew checked the gash in Ben's thigh, applying a sticky-looking, bright orange substance to the wound, then lifting him onto a stretcher and into the ambulance, I led Ahmed to where Josh, semi-conscious, was still lying recumbent between the rocks and being quietly clucked over by Freya. Seeing her bright head bent so close over his, I decided the red hair must come from their fathers' side of the family. Josh didn't have Freya's mop of coppery curls. His was more of a rusty crop, just long enough for her to run her fingers through. But I noted the familial similarity between them in a way I hadn't when they'd been yelling at each other at The Winter Palace. Ahmed cast a suspicious look at Josh and then lifted his head to look up and scan the cliff-side where I was pointing. 'Ah yes,' he said sagely. 'Dere are goat tracks and footpaths across de tops of dese hills. Dis one, I think, connects dis place wid de Valley of de Kings on de odder side of de cliff top. So, I am right, yes? You do not wish dat I should arrest dis man?'

I picked my way through the familiar jumble of Ahmed's mixed and broken English. 'That's right. I think the true villain escaped.'

Ahmed frowned at me. 'But dis is de man who shot de gun at de other man, no?'

'Er- yes.' It's quite difficult answering a no with a yes. 'At least, we think so. But he hasn't properly regained consciousness, so we haven't been able to ask him any questions.'

Freya sat back. 'There's no way Josh would have taken it into his head to shoot anyone,' she declared with an air of finality. She reminded me in that moment not so much of Bambi but of a lioness protecting her cub. I had no idea she could look so fierce. She glared at Ahmed as if daring him to disbelieve her. I could almost see her claws extending. 'It's even less likely he could get hold of a gun and actually know how to use it. No, Josh is a victim of this as much as Ben is. The person you should be arresting escaped over the cliff.'

Ahmed masked his disappointment with an effort and clipped his handcuffs back onto his belt. 'Dere is no point attempting to follow,' he said sadly. 'Dey will have made good deir run away by now.'

'Get away,' I murmured automatically. Adam and I were well practiced at correcting Ahmed's appalling attempts at colloquial English.

Unsurprisingly, what was left of the evening was spent at the hospital waiting for Ben and Josh to be patched up and to see if Josh would be declared in a fit enough state to be discharged.

That Ben had suffered a gunshot wound was obvious even without awkward questions being asked – although beyond this bald statement of fact the medical staff, with one eye on Ahmed, did not comment on it. But thankfully the bullet hadn't penetrated into his flesh. Instead it had gouged out a shallow furrow in his outer thigh. The copious quantities of blood he'd shed had made his injury look worse than it was. If it was indeed Josh's first and only experience with a gun then it was amazing that he'd hit his target at all, assuming that's what Ben had been. But none of us was thoughtless enough to say so in front of Freya. Instead we all murmured our thanks to God for Ben's lucky escape. I rather felt that if Josh had aimed a little higher then Ahmed might have had no choice but to arrest him on a murder charge, despite all the circumstantial evidence pointing to him as an unwitting accomplice. So, all things considered, it seemed Josh had had a lucky escape too.

The medical team decided Josh needed to be kept in overnight for observation. Ahmed volunteered to remain with him to stand guard. I'm not sure he'd entirely given up hope of making an arrest – whether of Josh, whom perhaps he hoped might yet be tempted into a confession; or of some unknown assailant who might possibly attempt to come and finish off Josh in the middle of the night to prevent him from pointing the finger at the true culprit, I couldn't say.

But it was Ahmed himself who delivered Josh, bandaged and befuddled, to our dahabeeyah the following morning. I assumed it was painkillers that caused Josh to seem so vacant and bewildered, or perhaps the effects of concussion. But Freya's relief was palpable to see him walking on his own two feet, however unsteadily, and she drew him down beside her on the settee in the lounge-bar and allowed me to ply him with tea and biscuits before she rounded on him. I could only assume, now it was clear he wasn't about to expire at a moment's notice, that normal relations between the two of them could be resumed. 'And you accused *me* of walking headlong into trouble!' she berated him. 'You *idiot,* Josh! What the Hell have you got yourself mixed up in? You're lucky you're not languishing in some police cell!' With a not altogether friendly glance at Ahmed, she added, 'If it had been left to the police officer here, you'd have been arrested! And you owe Ben an apology. I don't think he took too kindly to being shot!' It must have been obvious, even to someone in Josh's dazed and disorientated state who Ben was, since he was sitting with his extravagantly bandaged leg up on a stool, and with the walking stick the hospital staff had given him propped up against his chair. It was true he didn't look too happy. But I didn't think his ire was directed solely at Josh. It was Madam Gadalla I'd heard him muttering bitter imprecations about up on deck last night when he hadn't thought I was within hearing range. '...old witch was the death of the old man ... and nearly been the death of me...' Freya's attention snapped back to her cousin's wan face. 'Ok, Josh! You've got some serious explaining to do!'

I rolled my eyes at her accusatory tone, but settled myself on the sofa alongside Adam, glancing around at the others, since we were all assembled and agog; and waited to hear what the young man had to say for himself.

In the event, his tale was soon told. But it was woefully inadequate in satisfying our curiosity or the need for answers to the multiple questions we had. To say Josh stuttered and stalled his way through it would be to make him sound eloquent, when in fact his narrative had to be dragged out of him virtually monosyllable by monosyllable. Perhaps this too was owing to the after effects of the painkillers or maybe concussion. He'd seemed capable enough of lucid speech when I'd first observed him engaged in verbal fisticuffs with Freya in the lobby of The Winter Palace.

For the sake of simplicity, I'll summarise the essential points of his halting narrative. To seek to replicate it word-for-word would be simply too tortuous.

After we'd left him standing 'like a lemon' on the steps of The Winter Palace, he'd fallen into conversation with a friendly young Egyptian, who happened to be out on the terrace reading his newspaper. Soon the Egyptian's friend had joined them and Josh had been persuaded to tell them the embarrassing tale of the lack of a hotel reservation at the point of check-in. Both Egyptian men were smartly dressed in Western attire rather than the ubiquitous galabeyas, they both spoke good English and were friendliness personified, so Josh was inclined to trust them. Pressed for names, Josh said his new friends had introduced themselves as Hanif and Saiyyid.

The two young men expressed some horror about the way his female companion had taken herself off with strangers, leaving him high and dry. (You have to understand, Egypt remains a deeply conservative, male-dominated culture. Egyptian women were campaigning for emancipation in Cairo even as we spoke. For Freya to have behaved the way she had and in public was seen as deeply insulting to Josh's masculine pride). Anyway, once his two new friends had established that Freya was unlikely to be in any danger from the group of English people who'd whisked her away to their dahabeeyah so precipitously – almost to the point of kidnap – they'd suggested Josh should attempt to get back the upper hand by forcing Freya to be the one to make the first move. They advised him the worst thing he could do would be to follow her. Better to let her come crawling back to him. They'd promised to sort him out with somewhere comfortable to stay for the night, and to show him a good time in the meantime.

I'd heard him accuse Freya of being gullible, but it seemed to me Josh was a walking definition of the word. Although, in fairness, perhaps that's because my suspicions had already been aroused about the two newspaper-reading Egyptians. It was hard to account for the dent Freya had made in his fragile twenty-something-year-old ego and therefore his susceptibility to a bit of male bonding and solidarity.

Indeed, he clearly did enjoy himself that evening. Hanif and Saiyyid took him to a nice restaurant with spectacular views across the Nile, and he liked his first taste of Egyptian food, although he had no idea what it was he'd eaten. Saiyyid disappeared during the meal to scout out availability of the local hotels for him. The one he found was basic, to be sure, but it was clean with plenty of hot water and, more to the point, easily affordable within his meagre budget. He thought it a bit weird when Hanif and Saiyyid also checked in for the night, occupying rooms on the same corridor as his, since he'd assumed they lived locally, but by this time he was pleasantly inebriated on Egyptian beer, having gone on to a bar from the restaurant, so didn't ask questions.

Hanif and Saiyyid were as friendly as ever in the morning, and, after letting him sleep late, took him to a local coffee shop for brunch where they also persuaded him to try the local hubble-bubble pipe. That was the last thing he remembered. Everything was a blank after that. He had no recollection whatsoever of being taken across the river from Luxor to the Western Valley or, more importantly, being taught how to use a loaded firearm to shoot at Ben. Asked how he'd been persuaded to aim and fire at Ben at all he looked sick and miserable – as well he might – and said he had no idea. He'd never used a gun before in his life and since Ben was a perfect stranger, he couldn't possibly imagine why he might've taken it into his head to wish him harm. His first memory was of waking up with a crashing headache and finding himself slumped on stony ground outside in the open air among a pile of rocks and with the bright white sky above him. The first he'd known about a gun was when Adam called out to him to locate it and toss it away from him. That, and realising his hand was bruised and swelling, and hurt like hell.

'Do you believe him?' I asked as Adam and I escaped to the kitchen to make fresh coffee and top up the teapot.

'Well I don't know enough about his character or conduct to say if the lad's an accomplished liar or not but, on the whole, and given the dangerously wobbling chin towards the end, I'd say yes, I think I buy his story.'

'So they must have drugged him with something in that hubble-bubble pipe,' I said disgustedly. 'Poor kid! But how did they get him to fire the gun if he was completely out of it?'

'He may well have been functioning pretty normally while he was actually drugged,' Adam said. 'It might be a bit like being very drunk, where you think you're invincible while you're actually under the influence, but then have a complete blackout when you wake up in the morning about what happened the night before.'

'I've been drunk,' I admitted. 'But never to the point of memory loss.'

He smiled at me a bit sheepishly. 'There were a couple of occasions back in university days when I remember waking up and being uncomfortably blank about how I'd managed to get back to my digs.'

'Never in female company, I hope,' I said, frowning at him a bit primly.

'Thankfully not, but it's not a nice feeling wondering what happened and whether any apologies might be necessary.'

'Well, being drugged might help explain Josh's rather stupefied state now. It must have been pretty strong stuff they used on him. Mixed with painkillers it would account for his befuddled brain. But there's enough in what he told us to point the finger of suspicion very firmly at the two Egyptians I saw in The Winter Palace lobby. I always thought they were dodgy.'

He ginned at me. 'And your instincts have not been known to let you down yet, Merry.'

'Josh said one of them left the restaurant to scout out hotels. I'll bet in actual fact he was paying us a little visit for the purpose of stealing Freya's scarab. He'd probably already helped himself to the envelope Ben left for Madam Gadalla with our address on it.'

'Either that or they somehow relieved Josh of the scrap of paper you gave him with the name of the *Queen Ahmes* on it.'

'Mmm, that's a possibility I suppose,' I conceded. 'But I can't say I understand why they both booked into the hotel with Josh for the night.'

'They probably wanted to keep tabs on him and ensure he didn't have second thoughts about running off to join Freya – especially if they'd already hit on the idea of using him to take a pot shot at Ben. And, if Josh is right in thinking that they live somewhere locally, they probably didn't want him knowing where. He wasn't under the influence of drugs then; so they couldn't risk him remembering the location and leading us there.'

'You think they deliberately targeted Ben for the shooting?'

Adam shrugged. 'It's only a guess. But I'm not sure Josh could have been persuaded to shoot at Freya, even drugged up to the eyeballs. While I accept the Egyptian pair may have been on the lookout for Freya in The Winter Palace that day, they've seen she's barely more than a kid. Whereas when Ben went knocking on Madam Gadalla's door talking about a letter she sent to his father, the Egyptian who opened it – be it Hanif or Saiyyid – no doubt clocked that Ben's a great big strapping chap who's far more likely to pose a threat to whatever scam they've got going. They probably felt they could deal with Freya later – or maybe counted on her being so freaked out by the shooting incident that she'd jump onto the first flight home and save them the bother.'

'So that means both Ben and Freya are still in danger.'

'More to the point, I think it means *we're* in danger,' Adam said with a frown. 'It's not lost on me that if Josh had missed hitting his target, one of us could be dead right now, Merry. That's not a thought that's sitting comfortably with me, I don't mind saying. They know where we are and, no doubt that both Ben and Freya are staying with us. I don't much like the feeling of being a sitting duck. I wonder if we could persuade Ben and Freya to check into a hotel. The Jolie Ville is nice, and doesn't charge Winter Palace prices...'

'We can't do that!' I exclaimed. 'It would be like kicking them when they're down.'

'Well we need to think of something. I don't intend just sitting about waiting for some Egyptian nutcase to put bullet holes in our beautiful dahabeeyah.'

'I blame myself for letting you go trekking into the Western Valley unaccompanied,' Ted was saying as we carried trays of fresh tea and coffee back into the lounge-bar.

'No, it's my fault,' I admitted. 'I suspected a trap and allowed us to march recklessly into it. I'm sorry, Ben; truly I am.'

It wasn't the first time I'd said this. My apologies had been heartfelt and sincere, if a little repetitive, since the hospital staff patched up Ben's wound and deemed him fit for discharge.

His response was the same one he'd given countless times already to try to assuage my guilt and assure me he didn't hold me personally responsible. 'Please, Merry; forget it. There was no reason to suspect we might be personally in danger. None of us, including you, could possibly foresee a gun attack.'

I smiled at him, feeling better. But then frustration surged again. 'And we're no further forward than before,' I complained. 'We still don't know what's going on.'

'I always thought it was a damned strange place for an old lady to choose for a secret rendezvous,' Adam muttered. 'Out there in the hills in the scorching heat. Now we know for sure those two young Egyptians are involved it's all more perplexing than ever. I just can't imagine why they'd hit on the idea of using Josh to do their dirty work for them. I mean; it was opportunistic at best! And what on earth were they hoping to achieve? If they wanted Ben dead, they were leaving a hell of a lot to chance.'

These were unanswerable questions, of course. We'd gone over and over them last night, never getting beyond the bewildered, head-scratching stage. But this time, Adam had only paused for breath, and he went on: 'I've been trying to figure out why they'd want to target Ben for the shooting.' Then he levelled a narrow-eyed gaze on our wounded guest. 'Unless, of course, you know more about the stolen Dead Sea Scroll than you've told us?'

Ben met his stare unflinchingly and for a long moment they traded glares while I held my breath, feeling more and more uncomfortable. 'You know as much as I do about the scroll,' Ben said at last in a freezing voice that brooked no argument.

I let out my breath in a long sigh. 'Well, at least we've got Josh back with us now,' I said, eager to soften the rather charged atmosphere that had sprung up. 'But we're no closer to finding out what has happened to Madam Gadalla. Where is she, I wonder?'

'That's a very good question,' Ted said quickly, seeming equally relieved, and grateful for the change of subject. He adjusted his glasses and peered at me through them a bit myopically, then smiled. 'Well, Nabil Zaal is giving his lecture at the Mena House in Cairo this morning, and Shukura promised me she would go along. So if Madam Gadalla has taken it into her head to follow her nephew to the capital, we should know about it pretty soon. Shukura promised to call as soon as it was over.'

* * *

'Oh, my dears; you should have been here to see it for yourselves! It was quite thrilling and quite terrifying all at the same time!' We could all hear Shukura's excitable tones plainly since Ted had pressed the speakerphone button on the telephone. 'Nabil Zaal had just got to the part in his lecture where he was pointing out all the similarities between Amenhotep III and King Solomon. There had already been a lot of muttering from the audience, but now it broke out into open warfare! People started openly jeering, saying Zaal had no evidence whatsoever beyond a load of circumstantial conjecturing. Then a man jumped up and started shaking his fist at the dissenters. He said there *was* evidence but it had been lost when King Farouk was deposed and exiled from Egypt. There was a stunned silence at this pronouncement, and then all hell broke loose. Nabil Zaal leapt across the room, grabbed the man by his shirt collar and shook him until his teeth rattled demanding to know what he was talking about. As you know, Nabil Zaal is not a particularly large individual, so I thought the violence of his reaction spoke volumes about his strength of feeling. When the poor chap was finally able to catch his breath and speak again, he gasped out that his father had worked at the Cairo Museum back in the late forties and early fifties, and had told him that King Farouk had somehow come into possession of an ancient parchment scroll. It was rumoured by some to be one of the famous Dead Sea Scrolls - although Farouk apparently maintained he'd bought it from an antiquities dealer. Farouk took the scroll to the museum and demanded for it to be translated in deepest secrecy. According to the man at the lecture – speaking with Nabil Zaal's hands still locked firmly around his throat, I might add – his father said it told the story of the Biblical kings David and Solomon, and made it clear they were in fact pharaohs of 18th Dynasty Egypt, no lesser personages than Thutmosis III and Amenhotep III in fact! Nabil Zaal finally let the poor chap go and this sort of strange look came over his face, and he said, "So it's true! Mother was right!" Then he started shaking the poor man all over again, demanding to speak with his father. When it transpired the old man died five years ago, I thought Nabil Zaal was going to have a heart attack or a stroke or something. He let go of the poor man he'd been terrorising so mercilessly, and then with a crash he dropped to the floor and started wheezing and panting like a freight train. Anyway, an ambulance was called and he was carted off to hospital. Honestly! It's the best entertainment I've had in weeks!' Then, rather as an afterthought, she added, 'Although, of course, I do hope the poor chap will be alright.'

Adam and I stared at each other. It was Ted who managed to set this latest drama aside and ask the essential question. 'And Madam Gadalla? Was she there?'

A soft tinkling sound came from the telephone. I took this to be Shukura's dangly earrings moving as she shook her head. 'No. I observed no little old Egyptian ladies in the audience. But, my dears, I haven't told you the best bit yet!' Shukura's voice rose to a fever pitch of excitement and we all stared back at the telephone as if she might somehow materialise right there on the coffee table. 'After poor old Nabil Zaal was carried off on a stretcher, everyone gathered around the fellow who'd dropped the bombshell about the Dead Sea Scroll and who'd now managed to get his breath back. They were all demanding to be told what else he knew. I have to say I felt bit sorry for him to begin with. First Nabil Zaal nearly shook the living daylights out of him, and now he was being mobbed. I said to myself, "I'll bet he wished he'd kept his mouth shut". But then all that changed. After a while he threw off his diffidence and seemed to quite enjoy having an audience willing to hang on his every word; almost as if Nabil Zaal had been the warm-up act and now we were moving on to the main feature.'

I could feel myself growing impatient. I love Shukura to bits; but she's almost as bad as Ahmed when it comes to stringing out a story. Ahmed himself, strangely quiet since restoring Josh safely to us, was sitting ramrod straight, filling an armchair with his bulk. With his big hands resting on his knees, he was listening with open fascination, his dark eyes snapping with interest. Nobody loves a story quite so much as Ahmed, and he didn't know the half of it yet. It dawned on me we needed to bring our police pal up to speed on the events since Ben and Freya had arrived in Egypt. There'd been no time at the hospital yesterday for more than a cursory explanation. I could see he was itching to get a full account of what was going on. I could only wish we were in a position to give him one. As it was, we were still stumbling around in the dark. And I was far too interested in Shukura's tale to break off now to attempt to put things in context for him. He'd just have to wait a bit longer. 'So what happened?' I demanded eagerly, looking at the telephone.

Shukura's voice dropped almost to a whisper, as if she knew herself to be imparting something of the utmost importance. 'Well, my dears; it seems that despite King Farouk's appeal for the translation of the scroll to be done *under wraps*, as it were, in museum circles it was an open secret that the king had come into possession of a document purported to be one of the Dead Sea Scrolls. *"Idle talk costs lives"*, as they say, and it didn't take long for the rumours to start circulating... Firstly about what King Farouk had allegedly stolen – everyone knew the Jordanian Department of Antiquities had been in Cairo with the Dead Sea Scrolls – and secondly about what it revealed about the links between the

Bible and dynastic Egyptian history. You have to remember; by this time King Farouk had frittered away his popularity. And his reputation as "the thief of Cairo" was well known. His people had turned against him. And the powers that be were looking for a way to get rid of him. Anyway, the upshot of all of this according to the chap at the lecture – his name was Ali, by the way – was that King Farouk had basically set out on a path that not only toppled him from the throne of Egypt, but also signed his own death warrant.'

'Ali believed the Dead Sea Scroll was somehow relevant in terms of King Farouk being deposed and exiled?' Ted queried.

'Worse than that,' Shukura qualified in a thrilling whisper. 'Ali believes it was the reason King Farouk was assassinated.'

Chapter 10

'Assassinated?' Ben sat forward with a loud grunt. 'He said King Farouk was actually murdered?' His cheeks flushed and a strange look came into his eyes. 'But surely that can't be right. My father always said it was gluttony that killed him!'

'Well, yes.' Shukura's voice responded slowly. 'With a larger-than-life personality and lifestyle like Farouk's, he was never going to die quietly in his sleep. But now it sounds as if there might have been more to his death than we've always been led to believe. The suggestion is that the official story might have been circulated to cover up what really happened.'

'What exactly was the official story?' I asked, being completely ignorant of all the facts surrounding both the life and death of Egypt's last reigning king. I looked at Ben in some confusion. 'You say gluttony killed him? How is that possible?'

It was Shukura who answered, speaking volubly through the telephone receiver. 'The story that circulated in the press was that on 18 March 1965, when he was forty-five, he took his latest twenty-two-year-old fancy-piece for dinner to the swanky Ile de France restaurant in Rome (he was divorced from his second wife by this stage). It was a typically gargantuan meal. Farouk, who was enormously fat by now, ate oysters, lobster and heaven knows what else. After dinner, he lit up his giant Havana cigar, only to collapse at the table. He was taken to hospital, where he was pronounced dead. It was said he'd suffered a massive seizure, apparently brought on by over indulgence in rich food combined with his colossal weight putting an unbearable strain on his critical organs.'

Ted frowned. 'But as I recall it, there were mutterings right from the word go that he'd been poisoned. The trouble was there was no clear motive for anyone to want him dead – Egypt was well established as a republic by then – so nothing came of the rumours of foul play. It sounds to me as if the people at the lecture today were just flying kites. Sure, the Egyptians wanted to see him toppled from his throne, but I don't believe they wanted him dead.'

We all swung our gazes between Ted's face and the telephone. I remarked, 'And yet, after all these years, there's talk of assassination just at the same time as rumours about this mysterious Dead Sea Scroll Farouk is supposed to have stolen are surfacing.' Thinking quickly, I added, 'It seems to me we need to find out all we can about King Farouk and his last days. In the absence of anything else, it's all we've got to go on. And it may give us some kind of lead. Heaven knows, we need one.' I felt Adam's gaze come to rest on my face and I wondered if he was about to remind me that it wasn't our mystery. But when I turned my head to meet his glance it was to find him looking at me with that same soft look of indulgence I'd seen there many times before. I smiled at him, remembering what he'd said about being sitting ducks. Our experience in the Western Valley had evidently changed his perspective on things. We were involved now, like it or not. And it was better to have something to occupy ourselves with than to sit about waiting for someone else to make the next move. He smiled back and, reassured, I opened my mouth to speak. But Ben got there first.

'Remind me why exactly King Farouk was overthrown,' he prompted. This was very close to the question I'd planned on asking so I nodded to show my interest and noticed that Adam did too. Ahmed, Freya and Josh were sipping their drinks, letting the conversation unfold around them.

Ted sat forward and poured himself another coffee from the cafetière. 'There's no question that he brought it upon himself,' he said, settling back against the cushions. 'Farouk was an embarrassment to his government. He simply didn't take the business of rulership seriously. He avoided his advisers, preferring to remain a naughty schoolboy making mischief. His reputation as "the thief of Cairo" was a prime example. Whilst his tomfoolery might have been tolerated while he was still a teenager, the gloss soon wore off.'

Shukura's voice joined in with agreement. 'Ted's right. Farouk squandered his popularity for several reasons. He was unable to end the British occupation of Egypt, and his relations with the British government were particularly tense as World War II developed.'

'His support for the British cause was notional at best,' Ted added. 'He refused to stop using his Italian servants, even when the Italians were seeking to invade Egypt as part of the fascist offence. He's rumoured to have snapped at a British Ambassador, whose wife was Italian, *"I'll get rid of my Italians when you get rid of yours".'*

'How to win friends and influence people,' I murmured.

Shukura said, 'My father once told me the people were particularly offended by his decision not to put the lights out at his palace in Alexandria during a time when the city was blacked out because of German and Italian bombing.'

Ted was nodding in a way that suggested it was all slowly coming back to him. Shukura wasn't really old enough to be speaking from memory. She'd have been a child or, at most, a teenager during the latter days of King Farouk's exile and death in Europe. It was more likely something she'd learned about in the history books or heard her parents discussing. But Ted was old enough to remember the events unfolding during his lifetime. As a lifelong Egyptologist, he had more reason than most to pay attention to what was going on in the country whose ancient history he studied so avidly. He nodded, sipping his coffee. 'Apparently Farouk was known for harbouring certain fascist sympathies. He's alleged to have sent a note to Hitler saying an invasion would be welcome. He only declared war on the Nazis under heavy British pressure in 1945, when the war was almost over and the fighting in Egypt's Western Desert had ceased.'

I looked around the lounge-bar, trying to picture King Farouk here in this very room during the lavish picnic he and his party had enjoyed on board the *Queen Ahmes*. It was hard to equate the image of the teenaged king who'd come to the throne on a wave of popularity and had spent such a happy interlude on our dahabeeyah early in his reign with the older, despised despot being described now.

'He lost further popularity with his people in the conflict of 1948 when Egypt failed to defeat the new state of Israel.' Shukura added. 'The Egyptian's army's poor performance was blamed squarely on Farouk's lack of proper leadership. It led to Farouk's most famous quote...' Even though I couldn't see her, I had the strongest impression she was making speech marks with her fingers. '"*The whole world is in revolt. Soon there will be only five kings left – the King of England, the King of Spades, the King of Clubs, the King of Hearts, and the King of Diamonds*".'

'So, he was quite a wit,' Adam remarked.

'Perhaps,' Shukura conceded. 'But the rot had long since set in with the Egyptian people. The failure in the war against Israel just added insult to injury. Farouk had already damaged his standing in the eyes of his people by his failure to do anything to alleviate the suffering when Egypt was stricken by a cholera epidemic in 1947. More than 35,000 people died, but Farouk just went on with his partying, gambling and womanising as if nothing was wrong.'

She added, 'I think the final straw was when he married his second wife in 1951. She was considerably younger than him and the newlyweds went off on an extravagant European honeymoon and gambling spree, just as the holy month of Ramadan was starting here in Egypt. Fed up with the corruption, the Egyptian people took to the streets in Tahrir Square in January 1952 in mass protests against the government. A few months later the nationalistic Association of Free Officers led the military coup which toppled the monarchy and led to Gamal Abdel Nasser becoming president.'

'Funny how history has a habit of repeating itself,' I murmured, referring to Egypt's more recent revolution that had brought down the Mubarak regime. 'The names and the characters may change, this time the Egyptian people rising up against a corrupt dictator instead of a monarch; but it's essentially the same story.'

'So what happened after Farouk was forced to abdicate?' Ben asked, steering us back to the point.

Shukura's voice filled the room. It was obvious she was thoroughly enjoying this long, gossipy chat about Egypt's last king, given the chance to lecture from a position of knowledge the rest of us except Ted lacked. 'Well, his new baby son was officially proclaimed King Fuad II, but not for long. A year later the revolutionary government formally abolished the monarchy, ending one-hundred-and-fifty years of the Muhammad Ali dynasty's rule. Egypt was declared a republic. Farouk went into exile in Monaco and Italy, where he lived for the rest of his life until that fateful night at the Ile de France restaurant in Rome. His will stated that his burial place should be in the Al- Rafa'i Mosque in Cairo, but the Egyptian government initially denied the request, and it looked for a while as if he was going to be buried in Italy. But King Faisal of Saudi Arabia stepped in and stated he'd be willing to have King Farouk buried in his country whereupon President Nasser relented and agreed for the former monarch to be buried in Egypt, not in the Mosque of Al-Rafa'i but in the Ibrahim Pasha Burial Site.'

Adam was looking perplexed. 'But I still fail to see where the Dead Sea Scroll fits in,' he frowned. 'It doesn't appear to have played any part in his being toppled from his throne despite what those people may have said at the lecture today. So I'm struggling to understand how it might have been instrumental in anyone wanting to assassinate him.'

Ben sat forward. 'Madam Gadalla's letter said he was running out of money,' he reminded us. 'So he started to sell off his cars and yachts. But when even that wasn't enough to maintain his lavish living standards, he started letting it be known that he was in possession of a pretty explosive historical relic that he was willing to sell for the right price.'

'Well I can certainly imagine how word of the scroll leaking out would have caused all sorts of consternation in certain religious circles,' Ted remarked. 'Especially since Farouk was ensconced in Rome so close to the Vatican. I remember reading one of those conspiracy theory-type books a few years ago. It claimed the Vatican was suppressing publication of the Dead Sea Scrolls because they were found to contain information that challenged Christian dogma.'

'But now they've been published that's all found to have been stuff and nonsense, isn't it?' Adam queried.

'It would seem so, my boy. But let's just suppose King Farouk did happen to have the one scroll that blew some of the tenets of Christianity out of the water. I can well imagine that may have made him an assassination target for those of a mind to be overly zealous. Especially in view of how recently thousands of innocent Jews had been killed under Hitler's religious persecution.'

I felt a shiver go through me. Like Ben and Ahmed; I was following the conversation closely. It seemed a bit lost on Freya and Josh. Freya looked a bit as if she were watching a tennis match, her head swinging from side to side to concentrate on whomever was speaking, but there was a frown on her face that suggested she wasn't quite following the ball as it bounced back and forth. Josh was staring rather vacantly out of the window, watching a man on a fishing skiff alongside the dahabeeyah slapping the water with his rod to attract the fish up to the surface. Poor Josh! I couldn't help but wonder if he didn't fervently wish he'd stayed at home instead of bullying Freya into letting him accompany her on this trip. He'd got a whole lot more than he bargained for already. And I'm not sure listening to conspiracy theories about a king who was long dead before he was born was high up on the list of things he'd really like to be doing right now.

'What I don't understand is why Farouk would have needed the money,' Shukura said. 'There's a fascinating story that while he fled to Europe in great haste and abandoned his collections of trinkets and treasures – which became objects of curiosity and ridicule, with the valuable pieces being auctioned off by the revolutionary government – he nevertheless managed to get away with crates and crates of fine champagne...'

'I thought as a Muslim he wasn't supposed to drink alcohol,' Adam interrupted.

'That's quite right, my dear,' Shukura voice resumed its usual gleeful tone. 'Apparently he drank nothing but orange juice and fizzy drinks. It's said the champagne crates were actually packed with gold bars! These represented the bulk of the fortune he was able to smuggle out of Egypt with him. They kept him in the sumptuous style to which he was accustomed for a good many years.'

Ben sat forward with another grunt. 'But obviously not forever,' he said darkly. 'And so he took a risk on the scroll; and someone took it into their head to murder him before the scroll became public knowledge. You know, my father became very agitated remembering Farouk's last days in Rome after Madam Gadalla's letter arrived. I'm guessing there has to be a link.'

I felt another shiver snake down my spine. I also felt that something significant had been said; something that snagged on that bothersome little inkling that had been nagging away at me for days – the feeling that there was something in the letters Madam Gadalla had sent to Ben and Freya that was a bit incongruous. I did a quick mental re-run of the conversation, trying to pinpoint what it was.

'The champagne!' I exclaimed.

My sudden shout brought all heads snapping in my direction.

'Merry? Was that you?' Shukura queried from the other end of the country.

'Yes! I think I've had a brainwave! Something always struck me as odd and a bit out of place in those letters Ben's father and Freya received... Have you got them with you?' I demanded of our two guests.

Ben reached into his inside breast pocket, drawing out the floppily folded sheets, which he passed via Adam to me. Freya's letter was in her cabin. But, hearing something in my tone, she immediately jumped up and offered to go and retrieve it for me.

Once she was back and seated again alongside poor, befuddled Josh, I passed both letters across to Ted. Everyone stared at me expectantly.

'There was something in the letter she sent to Ben's father about Gregory Hunter arranging for a crate of champagne to be sent to Madam Gadalla on King Farouk's behalf every year on her birthday while Farouk was in exile. Can you find it, Ted?'

Ted propped his glasses on the bridge of his nose with a forefinger and scanned the intricate loops, swirls and dots of Arabic on the sheet unfolded on his lap. He cleared his throat. 'Yes, this is the paragraph,' He proceeded to read it aloud. '"*I choose you to write to since you were the man tasked by our dear Freddy each year during your exile with sending me a crate of champagne on my birthday. Perhaps you do not recall it. No doubt it was a small administrative duty for you. But to me receiving the annual gift of champagne was the highlight of my year.*"'

'That's it!' I cried in mounting excitement. 'And I'm sure there was also some reference to champagne or her birthday in the letter she sent to Freya.'

Ted switched the two sheets and frowned over Freya's rather more pristine letter. 'Is this it? "*Freddy looked after me, you know. Yes, even from exile. He never forgot my birthday."'*

'Yes, that's it.' I stared round at my audience with as much loaded expectancy as they were viewing me with. 'Don't you see?'

'The champagne,' Adam said slowly.

'Exactly!' I pounced. 'If our Madam Gadalla is a devout Muslim lady – and she certainly has the appearance of one from the glimpses I've had of her – then what was Farouk, or Gregory Hunter on his behalf – doing sending her a crate of champagne each year on her birthday? As you said earlier, Adam, it is forbidden under the religious laws of Islam for Muslims to drink alcohol!'

He was quick to catch on. It never takes Adam long to tune into my wavelength. 'You're saying it's possible those champagne crates sent to Madam Gadalla on her birthday each year contained something other than champagne?'

'Well, if it's true Farouk smuggled stuff out of Egypt in champagne crates, it strikes me he may have smuggled stuff back into Egypt in exactly the same way – whether just as a gift for Madam Gadalla or for some other purpose, who knows? But there's something suggestive in the phrase *"Freddy looked after me"* in Freya's letter, don't you think? I don't imagine Madam Gadalla could afford the luxury of her own suite in The Winter Palace all these years on any savings she might have put by from her singing and dancing days as one of Farouk's Fancies. Those champagne crates are significant. I'm sure of it.'

Ahmed spoke up. He'd been incredibly forbearing while our conversation had batted back and forth. But now he looked as if he was about to explode with impatience to find out exactly what was going on. 'My friends,' he said imperiously. 'I think de time has come for you to tell to me what dis is all about. I am in de black about what you are talking about.'

Adam rather surprised me by being the one to sit forward to tell the tale and help poor Ahmed out of the dark. I didn't stop him since it forestalled the comment about my instincts I felt sure had been on the tip of his tongue. Ben, Ted and Freya all added a comment or two here and there. The other surprise was Josh seeming to come back to life again while the story of the two letters, the stolen Dead Sea Scroll, the theft of the scarab – both in Rome and more recently from Freya's cabin – and the mysteriously missing Madam Gadalla was told. For the first time his eyes seemed to focus properly as he listened to Adam speak.

Shukura let out a little shriek when Adam got to the shooting incident in the Western Valley. She'd never met Ben, but she made lots of clucking sounds about his injury and assured him she would pray for a speedy recovery. Hearing about Josh's part in the mishap, her cries of alarm became even louder. 'Oh, my dears, I don't like the sound of this at all!

Those two young Egyptians sound like perfect villains. I don't like to think of you being in danger.'

'I will make it my mission to arrest dese men,' Ahmed vowed, sitting up even straighter, his dark eyes flashing. 'And when I do dey are in deep trouble. It is a very bad thing when Egyptian people make crime on de tourists. I will toss de book at dem. And den I will lock dem up and throw away de key!'

I didn't doubt that he would. And he was right. The Egyptian authorities took a very dim view of their countrymen targeting tourists. These were troubled times enough in Egypt without adding a further reason for holidaymakers to stay away. Drugging and shooting at tourists were serious crimes indeed. But it did add an awful kind of credence to the story of the Dead Sea Scroll. Some people were obviously willing to go to considerable lengths to track it down ... or to ensure that we didn't.

'They used me, didn't they?' Josh said bitterly. 'And I was stupid enough to let them lead me like a lamb to the slaughter. If I ever get my hands on either one of that pair, or preferably both of them, then, so help me, I don't think I'll be responsible for my actions.'

It was the first full statement he'd made without tripping over his words or getting tongue-tied. I could only applaud this return of his mettle – although it didn't necessarily bode well for our chances of peace and quiet on board the *Queen Ahmes*. He sat there with a rather vicious-looking expression twisting his handsome young face, no doubt contemplating the various ways he'd like to even the score should the opportunity ever arise.

'I wonder how they're connected to all of this,' Shukura mused. 'And to this Madam Gadalla. You say she is still missing?'

'Mohamed, the front desk manager from The Winter Palace promised to get in touch with us if she returned,' Adam said. 'So, we can only assume she still hasn't put in an appearance at the hotel.'

'How frustrating. She seems to be the key that will unlock this whole mystery. If she really does know the whereabouts of the fabled Dead Sea Scroll, she's in possession of information people are clearly willing to kill for. Now we know she hasn't turned up here in Cairo, let's hope and pray she's somewhere safe; and somewhere those two young thugs can't find her.'

'I wish I could think of something we could *do*,' Adam said, clearly still chafing at what he saw as our current status as sitting ducks. 'There must be some action we can take to flush them out before they take it into their heads to get really nasty.'

'If you ask me, they've already taken it into their heads to be really nasty,' Josh said with feeling. 'If there's anything I can do to help, then count me in. I reckon they deserve a taste of their own medicine for the way they've treated me!'

Sadly, he immediately ruined the effect of this show of strength by turning to his cousin with a supercilious stare, 'See, Freya? If you'd only listened to me, like I begged you, we could have avoided all this! I knew that letter spelled trouble. But you had to dig your heels in and get your own way.'

She shot him a truly evil glance. 'Shut up, Josh. We're here now, so it's too late for all that. I agree with Adam. There must be some action we can take.'

Adam and I exchanged glances and I knew he was hoping these first guests wouldn't prove typical of those we might have on board our dahabeeyah in the future.

Ahmed levered himself out of his chair in one great big heave. 'No, Adam and Merry. Dis is a job for de police. Dese men, dey are dangerous. I will return to de Western Valley to check dis Madam Gadalla has not somehow been trapped out dere. And den I will make enquiries in de Luxor hotels to see if I can track down dis Hanif and dis Saiyyid.' He turned his dark, snapping eyes on Josh. 'You do not remember de name of de hotel where dey took you, or de restaurant? Someone may recognise who dey are from a description.'

'The restaurant was on the lower bank of the Nile near The Winter Palace Hotel,' Josh said with a frown of concentration. 'We crossed the road and went down some stone steps to reach it. The hotel was a bit further away. I went on the back of Saiyyid's moped to get there. I don't remember the name – but I could see the sign of another hotel from the window. I'm sure the other hotel was called Hotel Joseph. I wouldn't have remembered, only when you were talking earlier about the scarab perhaps linking to the Biblical Joseph, it reminded me. The one I stayed in with the two Egyptians was more like a hostel than a hotel, and it was down a side street.'

Ahmed moved towards the doorway. 'Ah, I know de area where you mean. I must start making my enquiries.'

Adam jumped up. 'But we can't just sit here and wait for one of those young savages to make the next move. I'm not prepared to run the risk that one or both of them might decide to pay us a visit here. They clearly know how to find us since they left that note pinned to the door.'

'But dey haven't got de gun anymore,' Ahmed pointed out. 'You gave it to me in de Western Valley, remember?' He patted his pocket with one big hand, looking satisfied.

Adam didn't look any happier for being reminded. 'How do we know that's the only gun they've got? No, Ahmed; I don't think it's safe for us to just sit here impotently and do nothing. And I'm not sure my nerves can stand it.'

I'd been watching and listening to this exchange, feeling as anxious and frustrated as Adam, even while silently applauding the return of his more action-orientated self. Like it or not, all the time Ted, Ben, Freya and Josh were on board our dahabeeyah they were our responsibility and needed our protection. I wasn't confident Adam and I could do a sufficiently effective job of it should the need arise, especially in view of the injuries Ben and Josh had sustained. Besides, I'd thought of something Adam and I could usefully do, which necessitated us leaving the *Queen Ahmes,* and I was itching to get to it. A memory had stirred and my own detective instincts were humming. Ahmed wasn't the only one who wanted to make some enquiries. I was keen to do a bit of investigating of my own.

'Ahmed, when you patted your pocket just now, was that a sign that you still have the gun with you… the one Adam gave you in the Western Valley … the one Josh used to fire at Ben?'

Ahmed's big paw-like hand went once more to his pocket and lovingly patted it. 'I do. I have not yet returned to de police station to log it as evidence in dis matter.'

I smiled sweetly at him. 'Do you think it might be possible for you to leave it here while you go about your investigative police duties?'

The frowning look he turned on me was full of suspicion and dark with misgiving. 'Mereditd, why is it dat you ask me such a thing as dis?

'I was just thinking that if a certain pair should take it into their heads to pay the *Queen Ahmes* a visit, they might think twice about trying anything on if those on board were able to wave a gun at them – as a deterrent, you understand.

I'm certainly not proposing anyone should actually pull the trigger'.

Adam eyed me critically. 'I take it from the way you phrased what you just said that you yourself are not proposing to be one of those who remains on board,' he said, with a look almost as suspicious and dark with misgiving as Ahmed's. 'Ok, Merry; what have you got in mind?'

I cast a quick glance of appeal at Ben. 'Do you think you can manage to look menacing with a deadly firearm should the need arise?'

He looked a bit shocked but recovered himself quickly. It was almost as if I'd asked him if he was a man. And for one blessed with extra helpings of masculinity such as he, I can only imagine he took my question as a bit of a personal affront. 'Of course,' he said decisively. 'But if those two Egyptian devils turn up bent on causing trouble, I won't promise not to fire.'

'I think for Ahmed's sake you'd better promise not to fire,' I frowned at him. 'Perhaps, to be on the safe side, we should remove the bullets. We don't want to lose poor Ahmed his job by re-using the single piece of evidence we have that may lead to a conviction, even if it only has Josh's fingerprints on it. Believe me, with some of the shenanigans he's been involved in during the last twelve months, he's lucky to still have it. And I think Freya and Josh have had quite enough of shooting incidents in the last twenty-four hours. Ted, I shall have to count on you to be the voice of reason.' He snapped to attention, pushing his glasses up his nose. My gaze lingered on him as another thought occurred to me. 'And I have another task for you, if you don't mind. It strikes me we could do with a locksmith over here to put locks on the cabin doors, just in case those two Egyptian crooks should take it into their heads to pay us a nocturnal visit. Do you think you could arrange that? Your command of the language is so much better than Adam's. Thank you.' Then I looked at Freya. 'There's bread and cheese and salad in the kitchen. Do you think I could put you in charge of feeding everyone some lunch? She looked as if she was about to argue, then glanced at Ben and nodded, so I moved my gaze onto her cousin. 'Josh, if you feel up to it, I suggest you write down everything you can remember from the point we left you on the steps of The Winter Palace to the point you came to after your – er – experience in the Western Valley. When Ahmed succeeds in tracking your new friends down, the police are going to need a statement from you. It makes sense to make a start while it's all still fresh in your memory. And you never know; it might help to fill in some of the blank spaces left by your blackout. Writing it all down might just trigger something you thought you'd forgotten.'

    I turned back to Adam and Ahmed with what I hoped was a reassuring smile. Ahmed was shaking his head and muttering to himself, something about riding roughshod over rules and regulations. At least, I think that was the gist of it. He didn't actually use the word roughshod. But I took his meaning. Adam was simply watching me in silence, his eyebrows tilted at an ironic angle to convey his amusement at the volley of orders I'd issued to our guests; but his lovely blue eyes were troubled as he waited for me to elucidate what I had in store for him and me.

I decided to place my faith in his own stated preference for something to do over the inertia of sitting here waiting for someone else to make the next move. 'Adam and Ahmed,' I said. 'I would like you both to come with me into Luxor. I think we need to reprise our roles as the three musketeers and indulge in a spot of breaking and entering.'

Chapter 11

'I have a bad feeling about this,' Adam's voice was deep with foreboding as we followed Ahmed down the gangplank onto the crumbling causeway.

I sidestepped a sleeping feral cat, which opened one eye and lazily observed me as I passed, and then turned on Adam with a bright smile. 'Where's your sense of adventure? Come on, Adam, it's not as if it will be the first time we've visited The Winter Palace with nefarious intent. I don't remember you raising any objections when we unscrewed the picture of Queen Ahmes from the wall last year.'

'But we'd at least had the decency to book legitimately into the hotel as guests for the night. I'm not sure that's quite the same as what you have in mind now.'

'Perhaps not,' I admitted.

'So, you really are planning on us breaking into Madam Gadalla's suite?'

I looked at Ahmed's broad back as he walked on ahead of us. 'Well, I was rather hoping we might not actually have to *break* in, as in picking the lock or smashing a window.'

He caught my meaning straight away. 'And you had the damn cheek to scold Ben about the possibility of getting Ahmed fired from the local police!' But he was grinning, so I knew I had him. He can demur as much as he likes, but I know he loves being on a quest to solve a mystery as much as I do. And as he'd already said, he far prefers action to inaction; if he can play act at being Indiana Jones, so much the better. I wasn't sure there'd be much call for him to assume his alter ego with what I had in mind for today, but one never knew. I reached for his hand, giving it a little squeeze, and we followed Ahmed along the stone jetty.

It's fair to say Ahmed had not been at all happy about handing over the gun to Ben, despite taking the precaution of removing the bullets. I deduced from the way he kept patting his side pocket as he climbed the steep steps up onto the riverbank that he felt decidedly uncomfortable to have given away his only piece of concrete evidence in this strange case, even if only temporarily. Ahmed is generally fairly happy to play fast and loose with some of the strictures imposed by his profession. I've always assumed this is his tomb robbing instincts coming to the fore. He seems to have them hot-wired into his DNA thanks to his dodgy ancestry. Ahmed is, after all, descended from one of the most notorious families of antiquities thieves ever to operate in the Theban necropolis. I've always thought this makes his current status as a serving member of the Luxor tourist and antiquities police department rich with a delicious sort of irony. But in this instance his professional scruples seemed to have the upper hand. It had taken a good deal of energetic persuasion to convince him to part with the firearm. The trouble was I just didn't see how we could abandon the others on board the dahabeeyah with no means of protecting themselves, even if it was only to use the gun as a threat rather than actually to fire it. I was confident we'd have no need of it to execute the little scheme I'd hatched. Ahmed's police badge should suffice. And he could collect the gun when we returned later and still submit it as evidence as necessary.

He drove us into Luxor in his police car, parking it in a side street, and the three of us walked past Luxor Temple and along the Corniche until the impressive façade of The Winter Palace once again stretched in two long wings before us.

'This place is starting to feel like a second home,' Adam murmured. 'It seems to me we've spent more time here than on board the *Queen Ahmes* in the last few days. We'll have to watch out or else they'll start charging us rent.'

I smiled at his little joke, knowing his nerves were starting to jump as much as mine. This time we didn't climb one arm of the sweeping curved staircase up to the entrance lobby. Ahmed was the only one who was going to enter through the revolving door. He turned to me before putting his foot on the first step.

'Tell me again what I am to say to de person on de front desk.'

'You need to stride in there with as much authority as you can muster,' I said. 'I suggest you ask to speak to the general manager to make it as official as possible. Say you're there on police business. Then tell the truth. There's been a shooting involving tourists on the west bank. You're investigating. You've interviewed both tourists who claim they came to Egypt at the invitation of Madam Gadalla, whom they understand to live in a suite of rooms here. They told you they came to call on her at the hotel, only to find that she seems to have disappeared. You're concerned for her safety and you want to search her rooms to see if there's anything that might give you a clue as to her whereabouts.' He was nodding as I spoke, committing the words to memory so he could repeat them verbatim. 'Just, for goodness sake, don't allow him to accompany you. You need him or the housekeeping manager to unlock the door for you and then leave you to it. When he's gone, and you know the coast is clear, you can come and get us. We'll be waiting in the service stairwell.'

Adam stared at me. 'You've got it all worked out, haven't you?'

'I hope so.' But the truth was nerves were like a troupe of acrobats performing cartwheels in my stomach.

'There's just one thing that troubles me.' Adam frowned.

'What's that?'

'What if those two Egyptians are back here staking out the joint? I'm not really in the mood for another close encounter with that pair.'

221

'Then Ahmed will have the perfect opportunity to arrest them,' I said with far more confidence than I felt. The truth was it hadn't actually occurred to me that they might turn up. 'I can't believe they'd show their faces here,' I was thinking on my feet. 'If they've got any sense at all, they'll lie low for a while.'

'But I got the distinct impression one of them might be related to Madam Gadalla. How else did he manage to be inside her room that day when Ben knocked on the door? Ben made an assumption he was her son or grandson, or something, and even though we now know she doesn't have children of her own, I don't remember the chap disabusing him of the idea. Those Egyptians have got some connection to her. What if they've had the same idea you have?'

I looked at Ahmed's big, burly frame. At my mention of the chance of an arrest, his eyes had started to gleam with excitement. 'Den I will snap my handcuffs on dem quicker dan you can say "You're under arrest".' He threw back his shoulders, straightened his beret, then lifted his chin and marched up the stone steps with a purposeful stride, looking every inch the smart policeman on an important mission in his crisp white uniform with black beret, belt and boots. His love of the dramatic was to the fore again and I had no doubt he would play out the role I'd given him for all he was worth – with or without the chance to make the longed-for arrests – following his script to the letter and no doubt imagining himself in some Hollywood screenplay. All Adam and I could do was place our faith in his ability to carry it off.

I took Adam's hand again and we retraced our steps along the Corniche, past the row of shops selling tourist souvenirs and on to the separate entranceway leading to the reception of the Pavilion Wing hotel, built into the grounds of The Winter Palace. It led us through a tall gateway into the beautiful gardens shared by both hotels. Nobody paid us much attention. Once in the gardens, we skirted back on ourselves and climbed the stone steps leading to the rear entrance into the Winter Palace. It brought us through another revolving door into the dim coolness of the entrance lobby, but at the opposite end of that vast space from the reception desk. One glance was enough to show Ahmed standing there, legs akimbo and with his feet planted firmly on the marble floor, his chest puffed out with self-importance. He was flashing his identity card, speaking in full throttled Arabic. Mohamed, the receptionist, looked mildly intimidated and reached at once for the telephone to no doubt summon the general manager.

'Come on,' I urged Adam. 'We don't want him to see us and put him off his stride. He's obviously giving the performance of his life.'

We'd entered underneath the ornate staircase that curved around the back three walls of the lobby. I was keen not to draw the attention of the hotel's security staff to us. So we'd dressed up for our visit; Adam in pressed trousers and a rather nice cotton shirt, and me in a pretty summer dress. I very much hoped we looked like a couple of well-heeled guests returning from a stroll around the hotel's lovely gardens. As it was, the security guard posted near the front entrance seemed engrossed in Ahmed's performance and didn't even glance our way. This time we didn't want to take the direct route upstairs via the fancy staircase. So, dragging Adam after me, we darted across the lobby and into the huge corridor on our right, lined with guest bedroom doors. The shoeshine boy looked up as we passed, still decked out in his smart red uniform and matching tarboosh. But a single glance at our footwear told him he'd get no business from us today. My strappy sandals weren't the type one cleaned with a brush. And Adam's deck shoes were made of soft navy blue suede. So he returned his avid attention to Ahmed's play-acting instead, and we hurried on our way.

At the end of the corridor a set of heavy glass panelled doors led to the staircase we wanted. Rarely used by guests, it lacked the lavish décor of the rest of the hotel. A simple uncarpeted staircase led up to the first floor, and then on up to the second. A couple of housekeeping cleaning trolleys were parked on the top floor landing. They were laden with towels and posh toiletries, and with bright feather dusters, which extended on poles from little slots in their sides. But no housekeeping staff were about.

'If anyone comes, just smile and we'll walk back down the stairs again,' I advised. 'The worst thing would be to look as if we're hanging around out here.'

'Even though that's exactly what we are doing,'

'Well, yes; but hopefully not for too long.'

'You know, Merry; I adore you and I adore your willingness to take a risk in order to steal a march on things, but I do hope you've got a convincing story lined up just in case we get caught loitering with intent.'

I pressed a quick kiss against his lips. 'I'm sure I'll think of something, should the need arise.' But his words made me realise how far I'd come – or perhaps I should say how far I'd fallen – over the last twelve months of my adventures, some might say *mis*adventures, in Egypt. A scant year ago I was accepting redundancy from my job as a communications executive with a local charity back home in Kent. The Meredith Pink who'd worked there would never have dreamed of doing something like this. I'd always been the kind of girl who paddled safely in shallow water. During this last year I'd plunged head first into the deep end more times than I cared to count. But it was impossible to regret the change. The simple fact was I'd never looked back, not for a second. True, I was treading a fine line between adventure and outright criminality, but the blood pounding through my veins and my increased heart rate made me feel more fully alive than I'd ever felt during the fifteen long years of my so-called professional career. And to have Adam as my partner-in-crime for so many of my walks on the wild side was more luck than I'd ever expected or probably deserved. I reached up and kissed him again.

'What was that for?' he asked in surprise, his arms coming round me in a spontaneous hug.

'Just thinking there's no one in the world I'd rather be sharing this with.'

'Yes, well; if we make it out of here without being banged to rights, you can show me later exactly how much it means to you to have me tagging along on these perilous exploits of yours.'

'That's a promise,' I vowed.

The minutes crawled by painfully slowly. It was hot and airless in the stairwell. I was just contemplating helping myself to a bottle of water from one of the housekeeping trolleys and wondering whether Adam and I might have to break in to the hotel laundry and pinch a couple of housekeeping uniforms and perhaps a set of keys, when a familiar bulky form loomed into view on the other side of the glass panelled doors on the second floor. I breathed a heartfelt sigh of relief and pushed open the nearest door. 'What took you so long?'

You were correct about de general manager wanting to come wid me to search de lady's room. He was very consistent.'

'Persistent,' Adam murmured with a small smile. 'But you managed to dissuade him; that is, you said no?'

'I telled to him dat I must concentrate on my work in silence because my superior officers will come down on me like an avalanche of rock if I miss a vital clue dat might help me to find her.'

'I think you mean like a ton of bricks,' Adam said mildly.

'Ah,' Ahmed acknowledged with a pause. 'Dis man, de general manager, he is very worried about de Madam Gadalla. She is a very old lady, yes? And she has made her home in dis hotel for many years. I made a promise to him dat I would report to him on my way out. So, come now. We must be quick.'

The general manager had gone one step further than opening the door for Ahmed or calling the housekeeping manager to do so; he'd actually given him the key.

We hurried into the corridor, our feet sinking into deep pile carpet once more, and soundlessly approached Madam Gadalla's door.

'I suppose we ought to knock,' Adam suggested. 'Just in case she has somehow returned without anyone spotting her.'

'De receptionist said she has been gone for perhaps three days,' Ahmed said.

'Yes, but it's possible she's sneaked back in the dead of night.' I reached out and rapped on the door. My knock was greeted with a profound silence so after a pause Ahmed stepped forward and inserted the old-fashioned key into the lock.

He gave the door a gentle shove and it swung slowly back across the carpet to reveal a room in semi-darkness. The heavy curtains had been pulled across the tall windows, leaving only a little triangular dart for light to filter through at the top.

I sucked in a deep, steadying breath, acknowledging myself as the trespasser I undoubtedly was; and then with a nervous and, I hoped, comradely smile at Adam and Ahmed, flanking me on both sides, I looked both ways along the corridor to ensure no one was watching and stepped decisively across the threshold into Madam Gadalla's private suite of rooms.

As I'd registered once before during the only other brief glimpse I'd had of the place, the overall impression was of a large, lofty room, overstuffed with bulky and rather old-fashioned furniture, from the brocade settees and armchairs to the inlaid sideboard and occasional tables all groaning under the weight of lamps, flower displays in huge vases, decorative ornamental china plates displayed upright on invisible stands; and quantities of photographs, mostly black and white and displayed in heavy silver frames polished until they gleamed even without the benefit of light.

'I see no reason why we shouldn't open the curtains,' I murmured. 'After all, the general manager knows one of us is here to search the place. I don't imagine he expects you to do it in darkness, Ahmed.'

Ahmed went across to the windows and pulled back the weighty curtains, revealing tall windows with a spectacular view across the Corniche and the river Nile to the Theban hills glowing in golden sunlight on the west bank.

'When she said she watched the Nile flow past her window, she wasn't kidding, was she?' Adam said as light flooded the room. 'What a great view.'

But I was far more interested in the photographs than looking out of the window. 'Ahmed, perhaps you'd better take a look around and see if you can spot anything with your trained policeman's eye that might give us an inkling about where Madam Gadalla has disappeared to,' I said over my shoulder as I bent over a selection of pictures displayed on a side table set alongside the settee.

He grunted and crossed the space to enter another darkened room, which I guessed to be the bedroom.

I turned back to the photographs as Adam came to join me. 'If this is Madam Gadalla, she was very beautiful as a young woman,' I murmured.

'And look; this can only be King Farouk,' Adam pointed to the figure in several of the pictures. 'These must have been taken before he was deposed, but he was already gaining a huge amount of weight, wasn't he?'

'Mm, hardly the handsome, blue-eyed boy Shukura described when he first came to the throne. The fez and the closely trimmed moustache rather accentuate his round, chubby face, don't they?'

It was fair to say Farouk appeared in nearly all the photographs, and so did the exotically beautiful woman I took to be a youthful Madam Gadalla. 'I wonder what her first name is.'

'I think I've found the answer! Here, look!' Adam pointed to a large black and white photograph of three young women posed in a row with their arms encircling each other's waists. They were dressed a bit like English debutantes, in pale, probably white figure-hugging dresses with neat, nipped in waists and skirts which swept the floor, and with sparkling tiaras in their coiffed hair. They looked to be barely out of their teens. What distinguished them as Egyptian rather than English beauties were their sultry Middle Eastern looks, accentuated by skilfully applied make-up. Scrawled across the top of the picture in black ink in a hand I recognised at once since we had a fine example of it in our old visitors book on board the *Queen Ahmes* was the message *"To my adorable fancies, Sofia, Layla and Rosa. Ever yours, Freddy."*

I stared at the photograph for a long time. Madam Gadalla – Layla – was the one standing in the middle of the threesome, smiling rather coyly at the camera. She had wide, full lips, seductively made up eyes, painted with the outer corners tilting up, and quantities of dark hair piled on top of her head secured with her tiara. So, one of these other lovely young women was Freya's grandmother, and the other was the mysterious Rosa mentioned with apparent reluctance by Madam Gadalla in her letter to Freya. Allowing for the fact that the photograph must have been taken in the late 1940's or early 1950's, judging by their hairstyles and costumes, all three nevertheless exuded a timeless allure as they gazed out of the photograph, captured and forever frozen in their prime. There was a similarity in the curve of their smiles that hinted at the sibling relationship. I pictured the rather wizened old lady I'd glimpsed beneath the hijab headscarf the other day and wondered how she could bear to look in the mirror and then at these photographs and be reminded of the stunning beauty she had once been. The sheer quantity of photographs, all seemingly from the same era, suggested a lady who perhaps preferred to live in the past. And what a glittering past it was: doted on by royalty and invited to all manner of lavish banquets and receptions, even if only as part of the entertainment. The photographs spoke of a lifestyle I could barely imagine, of wealth, luxury and decadence beyond my wildest dreams. To have had all of that, and then to have lost it so cruelly when Farouk was toppled from his throne as Egypt became a republic. I could sympathise with Madam

Gadalla's apparent reluctance to move on, her determination to cling to the old life that had once been hers.

'She must have been lonely all these years,' I murmured. 'She said her sister Sofia went to England as there were people there who could look after her *in her condition*. So she must have been pregnant. Although I wonder why an Egyptian girl would go to England and whom she went to? And Rosa went to Europe if I remember rightly. I wonder if she followed Farouk there with a view to holding onto the vestiges of her old life? And, if so, I wonder why Layla stayed behind? It seems to me that she's lived through the last sixty years since Farouk's death-in-exile in a kind of self-imposed exile of her own, with just these memories and mementoes to sustain her. I wonder why?'

'Unless we can find the old lady, those are unanswerable questions,' Adam pointed out. He lifted his voice slightly and called over his shoulder. 'Ahmed? Any luck?'

Ahmed appeared back in the doorway, his bulk filling the frame. 'It is very difficult to say for sure, but I have found no overnight bag or suitcase in de cupboards. And dere is no toothbrush in de bathroom. Dese clues suggest to me dat Madam Gadalla she packed a bag and took it wid her, expecting not to return perhaps for a little while. But where she has gone. Dis is a mystery dat anyone can make a guess.'

Adam narrowed his eyes on my face. 'What exactly have we come here for, Merry? I can't believe for one moment that you harboured a belief Madam Gadalla would have left us a nice friendly note telling us where to find her. And while these photographs are fascinating, they don't tell us anything we don't already know. She's already revealed that the three sisters – Farouk's Fancies – sang and danced for the king at his parties. And who can say what other services they may have provided.'

I glanced sharply at him. 'You think they were high class prostitutes?'

He smiled at me. 'Perhaps *courtesans* would be a kinder way of putting it. I mean, thanks to Shukura and Walid, we know all about Farouk's reputation as a playboy and philanderer. And we know he favoured very young women. I find it hard to believe three gorgeous young ladies like that,' - he indicated the photograph, - 'wouldn't have tickled his fancy.'

'No pun intended,' I murmured.

He grinned at me. 'Quite. I mean, why would he remember Madam Gadalla's birthday and send her champagne every year if she wasn't more than a good friend?' He must have listened to himself as he uttered these words, hearing something suggestive in them, because suddenly his expression changed as he looked at me and that familiar stillness settled over him. 'The champagne? Merry, we're here because of the champagne?'

'It's just that while we were talking to Shukura, I suddenly remembered something I'd noticed about this room during the little peak we had of it when the housekeeping guy unlocked the door the other day. I glimpsed the mantelpiece.' I turned towards it as I spoke, 'And look; how many people do you know who line their mantelpieces with champagne bottles – especially what look like unopened ones?'

It was true. Along with the ubiquitous black and white photographs in silver frames, there were at least a dozen champagne bottles neatly lined up on the shelf still with their golden seals intact.

'But Shukura said Farouk smuggled gold bars out of Egypt in champagne *crates* – not in champagne *bottles*.'

'We've got to at least take a look, haven't we?' I coaxed. 'I mean; don't you think it's a bit weird that a Muslim man should send a Muslim woman champagne on her birthday, when the Qur'an strictly forbids the consumption of alcohol?'

Adam raised one eyebrow. 'From what I understand, the Qur'an strictly forbids gambling, too. And yet King Farouk was a notorious gambler. From what Shukura said, it was part of the reason his people turned against him.'

But I was determined not to be put off and, for all his arch look and dampening words, Adam was quick to join me as I moved towards the tall mantelpiece.

'Ahmed, can you stand guard by the door please? We don't want to be interrupted. And the general manager may take it into his head to come and check how you're getting on.' Ahmed obediently moved towards the door and opened it just a crack so he could see along the corridor.

I was painfully aware of my heart thudding in my chest as I reached out for one of the champagne bottles. A photograph of Layla Gadalla and King Farouk stood in front of it and my fanciful brain imagined them watching me as I sought to discover if there was a secret they shared.

It was a breathless moment as I lifted the bottle down from the shelf. It's fair to say it looked and felt exactly how an unopened champagne bottle ought to look and feel. My first reaction was a puff of deflation as I felt the liquid contents shift inside the glass bottle. I passed it to Adam with a small, deflated sigh. 'Forget it. I was wrong. This is exactly what it appears to be. Just a bottle of a very nice vintage champagne – probably worth a fortune and quite possibly undrinkable unless it's supposed to be stored for more than half a century – but not a place for hiding secret messages, or anything else for that matter.'

Adam took the bottle and turned it in his hands, studying the label. 'Mm; very nice. Dom Perignon – vintage

1960. This was bottled half way through the years of Farouk's exile in Europe.' He turned it upside down and I watched the champagne shift through the dark glass. 'Wouldn't you love to open it and try just a small sip?'

I stared at him. 'Breaking in and searching Madam Gadalla's room is one thing. Drinking her birthday champagne is quite another. I know I can be accused of leading you astray, Adam; but even I baulk at that.'

'Shame. I was starting to think I could resist everything except temptation. But I won't do it without your permission, Merry.'

'Perhaps we should just put it back and get out of here,' I muttered. 'The whole thing's been a hare-brained scheme. I don't know what I was thinking really. I just got the idea into my head that it was significant the way she kept mentioning the champagne in her letters, yet not being able to drink it because of her religion.'

Adam was staring down at the bottle in his hands. 'It does seem odd,' he agreed musingly. 'And to find them still unopened after all these years. Unless she's hoping to sell them for some extortionate amount of money at some future point, I agree with you it's a strange thing to hang on to; and even stranger to display them unopened on the mantelpiece in her living room. I mean; I know some people stick candles in used champagne bottles. But I've never known anyone to consider them particularly ornamental outside of that.'

'And where did she get the money to afford to live here in the lap of luxury all these years?' I added. As I spoke Adam was running his fingers over the surface of the bottle and pressing the top where the cork was set into the neck underneath its fancy gilt seal as if it might release a catch. 'It can't be anything to do with the cork or the wire that holds it in,' I said, 'otherwise she'd have taken the seals off. Every single one of these bottles has its seals intact.'

Adam glanced into my eyes and transferred his attention to the bottom of the bottle with its depression underneath for a wine waiter to stick his thumb into. I watched, biting my lip, as he felt all round the base. 'There's a small ridge here,' he said in hushed tones. 'It's all but invisible, but I can feel it.' I saw him grip the body of the bottle around the label with one hand and attempt to twist the base of the bottle with the other. I held my breath and felt my chest tighten. 'My God, it's stiff,' he grunted.

But I could see he'd found the secret hiding place within the bottle. With my heart pounding as he unscrewed the base from the bottle, I half expected to see a gush of liquid spill in frothy bubbles all over the carpet. But the glass base came off cleanly in Adam's hand with a final twist and I let out a long shuddering sigh, feeling my heartbeat thump back to life.

'It's empty,' he declared, turning it over and peering inside, then inserting his hand inside the cavity within the bottle just to be sure.

Ahmed was craning back over his shoulder to look at us from the door. 'You have finded something?' he called gleefully in what he may fondly have imagined was a whisper. All I could say was I sincerely hoped there was no one approaching along the corridor. He'd have given away our presence as clearly as if he'd announced us through a loudspeaker.

'We don't know yet,' I whispered back. 'Oh my God, Adam; open the others.'

He didn't need any further encouragement, and lifted another bottle down from the mantelpiece. I decided I couldn't wait and watch breathlessly while one by one he investigated the bottles. So I reached for one too. Like the first, the base was tightly screwed into the bottle. It took all my effort to twist and prise it open. Like the first it was empty. But I paused before putting it back together and spent a moment admiring the workmanship that had transformed a vintage champagne bottle into a receptacle for smuggling who-knows-what from King Farouk to Madam Gadalla. The cleverest thing about it was the thin skin that had been left within the bottle. A skin containing liquid, so that when the bottle was turned it gave the appearance of being full of champagne. 'Very ingenious,' I murmured, and screwed the base tightly back into the hole at the bottom of the bottle.

'Your hunch is on the money yet again,' Adam smiled, a soft expression in his blue eyes as he looked at me. 'One day you must let me know how you do it.'

'It's just luck,' I said.

He grinned at me. 'Well, you have the Devil's own.'

'Thank you,' I said demurely. 'But I'm not sure we're any further forward. If these bottles are all empty then all we've done is prove that King Farouk did indeed look after Madam Gadalla during the years of his exile, probably by sending her money.'

'What were you hoping for?' His lovely eyes narrowed on my face and he guessed it in one. 'No, don't tell me. You thought she might have the fabled Dead Sea Scroll rolled up inside one of these bottles?'

'Well, she said she knew where it was hidden,' I responded a trifle defensively. 'And, as we've had cause to remark before, the best place to hide something is in plain sight. At least here she could keep an eye on it.'

'But if King Farouk was letting it be known towards the end of his life that he had the scroll and was willing to sell it to the highest bidder, don't you think he'd have wanted to keep it somewhere close by where he could lay his hands on it, rather than shipping it back to Egypt?'

'I guess it depends whether he felt it might be at risk of being stolen,' I said reasonably. 'That was a chance he couldn't take. I'd say it was a very sensible precaution, particularly if for any reason he felt his life might be in danger.'

'You think he knew someone might attempt to assassinate him?'

'If he knew the scroll contained information to challenge the teachings of Christianity, then it was a dangerous game he was playing to start drawing attention to the fact that he had it in his possession in Rome so close to the Vatican.'

Adam was scanning the labels on the remaining bottles. 'Well, if you're right, Merry and, as you know, I have the utmost respect for your instincts; then these bottles are all too early. Farouk died in 1965. So assuming he smuggled the scroll out of Italy towards the end of his life and also assuming he didn't have a job lot of these adapted bottles, but had them custom made each year for Madam Gadalla's birthday, then we need to find a later year.'

'There are two bottles here from 1964.' I said excitedly, reaching out. I took one and Adam lifted down the other.

'You know, if you're wrong, we're going to be bitterly disappointed,' Adam breathed.

'I don't think I'm wrong,' I said with brazen self-confidence, swallowing hard to suppress the nervous tension pressing up my windpipe and nearly choking me.

Murphy's Law being what it is, I don't suppose I should have been surprised when the longed-for and tightly rolled scroll of parchment turned up inside Adam's bottle, not mine.

In awed silence we both stared at it, snugly fitted inside the cavity within the bottle, and I willed my heart rate to slow down. Then Adam reached in with his fingertips and gently eased it from its hidey-hole. He gave a low whistle. 'Well, wherever our mysterious Madam Gadalla has vanished to, she was willing to leave this behind.'

'Which makes me think either she's not gone far, or she's not intending to be away for long. And hopefully she's confident that our gun-toting Egyptian friends have no idea it's here.'

Adam carried the scroll across to the settee while I screwed the bottle back together and replaced it, along with the one I'd opened, on the shelf, so the bottles were once more lined up looking innocently like a row of unopened vintage champagne bottles. Then I went to join him.

Very carefully, he'd unrolled the parchment. It was dry, cracked and brittle, reminding me very much of some ancient papyrus we'd had the privilege to study not so long ago. But this time the lettering was not in the ancient Egyptian hieratic script I'd come to recognise. 'Ted would be able to tell at a glance, of course,' Adam said. 'But my money's on Hebrew.'

'Do you think it's genuine?'

'If it's a fake it's a damned good one.'

I drew in a shaky breath. 'Oh my God, Adam; we've found it! We've got the missing Dead Sea Scroll!'

'You mean the stolen Dead Sea Scroll,' he amended.

'So, what are we going to do with it?'

'You mean to say you don't have it all worked out?' he asked with exquisite sarcasm.

'I hadn't quite thought that far,' I admitted.

'Well, I suggest our first plan of action must be to show it to Ted. He'll be able to vouch for its authenticity, or otherwise – and tell us what it says. After that – and always assuming it does prove Nabil Zaal's wildest fantasies concerning the Biblical kings and the pharaohs of the 18th Dynasty of ancient Egypt – I think all we can do is step up the search for Madam Gadalla in earnest and see what more she might be willing to tell us about it.'

I stared at the ancient scroll with its scratchy writings wondering if, once again, we'd been lucky enough to stumble across a genuine historical artefact, one historians and scholars would give their eye teeth – or possibly kill – for.

Adam's darkly lashed eyes came to meet mine. 'Oh well, considering this wasn't our mystery, it seems to me we're in it now up to our necks.'

I couldn't help but smile. But a sudden urgent motion from Ahmed by the doorway made it freeze on my face. 'Quick! Hide! Someone comes!'

Chapter 12

Ahmed clicked the door closed and stood there looking as sick and panicky as I felt. He'd been watching and listening to us intently, but had obviously turned back to his task as look-out-scout just in time. It flashed across my brain in a moment of horror that maybe by mentioning the two gun-toting Egyptians I'd somehow conjured them into being in the corridor outside Madam Gadalla's room. But the voices that reached us through the closed door were speaking in English.

One made itself plainly heard. 'Do you mean to tell me my aunt has been missing for three whole days and nobody saw fit to notify me?' The American accent gave away his identity if what he'd actually said left room for doubt. 'I need to speak with her urgently on a matter of the utmost importance.'

Nabil Zaal sounded, I thought, rather pompous. I decided he spoke the way he lectured, as if for the benefit of an audience – although he surely couldn't begin to imagine the one he had listening in to what he was saying just now. I opened my mouth to protest my belief that he was in hospital in Cairo being treated for a heart attack or a stroke or something, only to find myself prevented from uttering more than a squeak as Adam clamped one hand over my jaw and started manhandling me towards the bedroom. 'Hold that thought, Merry,' he whispered urgently, snatching up the parchment scroll from the settee and half pushing, half pulling me along with him. 'Ahmed's got an excuse for being in here. We haven't. C'mon; I have no desire to be caught red-handed with this potentially explosive document.'

At the sound of voices outside, Ahmed leapt away from the door as if he'd been scalded. For some reason best known to himself he pulled a notebook from his breast pocket and stood with a pen poised over it as if interrupted in the course of making some important note.

Still from the other side of the door, I heard: 'Sir, we had no reason to believe there was anything suspicious in your aunt's disappearance until the police officer turned up here this afternoon and told us he was investigating an incident involving British tourists. It seems your aunt may know these people. The officer says they have come here to Luxor at her invitation. It is this, I understand, that gave some cause for alarm. I await the policeman's report. Although, now you are here...' The general manager's long-winded explanation was cut off mid-flow as Adam swept me into the bedroom and pulled the door tightly closed behind us.

Just in time. A hasty and theatrically over-loud greeting from Ahmed – for our benefit no doubt – informed us Nabil Zaal and the general manager had opened the door and entered Madam Gadalla's suite.

I stood with my ear pressed against the door and with my heart thudding loudly and painfully in my chest.

'This is the officer investigating the case,' I heard the general manager say.

'Ahmed Abd el-Rassul,' Ahmed introduced himself, rolling the R with great gusto. I could see him clearly in my mind's eye, his chest puffed out with self-importance.

If Madam Gadalla's illustrious nephew registered anything familiar about Ahmed's name he didn't say so. As an historian I'd have thought Nabil Zaal might have been acquainted with the Abd el-Rassuls, by their tomb-robbing reputation if nothing else. But I was forgetting Mr Zaal had found fame and fortune churning out what Adam had rather unkindly referred to as pseudo historical psychobabble. Whatever, he made no comment and I pictured him looking Ahmed up and down as the general manager completed his introductions. 'Officer, this is the renowned author Mr Nabil Zaal. You may have heard of him. He also happens to be Madam Gadalla's nephew.'

'But I thought dat you were in C-,' Ahmed cut himself short just in time. Of course, I thought, Ahmed had been present and all agog listening to Shukura's report about Nabil Zaal's lecture at the Mena House earlier on. He knew all about the author being carted off to hospital.

'What's all this about British tourists?' Nabil demanded. He sounded decidedly put out. 'You say they're here at my aunt's invitation?' He added, under his breath but distinctly audibly, even through the closed door separating him from

Adam and me, 'What the hell does the old witch think she's playing at now?'

I can only imagine the general manager must have shrugged as there was no audible response from him so Nabil Zaal addressed his next question to Ahmed. 'Officer, I take it you know the whereabouts of these tourists?'

As an awkward silence drew out I pictured Ahmed opening and closing his mouth like a goldfish wondering what to say. I prayed he wouldn't betray our presence by darting an involuntary glance at the bedroom door.

Nabil Zaal clearly took the lengthening silence as an invitation to explain himself, and went on, 'I would very much like to speak with them. Do you know where I can find them?'

I took it he'd switched his focus back to the general manager for that gentleman responded, in my opinion over-reaching himself in his desire to be helpful. 'My receptionist Mohamed mentioned that he has contact details for how to reach them where they are staying. With the officer's permission of course, I shall be happy to give them to you.'

I sagged against Adam with a silent groan. What could poor Ahmed do? It sounded to me as if he had little choice but to consent. Our police buddy excelled himself once again, however. 'If dis gentleman wishes to visit de British tourists, I will be happy to accompany him.'

But even with Ahmed acting as bodyguard it would still lead Nabil Zaal directly to Ben and Freya on board the *Queen*

Ahmes. And with everything so uncertain I wasn't at all sure how I felt about that. I had no idea what was going on although I thought I could probably imagine what had brought Nabil Zaal haring from his hospital bed to Luxor. I wondered how much of a spanner it threw in the works for him to find his aunt had vanished into thin air and thus avoided his interrogation. I stood silent and statue-like behind the bedroom door thinking at least we'd be able to follow hard on their heels back to the dahabeeyah once Ahmed led Nabil Zaal away and we were freed from our hiding place. I could only hope that the scroll of parchment Adam was holding so carefully might prove to be a trump card we could play should it become necessary. But Nabil Zaal surprised me by not wishing to head off straight away.

'With your indulgence Hamid, I shall just take a few moments to look around my aunt's suite on my own. I'm more familiar with her belongings than the officer and may be able to spot what, if anything, is missing. I'd also like to leave a note for her, just in case she should return. Can you allow me a few minutes alone?'

I stopped breathing and shot a terrified glance at Adam. His eyes were darting around Madam Gadalla's rather fussy bedroom searching for somewhere to hide. With even the most cursory inspection Nabil Zaal could hardly fail to discover us. I joined Adam in glancing frantically around the room for potential hiding places and drew a blank. There was no way we could crawl under the bed as it was a wooden-framed divan with deep drawers in the base and barely enough space underneath it for a spider to go undetected let alone Adam and me. The wardrobe, one of those fancy armoire types, wasn't big enough for both of us. And while there was a nice balcony outside, affording the same great view across the Nile as from the living room, I could hardly see us attempting to shimmy down the nearest drainpipe without drawing the attention of the hordes of caleche drivers on the Corniche – or more probably falling and breaking our necks.

The general manager's voice sliced into my panic like a knife blade. 'Yes Mr Zaal, of course. The officer and I will wait downstairs in my office. Just let us know when you are ready to go. I'll leave you to lock up and ask that you please bring the key down with you.'

To my way of looking at it the general manager was really way too accommodating. I'd say it's definitely possible to take customer service training too far. It also occurred to me that even if Nabil Zaal should somehow fail to discover us, if he locked up behind him and took the key away with him there was a fair to middling chance Adam and I would find ourselves locked in. I doubted Ahmed's ability to dream up an excuse for returning to Madam Gadalla's suite for the purpose of setting us free.

'I will stay,' Ahmed announced staunchly. I imagined him standing there, as solid and immoveable as one of the granite Pharaonic statues that adorned the temples around here.

'No, no, officer, I'm sure there is really no need,' the general manager argued. 'It is a shock for Mr Zaal to find his aunt is missing. We must allow him a few moments alone.'

'But –'

I heard the outer door click and tried to imagine how Ahmed felt about being escorted firmly from the room knowing he'd tried and failed, so had little choice but to leave us stranded inside Madam Gadalla's rooms. I gave it up in the dawning awareness of my own feelings at being left high and dry.

Adam didn't waste another moment. He grabbed my arm and hauled me across the room, shoving me into the en suite bathroom, where he joined me a split second later and quickly pushed the door closed. So now there were two closed doors separating us from Nabil Zaal. But I really didn't see what difference it would make to our inevitable discovery. The author was sure to want to use the loo while he was here. I supposed, for now, I ought to be grateful for the soundproofing qualities of deep pile carpets. If Madam Gadalla had preferred stripped wooden floors we'd be goners by now.

I stared at Adam and Adam stared at me. 'I told you I had a bad feeling about this,' he whispered. 'Now what, Merry? Any bright ideas?'

I realised I had once again submitted to my amazing penchant for getting trapped. It was a very bad habit of mine, and one about which a certain ex-boyfriend had once waxed lyrically and critically. I knew there was no chance of Dan Fletcher turning up miraculously, as he'd done once or twice before, to rescue me just in the nick of time and with a pithy put-down on his lips. Adam and I were on our own this time; and without any possible explanation we could offer for being here.

I shrugged. 'All we can do is pin our hopes on Ahmed.'

He looked at me a bit quizzically. 'I was afraid you might say that. Somehow I don't find it especially reassuring.'

I perched on the toilet seat with my legs crossed and my right foot jerking nervously up and down. Madam Gadalla's bathroom was a perfect extension of the rest of her suite, with a big old-fashioned roll top bath, a ceramic toilet with a wall mounted cistern and a proper chain, a bidet and a matching sink with a round bowl and fancy taps. Her towels were pink and fluffy, hanging in tiers on the bars of a wall-mounted radiator. I imagined her rooms might not have been included on the last modernisation and refurbishment schedule in the hotel. Adam propped the scroll on the vanity unit above the sink, then went to the window, eased it up and leaned out. 'We're on the end-side of the building,' he whispered, pulling his head back in again. 'There's a vine growing up the wall, but I'm not sure I rate our chances of reaching it from the window ledge. I went and joined him and peered out. We were indeed on the side-end of the building which would have had a view across towards Luxor Temple a little further along the Corniche had the view not been obscured. But as it was, there was a flippin' great hoarding facing us. Before the Egyptian Revolution there had been plans to build a deluxe extension to The Winter Palace. The expansion plans had ground to a standstill in the aftermath of the Arab Spring. With tourist numbers so low I guess the investment was no longer seen as worthwhile. The hoarding covered what I imagined was just an empty space of waste ground behind it, not yet a building site. But at least it meant if we made an attempt on the vine we'd be hidden from passers-by on The Corniche. Not that I relished my chances with the vine. For all that it was gnarled and twisted and pretty sturdy looking, reaching from the ground up to the top of the building somewhere above us; it was also growing at least a metre away from the window ledge. It would mean edging along the ledge, with a sheer two-storey drop below, and then leaping with the hope of attaching to the vine like Spiderman. I didn't fancy it, myself. Especially wearing my figure-hugging dress and strappy sandals.

    Rap ... rap... rap...

    I nearly fell out of the window altogether as the sudden sound of knocking shattered the quiet. I jumped violently, bumping my head on the window sash; swore, and pulled back inside quickly. 'What's that?'

Luckily the noise of the peremptory knocking coming from Madam Gadalla's suite drowned out the sound of my minor head injury.

'Sounds like someone's bashing on the outer door.' Adam eased the bathroom door open a crack so he could hear better. I joined him and stood pressed up against him in the narrow space, listening intently.

There was a click, which I took to be the sound of the outer door opening, and then I heard Nabil Zaal exclaim, 'Ashraf! What the hell are you doing here?'

I leaned back and stared round-eyed at Adam. According to Mohamed the receptionist Ashraf Zaal, Nabil's brother, was the one who'd cancelled the hotel reservation Madam Gadalla made for Freya. I had good reason to be highly suspicious of him.

'Hello Nabil; I might ask the same question of you. I passed Hamid and a police officer on the stairs and Hamid told me you were here. I'd like to know how you got here so quickly. The last I heard, you'd been rushed into hospital in Cairo; and that was only this morning.'

I presumed since Nabil Zaal had opened the conversation in English he'd set the expectation it would continue that way. His brother spoke with a pronounced

252

Arabic accent but his command of the language was impressive.

'Spying on me again, eh, Ashraf?'

'It's always worth knowing what goes on at your lectures. You never know when someone might say something interesting. So I asked my old university pal Saleh to go along. I understand this morning's session got the fur flying a bit with all that talk about a Dead Sea Scroll King Farouk supposedly spirited out of Egypt when he was deposed. I imagine that's why you've come racing back here. Hit on the idea of interviewing Aunt Layla, did you?'

I strained my ears to hear the response since I was more than a little interested in what had motivated Nabil Zaal to make this trip.

'I was lying in hospital when it suddenly struck me she must know more than she's ever been willing to tell us,' came the response. There was a slight pause, then Nabil went on in a musing tone, almost as if speaking to himself, and I strained my ears even harder to catch what he was saying. 'Mother always said there was a scroll. Oh, I know she made it sound like a children's fairy-tale when we were kids. But I was listening at the door one night in Rome when she was reporting back to that military-looking gentleman friend of hers. She said she'd searched Farouk's rooms and failed to find whatever it was she was searching for. She'd even searched the apartment of that British side-kick of Farouk's the night she stole the scarab from him, thinking perhaps the king had given it to him for safe-keeping. But found nothing. She speculated then that Farouk had somehow smuggled it out of Italy. She never actually referred to it as a scroll, but what else can she have been talking about? And it dawned on me that possibly the only one devoted enough to Farouk to keep a secret like that was Aunt Layla. There was no way I could stay in hospital once I'd cottoned onto that. I discharged myself; against doctor's wishes, I might add. They're concerned about my blood pressure. I jumped in a taxi to the airport and was lucky enough to get a last-minute seat on the late morning flight. I wanted to catch Aunt Layla unawares.'

I barely had time to assimilate all this, since Ashraf Zaal's response was immediate.

'Well as you can see, the dear old bird has done a disappearing act.'

'Do you know where she is?'

'I have no idea. She seems to have vanished into thin air. But I can see you thought you'd take advantage of her absence to have a good old snoop around.'

'If you already know she's missing, then I can only imagine you had the same idea.' Nabil spoke with a distinct chill in his voice. Ah, I thought to myself, the brothers don't get along. 'Why else would you be here?'

'Well, we know she's had the scarab hidden away here for years. Yes, I'll admit it occurred to me too when I heard someone had been sounding off about a Dead Sea Scroll that Aunt Layla might know something and perhaps have stashed it in the same place. It would certainly explain why she's been sending letters to England. She'd rather die than let you or me inherit something like that since, the way she sees it, our mother betrayed Farouk, possibly to his death. I didn't think it could hurt to have a quick scout about. Great minds, eh? So, where shall we start looking? It can't be underneath the mattress because the housekeeping people come in to change the bed linen every few days. Perhaps it's sewn into the curtain lining or pressed behind a picture frame, or something. Any ideas?'

'If it's with the scarab, then I hardly think either of your suggestions are credible,' Nabil sneered. 'And anyway, I want you to tell me what the hell you know about the goddamned British tourists Aunt Layla has apparently invited out here?' I thought I detected a note of deep suspicion in his voice.

There was a short pause and then Ashraf spoke in what I could only describe as gleeful tones. 'Of course! You're here to search for the scarab as well as the scroll! Well, I'm pleased to say I can save you the trouble! And as for the British tourists, well, I think it's fair to say we have one of them to thank for that in a roundabout way.'

There was a moment of deathly silence. Then Nabil spoke in strangely strangled tones. 'You've got the scarab?'

'I have indeed.' His brother sounded impossibly smug. In the loaded pause that followed, I gaped at Adam, starting to fit the pieces together in my mind. He gazed back at me and I could see he was slotting the same bits of the puzzle into place.

'So where is it?' Nabil demanded in a rising pitch. 'Please don't tell me you've finally murdered the old witch for it and that's why she's missing!'

'I didn't need to murder her, much as I've been tempted. I just needed to outwit her. As it turned out, she was a bit careless.'

'So where is it? Where's the scarab?'

'Not here,' was the smooth reply. 'But, now I come to think of it, I suppose it might be the decent thing to offer you first refusal to buy it from me. You're my brother after all. But if you don't want it then it strikes me there may be another couple of potential buyers right here in Luxor thanks to our revered aunt. One of them is the son of that British lapdog of Farouk's. So I'm guessing he'll consider he has a right to stake a claim to the scarab since Farouk gave it as a gift to his father. The other one, believe it or not, is Aunt Sofia's granddaughter, which must make her some sort of cousin of ours. Perhaps I could start a bidding war.'

'You know I want it, you bastard!' It sounded like Nabil Zaal's blood pressure was on the rise again. 'I begged Aunt Layla to let me buy it from her after she brazenly stole it back from Mother all those years ago. I told her she could name her price. I tried cajoling and even threatening her. But she just looked at me with that coy expression of hers and said she'd hidden it somewhere safe, and that she'd rather burn in the blazing fires of Jahannam than see a son of Rosa's profit from her beloved Freddy's downfall. You know, she sat at the back of the lecture I gave here at The Winter Palace the other day. I think she came along just to taunt me. She takes a cruel and twisted delight in knowing she has something I'd give my right arm for. I believe she positively relished hearing the jibes I got from the audience while she sat there calmly withholding, out of pure spite, the one piece of incontrovertible evidence that would make them laugh on the other side of their faces. She really is an evil old buzzard'

'The trouble with Mother and Aunt Layla was they ended up hating each other because they had fundamentally different ideologies about what was right for Egypt, and loved such different men.'

'Never mind all that,' Nabil cut him off impatiently. 'How much do you want for the scarab?'

'Aren't you interested to know how I got it back?'

'You can tell me all the sordid details later,' Nabil said snappishly. 'For now all I want to know is where it is and just how much those goddamned British tourists might happen to know about it. If you're playing both ends to the middle, so help me Ashraf, I'll kill you!'

'Temper temper,' Ashraf responded tauntingly. 'You need to calm down brother. Remember the doctors' concern for your blood pressure.'

'How can I calm down, you fool? That scarab gives me the chance to vindicate the beliefs I've built my entire career on! You drivel on about the different ideologies of our mother and Aunt Layla. But we're just the same, you and I. I've dedicated the last twenty-five years of my life in a scholarly search for the truth, attempting to prove something the world claims is unprovable – and all based on some willo-the-wisp stories our mother used to tell and my certain knowledge a scarab existed that proved the identity of Joseph, even though I couldn't get my hands on it thanks to our malicious aunt. You're driven by nothing more than a mean-spirited desire to get-rich-quick. You make me sick! Your only interest in the scarab is its monetary value. So, come on, name your price and let's get it over and done with.'

'Perhaps you'd have been better off staying in hospital after all,' Ashraf mused. 'You really don't look at all well. And I have an inkling you'll feel even worse when I tell you that Aunt Layla sent the scarab to our British cousin in the international post.'

'She did what?' The horror in Nabil's voice vibrated even through one closed and the other almost-closed door between him and us.

'Oh yes, with instructions to come to Egypt and bring it back with her so Aunt Layla could tell her all about it. Aunt Layla booked a room for her here at The Winter Palace.'

'How do you know all this?' Nabil asked suspiciously. 'Are you taking up spying as a profession? No, on second thoughts, don't tell me. I probably don't want to know.'

'I've certainly been keeping my eye on our aunt. I had a feeling she might try something under-handed. She knows she can't last forever, and she can hardly take the scarab with her into the burning fires of Jahannam when her time comes. But she's quite determined neither one of us should inherit it, thanks to her hatred of our mother. I think she started to become suspicious about the frequency of my visits and felt I was watching her. I daresay she rumbled that my true motivation was the hope that she'd slide into senility and let something slip. So she tried to out-fox me. But she wasn't clever enough to cover her tracks. I knew all about the letter she'd sent to our young female cousin, and that she'd packaged up the scarab along with it, thanks to her need to write the letter in English. She was stupid enough to leave a draft copy screwed up in the waste paper basket. But I admit I had no idea about this son-of-Hunter character until he turned up here shouting the odds about a letter she'd sent to his father. Think about it, Nabil. It must be further proof that Aunt Layla has the scroll. I mean, why would you write to two people if you have only one item to bequeath? '

There was a deep groan from Nabil. 'So what's the point of us wasting our time searching this place for it?'

'What do you mean?'

'Only that if Aunt Layla's mad enough to send the scarab through the post to our young English cousin, who's to say she didn't also package up the scroll and mail it to this son-of-Hunter person when she wrote to him?'

'She didn't write to the son-of-Hunter. She wrote to Hunter himself. Think about it, he'd be a man in his nineties by now. Surely she wouldn't take the risk of him being dead before the package reached him. For all we know, she may have mentioned the scroll in the letter and used it as a lure to get him to come here, but I doubt she posted it to him. Come on Nabil, I just have a feeling it might be here somewhere. If we can get our hands on it then even if Hunter knows about it, there's nothing he can do. Let's get started.'

'Hang on; hang on,' Nabil protested. 'The bit I don't understand in all this is why Aunt Layla would take it into her head to vanish just as her invited guests arrive in Luxor. It doesn't make sense.'

'Ah, well I think Hanif and Saiyyid may have had something to do with that.' Ashraf's voice sounded a trifle sheepish. 'The trouble is, they didn't have the simple common sense to stay hidden behind their newspapers the day I sent them here to keep watch for our cousin's arrival. You see; I'd made it my business to cancel her hotel reservation, so I knew there'd be trouble at check-in. The sad fact is Aunt Layla spotted my two dear boys. I don't think they were expecting her to go downstairs to sit in on your lecture. Even though Saiyyid tells me he tried to reassure her, she obviously got spooked and vanished.'

'Knowing the scarab was at stake; you invited those two young buffoon sons of yours in on the act! Are you mad?'

'Yes, well, as things have turned out, quite possibly. But, you see, I knew I'd be recognised by the staff here. They were only supposed to waylay the girl for a while so I could get to her before Aunt Layla did, but it all got a bit out of hand when the girl disappeared off to stay on board some dahabeeyah on the Nile. It enabled me to get the scarab back, so it wasn't a complete disaster. Hanif got the name of the dahabeeyah from a young English lad our cousin left stranded here, so I paid it a visit after dark and found the scarab left helpfully ripe for the picking in one of the cabins.

I stared bug-eyed at Adam. But Ashraf Zaal had only paused for breath. 'My mistake was saying we needed to get rid of Gregory Hunter's son. I hadn't accounted for him, and I couldn't take a risk on how much he might know about the scroll. The boys took me a bit too literally and hit on some scheme to lure him into a deserted wadi on the west bank and frighten him off with a gun Hanif borrowed from his gun club.'

'They did what?' Nabil sounded as if he was about to suffer a seizure.

'Oh, don't worry. They – quite cleverly, I thought – managed to frame the young companion our cousin brought with her and then left him high and dry. I take it he's her boyfriend, or something. And Hunter's just slightly injured. I'm sure the whole thing will blow over.'

There was a sound I took to be Nabil Zaal slumping heavily into an armchair. At least, I hoped it was that and not a seizure after all. My fears were allayed when he spoke, although his voice was muffled, as if he were speaking with his head in his hands. 'This is a total nightmare. I am not prepared to come this close to getting hold of the scarab only to see it snatched away from me as evidence in some police investigation into the shooting of a British tourist. You've always been stupid, Ashraf. But even I wouldn't have believed you capable of this sort of lunacy. And it's not just lunacy – its outright criminality!'

'But I've got the scarab. Nobody else knows where it is. And if we can get our hands on the scroll too then we hold all the aces. There's no reason for anyone to suspect Hanif and Saiyyid. They both got away.'

'And what about the poor kid they framed?'

'They drugged him so I doubt he'll be able to give a coherent account of what happened. Come on Nabil; if there's a chance the fabled scroll is here somewhere, don't you want to look for it?'

'I can't believe you can speak so calmly about what Hanif and Saiyyid have done. Ashraf, if this ever comes to light they'll throw the book at them, and probably at you too by association. After all, you got them into it. And besides, surely if Aunt Layla's got the scroll she'll have taken it with her wherever she's gone,' Nabil objected.

Ashraf didn't seem too concerned with the possible implications of his actions or those of his sons. He was far more interested in the scroll. 'I think she left in a bit of a hurry when she realised her carefully laid plans had gone awry. She may not have had the time. Or she mightn't have wanted to take it with her wherever she was going.'

'And if Aunt Layla suddenly puts in an appearance again?'

'Then she'll realise the game is up and we've won.'

Nabil gave in. 'Then we'll have to be quick. Hamid is waiting for me to return the key to him downstairs and he still has a police officer with him, remember? After what you've just told me, I should think he's best avoided. And we'll have to be clever. We can't tear the place apart. You know, before you turned up just now, I was starting to think Aunt Layla's champagne bottles looked interesting. They've stood unopened on that shelf as long as I can remember. Wasn't there some story about Farouk smuggling his riches out of Egypt in champagne crates when he was exiled?'

Adam had heard enough. He sent me a look of raw and naked appeal and, pulling me away, eased the bathroom door closed again.

Our eavesdropping had proved quite fruitful. We had answers to a lot of questions, while, admittedly, many went still unanswered. But I agreed with Adam, we didn't dare stick around in the hope of hearing more. If the brothers found the empty hidey-holes inside the bottles, I could only hope they'd assume Madam Gadalla had absconded with the scroll. In the meantime it remained a very real possibility that either Nabil or Ashraf would need to answer the call of nature before they departed.

Chapter 13

Adam wasn't willing to submit to the inevitability of our discovery. He was already leaning out of the open window again. 'I think we're going to have to take our chances with that vine,' he whispered.

This was not an appealing prospect, but I had to admit it was probably preferable to being caught. While it was true we'd been trapped in worse places and without anything so handy as the vine to use as a potential escape route, there was something about the sheer drop that made me feel quite sick.

Adam eased himself out onto the ledge. 'Pass me the scroll, Merry, would you?' I handed it out to him. 'Ok, your turn; come and join me.'

I've never climbed out of a window two storeys up before. I can honestly say I didn't enjoy the experience. My head started to swim with vertigo before I'd even lifted my feet off the bathroom floor and gradually reversed my sitting position so my legs were dangling on the outside. It was quite a wide ledge. But somehow that wasn't the point. 'This is even worse than crawling across that pit shaft,' I muttered.

'And look how bravely you did that,' he reminded me. 'C'mon Merry, don't lose your nerve now.'

As I joined him so we were sitting alongside each other, he started shunting himself sideways, out of sight of the open window. 'See if you can pull it closed again behind you, can you?'

This required more movement than I was prepared to make with the hard ground so far away and no safety net between it and me.

'It's too stiff,' I protested after a token effort. 'It won't budge. And anyway I'm frightened of making a noise that will alert them to our presence.'

'We're going to have to move along as far as we can then. At the moment they've only got to open the bathroom door and they'll see us.'

I copied his technique, straightening my arms on either side of me so I could hoist my backside sideways and so slowly shift myself along the ledge.

Finally we were perched side-by-side like two sparrows right at the very end of the ledge. I looked straight ahead and tried to admire the view of the hoarding rather than glance down and submit to the terror of our precarious position. It was impossible now to hear anything that might be going on inside Madam Gadalla's suite of rooms. Whilst we were on the side-end of the building with the Corniche hidden around the corner of the hotel off to our left, the noise from the busy street below was loud and constant. We listened to the shouts of street vendors and taxi drivers blending with the clip clopping of horses hooves and the merry tinkling of the bells the caleche drivers adorned their horse-drawn carriages with as they all plied their trade along the Corniche. And of course there was the incessant honking of car horns that provides a constant background accompaniment to all things in Egypt.

It was hot on the ledge. We had none of the benefit of the hotel's air conditioning out here. The sun slanted high above us, just starting its slow descent towards the west bank, also off to our left on the other side of the river. 'I can think of better places for a spot of sunbathing.' I muttered, wishing I was wearing a hat. I pulled my sunglasses forward off the top of my head where they'd been perched since we'd come inside from the hotel gardens. I was thankful I could at least dim the glare of the slowly sinking sun.

I wondered if the brothers had discovered the secret hiding place within the champagne bottles, and found myself reflecting on everything we'd overheard. 'So the mysterious Rosa was the original thief of the scarab,' I said after a while. 'Which probably explains why Madam Gadalla told Freya she no longer wishes to speak of her. I wonder what Ashraf meant about their different ideologies, and their love for different men.'

'I get the sense of a bitter falling-out between the sisters,' Adam speculated. 'Didn't Ashraf say Madam Gadalla hated her sister for betraying Farouk, possibly to his death?'

'Mm, they certainly don't give the impression of a happy and united family; do they? And Ashraf's bombshell about stealing the scarab made it quite clear he's the father of those two unsavoury young Egyptians who lured poor Josh into the Western Valley.'

Adam pondered this for a moment. 'Clever of them to think of using the oblique references to Amenhotep III and hence the scarab to pique our interest. So they're not as stupid as Nabil seems to think them.'

'But I still don't understand what they were hoping to achieve or why they hit on the idea of using Josh to do their dirty work for them,' I frowned.

His voice was a bit detached as he made quotation marks with his fingers and said, *'Will no-one rid me of this troublesome priest?'*

'I beg your pardon?' I said, not immediately catching on to his reference.

'It's what Henry II is supposed to have said when Thomas Becket as Archbishop of Canterbury started making life difficult for him. Four knights took him at his word and rushed off to Canterbury Cathedral where they murdered Becket, which is what led to him being canonised as a saint.'

'And you think those two, Hanif and Saiyyid, took their father equally literally when he said they needed to get rid of Ben?'

'It sounded that way to me.'

'Then we're lucky Ben's still alive,' I said fervently. 'Perhaps it was a blessing they decided to use Josh as a patsy. It's clear he's never used a firearm before in his life. It's amazing he managed to hit the target at all considering they drugged him. We should count our blessings they didn't stick around to finish off the job.'

'They may have thought Ben's injury was worse than it was,' Adam mused. 'I, for one, thought the worst when I saw he'd been hit.'

'And they obviously wanted to make good their getaway,' I murmured. 'Damned cowards. But, even so, they can't have been thinking straight.'

He fell silent for a moment, and then said unhappily. 'I suppose you realise that when the Zaal brothers leave here they're going to make a beeline for the *Queen Ahmes*. Now they've worked out Farouk probably smuggled the scroll to their aunt, and once they find the champagne bottles are empty, they're going to want to know for sure whether or not she packaged it up and sent it to Ben.'

'Can you imagine it?' I asked rhetorically. 'Entrusting potentially priceless ancient artefacts to the notoriously unreliable Egyptian postal system! I've known it take months for a postcard to make its way home. She was taking an awful risk with the scarab.'

'Mm, well, it seems clear she feels that just about any outcome is preferable to her nephews getting their hands on those artefacts. You know, I feel a bit sorry for Nabil Zaal. I mean, his brother sounds like an unpleasant sort, but Nabil really has been on a mission all these years. His mother obviously knew just enough to get him started. But she didn't have the scroll and it's clear that she didn't have the scarab for long, since it seems her sister boldly stole it back and then probably hid it inside one of those champagne bottles. The bitterness between those sisters must've run very deep for Aunt Layla to continue to withhold the evidence even once her nephew started to make an international reputation for himself.'

'Maybe she really is an evil old witch after all. I wonder where she is. Probably holed up with a friend somewhere. Which explains why she didn't take the scroll with her. I mean, she can hardly turn up with a bottle of fine vintage champagne and not offer to open it, good Muslim or not. But I agree with Nabil her timing stinks. It strikes me all she's achieved with her disappearing act is to divert the danger she clearly fears for herself onto Ben and Freya.'

'And we've left them alone and unguarded on the dahabeeyah with just an unloaded gun to defend themselves,' Adam reminded me. 'I think it's time we were getting back there, don't you? And I want to get Ted to take a look at this scroll. We need to know just how potentially explosive it is.'

Without another word, he hoisted himself up onto his knees and started to stand. I let out a terrified little gasp and clung even harder to the ledge. Somehow having him standing alongside me made me feel even more unsafe and started the vertigo up again. 'For God's sake, Adam! It's too dangerous. Wouldn't it be better to just wait for the pair of them to go?'

'And let them get there ahead of us? No, I think we've heard enough.' He rolled the scroll tighter and eased it behind him into the waistband of his trousers in the centre of his back, notching his belt tighter to keep it in place.

'Please Adam,' I appealed. But I knew it was no use. Adam hadn't spent months lavishing love and cans of calico paint on our beautiful dahabeeyah just to allow two Egyptians who may imagine they had a score to settle to muscle their way on board.

His next words proved my point. 'I love you, Merry; but I am not prepared to spend what's left of the afternoon sitting out here on this window ledge. There's too much at stake. I used to be quite good at gymnastics when I was at school, so here goes...' And with that, he dropped a quick kiss on top of my head, crouched and leapt.

I think I may have let out an involuntary scream as his feet left the relative safety of the ledge alongside me. I know time didn't really slow down, but it seemed to me I watched him spring across the space in an awful sort of slow motion. For a heart-stopping moment that must have been just a split second – though it was long enough to turn the blood in my veins to sludge – he seemed to hang in a kind of suspended animation, no longer in contact with the ledge, but certainly not in contact with the vine climbing the wall a metre or so away. And then his reaching hands connected with a gnarled shoot that looked like a piece of twisted rope, and his feet clamped around another one a little further down. He'd made it. He clung there for a moment, securing his hold, and then grinned back at me. 'Easy!'

My heart jolted back to life again only to judder to a halt once more as I heard a noise through the open window and realised the bathroom door was being opened. I raised my finger to my lips in an urgent gesture to Adam. We both froze as the sound of movement reached us.

'It must have been a noise from the street,' Nabil's voice floated out through the window. 'For some reason the window is wide open in here.' This was a situation he sought immediately to rectify. I closed my eyes, sucked in a breath, flattened myself against the wall and tried to make myself invisible. As I did so, I heard the window being pulled closed alongside me.

When no shout of discovery greeted me, I opened first one eye then the other and let out a long shuddery breath. I sent a look of heartfelt relief at Adam and whispered, 'My God! That was a close shave!'

He waited for a few moments to give Nabil Zaal time to go back inside, and then started scrambling carefully down the vine. 'I'll lower myself down a bit more to give you room to follow.'

My heart did a painful somersault all over again as I realised he really did intend for me to make the same death-defying jump he'd just demonstrated. 'There's no way I can follow,' I squeaked, trying to keep my voice down. 'Unlike you, I was most definitely *not* good at gymnastics at school. I was one of those kids who sprinted up to vault across that horse thingy only to come to a grinding halt in front of it. The gym teacher despaired of me.'

His troubled blue-eyed gaze came to meet mine. 'But I can't leave you here, Merry. What if they decide to come back to investigate why the window was open and find you?'

'Yes, well, looking at the sheer drop between you and me I think I've revised my opinion and decided that might be the lesser of two evils. If I'm caught there's at least a chance I can somehow talk my way out of it. Whereas if I fail to emulate your monkey-like abilities, the only talking I'll be doing is to beg St Peter to overlook my many transgressions from the straight and narrow and let me in through the Pearly Gates. And you've got the scroll, so even if they do discover me at least I'll be empty-handed.'

'But –'

'Honestly Adam,' I cut him off before he could protest further. 'I'm staying put. I can spend the next few minutes entertaining myself quite happily by concocting a story to explain just why it is I've decided to spend the afternoon sunning myself on a bathroom window ledge when the loungers around the pool are so much more comfortable. Besides which, just look at what I'm wearing!'

He eyed my slim-fitting dress and the heels on my sandals with some appreciation. 'You could always take them off?' he suggested.

I sent him my best withering look. 'I hardly think I can emerge into the Corniche in just my bra and knickers! This is Egypt, remember?'

He tried to argue some more but in the end he had no choice but to give it up in the face of my unswervable determination to stay where I was and even grinned at me with one of the quick returns to humour that I find such an appealing part of his personality. 'I'll bet if anyone can come up with a convincing story, you can! Just sit tight and I'll think of something to get you out of there.'

I basked for a moment in this unexpected praise and watched as he reprised his monkey-impression, clambering with great agility down the vine.

He waved up at me when he reached the bottom and I blew him a kiss, trying to look perfectly at home and relaxed in my precarious position perched on the side of one of the most iconic buildings in Luxor. In truth I wasn't feeling nearly so nonchalant as I pretended at being left on my own on an outside bathroom window ledge, two storeys up. But I was genuinely terrified of attempting – and failing – the leap onto that vine. As Adam disappeared from my sight under the hoarding I contented myself with the thought that never again would I be able to visit the refined Winter Palace Hotel and think of it in quite the same way. I would always carry with me the mental image of myself sitting up here with all my nerve endings jangling.

I sat ramrod straight with my back pressed up hard against the wall and tried to interest myself in the hoarding opposite. Adam had said he had a bad feeling about this latest venture of mine. But now we had the scroll I couldn't see how we could possibly regret it. Even if Nabil Zaal and his brother should happen to catch me, the scroll must surely give us some bargaining power.

The sunshine warmed my skin and I drifted in a languorous kind of torpor for a while. I couldn't help but wonder how the world might react if the scroll did indeed prove that Kings David and Solomon of the Bible were, in fact, the Pharaohs Thutmosis III and Amenhotep III.

I wouldn't claim to be in anything like the same Egyptological league as Ted or Adam but they were names to thrill even the most recumbent of armchair Egyptologists. Thutmosis, nephew and stepson to the first female pharaoh Hatshepsut, was ancient Egypt's mightiest warrior pharaoh, expanding the borders of his empire up to the Euphrates in the north and way down into the Sudan in the south. His great-grandson Amenhotep presided peaceably over Egypt's golden age as the richest nation on earth as tribute poured into Egyptian coffers from its many vassal states.

I lost myself for a while in the wonder of the scroll's passage from antiquity, stored inside a clay jar in a cave in Qumran near the Dead Sea, into the modern world, then the years it had spent tightly rolled up inside a re-modelled champagne bottle.

I wondered, perhaps a bit cheekily, if I might be able to make any mileage from this new discovery on my website advertising our luxury Nile cruises to those with more than a passing interest in ancient Egyptian history. The story of how King Farouk stole it from the visiting Jordanian Antiquities Service was exciting enough, but to be able to embellish the tale with our personal involvement in helping the scroll on its way into the history books was something I felt might give us a unique marketing angle and help us win out over our competition.

In such happy daydreams the time passed quite quickly out there on the window ledge. I glanced at my watch and realised an hour had gone by. Surely it was enough time for Nabil and Ashraf Zaal to have made a pretty thorough search of their aunt's belongings, especially since they knew the general manager and Ahmed were waiting for them downstairs.

After sitting and dithering for a bit, I decided I could take my chances and started to shunt my way back along the ledge towards the closed window. I eased myself up onto my knees so I could get some purchase on the glass and tried to shift it upwards. It refused to budge. I put a bit more effort into it and let out a yelp as I lost my balance momentarily. With my heart thumping, I slumped sideways into a sitting position again and spent a moment concentrating on bringing my raggedy breathing and swimming head back to normal.

It occurred to me there must of course be a latch on the inside of the window that secured it closed and Nabil Zaal must have helpfully locked it in place. So I really was stuck out here on the ledge. I reminded myself that even if I'd been able to make it back inside, I'd still be trapped. The brothers would have locked up Madam Gadalla's suite behind them when they left and returned the key to the general manager. But I would have been a whole lot more comfortable inside. The shadows were lengthening and some of the heat was starting to go out of the sun. My muscles were beginning to protest at being bunched in one position on the hard stone ledge. It occurred to me I needed to use the toilet. The sight of one within a few feet of me taunted me with its proximity. But it was out of reach. I crossed my legs and tried not to think about running water.

I wondered briefly about Ahmed before it dawned on me that he was no doubt accompanying the Zaal brothers to see the British tourists as he'd promised. He'd know at once they hadn't discovered Adam and me. But he could hardly excuse himself for a few moments to come and let us out before heading off to the dahabeeyah. I really was on my own. I could only place my faith in Adam somehow getting back to me before nightfall. Until then I faced a long, uncomfortable evening ahead.

My daydreams were not nearly so happy now and the time passed considerably more slowly. Sitting in the late afternoon sunshine had made me drowsy but I didn't dare close my eyes. The prospect of relaxing, dropping off to sleep and sliding off the ledge was too real and too terrifying.

I started to agree with Adam that this whole thing was a really bad idea. While it was true that the advent of Ben Hunter and his letter in our lives had spiced things up over the last few days, I couldn't help but feel a bit nostalgic for the simple life Adam and I had been leading before he arrived. Adam had worried it might not be enough for me, just cruising up and down the Nile. But right now I couldn't think of anything I wanted to be doing more. The fringe of greenery along the riverbanks would be starting to change from dusty green to charcoal black as the sun sank behind the Theban hills. It was my favourite view on earth and I found myself longing for it with a pure and steady need. I stared at the hoarding in front of me and wished there was something more interesting to look at so I could distract myself from the downward spiral of my thoughts.

Assuming Adam had hopped into a taxi, he'd have been back on board the *Queen Ahmes* long since. Ted was no doubt poring over the scroll with all his scholarly fires alight. I wondered if Adam had allowed Nabil and Ashraf Zaal on board when they turned up. It was frustrating to be sitting out here on a window ledge when all the action was going on back on board the dahabeeyah.

And then all of a sudden I heard my name being called. At least it was the version of my name that passes for the real thing in Ahmed-speak. 'Mereditd! Adam! Are you here?'

I jolted back fully awake from the dull listlessness I'd been drifting in and started banging on the window as loudly as I could. 'Ahmed! I'm out here! In the bathroom! Quick!' I saw the shadows move inside the room as he opened the bathroom door, and then he saw me. I might have laughed at the look of stark horror on his face if I hadn't been so keen to get back inside.

He flung the window open and reached out for me so I half scrambled, half fell back into the bathroom and into his bearlike embrace. 'Mereditd! I have been mad wid worry! Are you alright? Why were you outside? You could have fallen and killed yourself! Where is Adam?'

I eased myself out of his clutching arms. 'I'll answer all your questions in a minute, Ahmed. But first, if you'll excuse me, I rather urgently need to use the loo.'

I joined him a few moments later back in Madam Gadalla's furniture-stuffed living room. The essentials such as Ashraf Zaal's arrival and Adam's departure were swiftly told. 'But, Ahmed, what are you still doing here? I thought you were going to escort Nabil Zaal back to the dahabeeyah.' I slapped the top of my head as I realised the stupidity of what I'd just said. 'Of course! Now Ashraf has turned up, Nabil doesn't need you to show him how to find Ben and Freya. Since Ashraf's the one who stole the scarab from Freya, he knows exactly where to go, all thanks to the helpful little note I left with Josh! And I'm quite sure he'd rather interview them without a police officer – that is, you – looking on.'

'I waited and waited,' Ahmed explained. 'But dis nephew of Madam Gadalla he didn't come. In de end I went to see de receptionist and he said de two nephews of Madam Gadalla had come downstairs and given him de key and den rushed off. I asked him to give de key to me. I telled to him dat I left something up here while I was searching de room.'

'Well, thank God you're here! I had visions of being stuck out on that ledge all night!'

'We go now, yes? De two men are ahead of us.'

'Yes. Ahmed, we need to get back to the dahabeeyah as quickly as possible.'

We retraced our steps to where Ahmed had left his police car parked in one of the side streets behind Luxor Temple. As he drove us back through the darkening outskirts of Luxor and across the bridge, I filled him in on everything Adam and I had learned listening to the conversation between Nabil and Ashraf Zaal.

By the time we arrived on the west bank dusk had descended. Ahmed parked up on the bank behind the knot of swaying palm trees and accompanied me along the track to the stone steps that led down to the crumbling jetty where the *Queen Ahmes* was moored.

'I will collect de gun to be used in my evidences and den I must leave you to pursue my invesdigations,' he said importantly.

Except there was just one problem with this plan. I blinked, did a quick double take, and said; 'I think you're going to have to manage without any forensics that gun may provide for a little while longer, my friend.'

The dark river gently lapped against the causeway in the space where the dahabeeyah should have been – but was no longer – tied to its mooring posts. The *Queen Ahmes* herself was floating at anchor a little way off in the middle of the river; her sails still neatly furled in so just the long poles were etched diagonally against the darkening sky. The only thing still connecting her to the bank was the long electricity cable strung like a tightrope across the dark waters of the Nile.

Chapter 14

But it wasn't only the sight of the *Queen Ahmes* at anchor in the middle of the Nile that made me gasp in surprise. In the gathering gloom, those on board the dahabeeyah had decided to switch on the lights. I could see the lounge-bar illuminated by the ambient glow of the lamps I'd set on side tables around the room. It seemed there was quite a gathering of people in there, although I couldn't tell exactly how many or precisely who. But I knew Ted couldn't be counted among their number, as I was also able to see into his cabin. It was located on the side of the dahabeeyah facing me where I was standing on the riverbank and he'd switched on his bedside lamp. As I might have predicted, he was sitting at the small Victorian bureau I'd installed, leaning forward in concentration. Not hard to imagine what he was doing. But it certainly wasn't the sight of Ted bending myopically over the scroll that accounted for my gasp of shock. No; that was drawn from me by the view I had into another cabin altogether; one which I might reasonably have expected to be in darkness, but in which a solitary lamp was glowing. It allowed me to see inside quite clearly. 'So *this* is where she's been hiding!' I exclaimed, staring into the porthole of one of the tiny cabins we'd fitted out for our as yet non-existent crew, situated below the kitchen at the back end of the boat. 'My God, she's got some gall! You know, I *thought* that loaf of bread I bought on the way back from the hospital yesterday had gone down rather quickly. It was nearly half gone when I went to slice it for breakfast this morning. I figured maybe someone had helped themselves to a few slices as a midnight feast. But now I come to think of it, our uninvited guest will have needed something to eat if she's been here for the last three days.' I could see her quite clearly, huddled up on the bed still swathed from head to toe in her enveloping black robes with her hijab headscarf wound around her face. 'Now there's an old lady I very much wish to speak to,' I muttered darkly. But it was a simple fact that out here on the riverbank I was as far away from whatever answers were to be found on board the *Queen Ahmes* as ever I'd been stuck up on the window ledge at The Winter Palace.

Ahmed was staring wide-eyed at the *Queen Ahmes*. 'Can we ask dem to bring de dahabeeyah back to shore?' he asked a bit uncertainly.

'I doubt it. She's out there for a reason. No, there's only one thing for it. I'll have to swim.'

Ahmed turned his incredulous and no less round-eyed stare on my face. 'But Mereditd, no – you cannot! I must go and fetch a boat. Dere is a dinghy we can use at de police station.'

'I've wasted too much time already,' I argued shortly, glancing back in through the narrow run of lounge-bar windows hoping for a glimpse of Adam. It went unrewarded. Ben I could see; and Josh – so I guessed Freya must be there somewhere too. And, more worryingly, Nabil and Ashraf Zaal were there. And so too were the pair I dreaded to see most, the two young Egyptians Hanif and Saiyyid. So my bright idea of using the gun we'd retrieved from the Western Valley as a deterrent clearly hadn't worked. The causeway where Ahmed and I were standing wasn't lit. So while I could see in through the dahabeeyah's windows I was confident those inside couldn't see us. They looked to be having some sort of intense powwow. 'Do you see Adam anywhere?' I started to unstrap my shoes. 'I'd have thought he'd break the moorings to *prevent* them boarding, not with them already on board. Something must be wrong!'

'I do not see him and I cannot let you swim out dere on your own,' Ahmed declared stolidly. 'But I myself am unable to swim, so I cannot offer to take your place.'

'Then go and get some help!' I rounded on him a bit desperately. 'He must be in trouble.'

I think the poor man nearly fainted on the spot when I kicked off my sandals and started to pull my dress over my head, treating my devout Muslim friend to an eyeful of me *en déshabillé*, as it were. 'I was never much of a gymnast,' I muttered, 'But I was always a strong swimmer.' And with that I stepped to the edge of the jetty and eased myself down into the dark waters of the Nile.

Despite the residual heat of the day lingering in the air temperature, the water was a clammy sort of cold as it enveloped me. I pushed out from the bank and started a measured breaststroke, keeping my head above the water and my mouth clamped tightly shut, concentrating on breathing through my nose. For all that the locals swim in the river quite regularly with no apparent ill effect, Nile water is renowned to be teeming with all sorts of nasties. I had no wish to contract a dose of dysentery just to round things off.

I didn't glance back to see if Ahmed had moved off the spot where he appeared to have taken root with his eyes bulging. All my attention was focused solely on reaching the dahabeeyah. I spared a momentary thought for crocodiles; heartily thankful they'd died out in the Nile after the Aswan dams were built. So, with no crocs to worry about there was little to impede my progress. My waterlogged underwear didn't hamper me and before long the flank of the dahabeeyah's starboard side was within reaching distance.

My first priority was to try to locate Adam. I couldn't settle to anything else before I'd clapped eyes on him and reassured myself he was ok. I swam around the prow, kicking out through the water some distance from the dahabeeyah so I could attempt to see in through the windows. The cabin Adam and I shared was in darkness. But two windows along from it the glow of lamplight shone from Ben's cabin. I knew Ben to be in the lounge-bar since I'd seen him there moments ago. Treading water, another glance confirmed it. I watched him hobble up and down for a bit, trying to get a sense of what was going on. His injured leg was clearly still paining him. Then a movement drew my attention back to Ben's lighted cabin window and I let out a long sigh of relief. Adam was inside. I watched him move away from the window and slump down out of sight, presumably onto the bed.

I struck out towards the boat again. Underneath the lighted window all I could think of to attract his attention was to splash water up at it. I didn't dare call out. It took several evermore tsunami-like splashes before Adam apparently noticed that someone was attempting to wash the windows with Nile water. The window opened and after a moment Adam poked his head out.

'Finally!' I exclaimed.

I watched the shock register on his face. 'Merry? Bloody hell! Is that you?'

I bit back a retort about the relative merits of swapping a precipice without a safety net for the murky waters of the river Nile. The situation was too serious for that. 'It's me. Ahmed rescued me.'

'Thank God!' Relief swept across his features. 'Are you ok? I've been driving myself nuts thinking of you stuck outside on that ledge and knowing I couldn't get back to you.'

'I'm fine.' I clung to a ridge at the waterline on the side of the boat rather than tread water interminably. 'Adam, did you know Madam Gadalla was hiding on board?'

'*What*?!'

'Yes – I've just spied her from the riverbank. She's stowing away in one of the crew cabins.'

'You're joking! Bloody cheek!'

'So can we assume the others don't know she's here?'

'I don't know. I've spent most of the time since I've been back locked here in Ben's cabin. You know, getting Ted to arrange for locks to be fitted on the doors today wasn't one of your better ideas, Merry.'

'What happened? Did you know Hanif and Saiyyid are here? I'd hoped they might want to avoid us like the plague after what they did to Josh.'

'They were here when I got back. I think they came to put the frighteners on Ben. To be fair, I don't think they had any idea Josh was here. Ben stood his ground well. He's not a man to frighten easily. But it seems when he started threatening them with the gun they just laughed at him. They said he'd need to learn how to release the safety catch first. I gather at least one of them is pretty competent with firearms. Anyway, it seems they'd just muscled their way on board when I got back. Nabil and Ashraf Zaal were only moments behind me, by the way, so they can't have wasted much time on searching Madam Gadalla's suite. I only just managed to hand the scroll over to Ted, who immediately shut himself away in his cabin. Nabil looked quite appalled at finding his nephews here, but Ashraf took it all in at a glance and, when he realised I was surplus to requirements, shoved me into the nearest cabin – which happened to be this one – and locked the door.'

'Is Ted locked in, too?'

'Yes, but at his own behest. He was clever enough to have already put his key on the inside of the lock.'

'So they can't get to him.' I said with relief. 'Do they know he's got the scroll?'

'I'm not sure they even know he's here. I don't think they had the rudimentary common sense to check the other cabins. And, so far, to the best of my knowledge, Ben has staunchly denied any knowledge of a scroll.'

'Just one more question. What the hell is the *Queen Ahmes* doing in the middle of the river?'

'They broke the moorings just after they locked me in here and when we'd drifted far enough out from the bank I heard the anchor drop. I imagine it's a tactic designed to make it clear to Ben and Freya in particular that they're now captive. Perhaps they hope it will loosen their tongues.'

It seemed we'd covered all the essentials. 'You'd better come inside, Merry. He leaned forward to haul me in through the window. 'You'll catch your death out there.'

'Not yet,' I said. 'First I want to pay a surprise visit to our uninvited house guest.'

He started to argue, but I was already pushing out again from the side of the boat. 'For God's sake, please be careful,' he called softly after me.

My mission was to get these damned people – all of them – off the dahabeeyah so Adam and I could have it to ourselves again. I'd make an exception for Ted, of course. If he could stay safely locked in his cabin with the scroll so much the better. But as for the rest of them, I wanted shot of the lot. Mysteries were all very well, I decided; but when it meant Adam was locked up on his own boat and I was forced to swim to find a way on board, it was time to draw the line. A return to our simple life was altogether more appealing. But I wouldn't demur at hanging onto the scroll.

I had no intention of reprising my splashing-at-the-window routine with Madam Gadalla. Trying to conduct an interrogation from the water would put me at a distinct disadvantage. Instead, I swam around to the back of the dahabeeyah and hauled myself up the couple of rungs of the mini stepladder fixed to a small landing platform at the stern. I think its purpose was for us to be able to tie up a small fishing boat or tender. Adam had sat there once or twice on lazy afternoons with his fishing rod stretched out across the Nile. The door at the back below the kitchen was unlocked and, shivering in my wet underwear, I stepped through it into a small dark space. To call it a corridor would be to grossly exaggerate its proportions. It was no more than a single pace wide and perhaps two paces long, although four doorways led off it. Khaled's ability to squeeze four crew cabins into this tiny space was quite possibly the most impressive part of his renovation of our beloved dahabeeyah. I already knew which room Madam Gadalla was camping out in, although the rim of light under the door would have betrayed her had I not. I ducked silently into the room opposite and pulled off the single sheet that adorned the small bed wedged up against the wall, drying myself with it as best I could. Conducting the interview I had in mind in just my underwear and with Nile river water cascading off me in torrents would also put me at a distinct disadvantage. And I had every intention of having the upper hand. Then I wrapped myself in the sheet toga-style. If being swathed from head to foot in a voluminous bolt of fabric was good enough for Madam Gadalla, it would serve equally well for me. My hair was plastered wetly against my head, but it was reasonably short so it would dry quickly.

Stealthy as a cat, I crept back into the corridor space. I flung Madam Gadalla's door open with a single twist of the door handle. 'Would you mind telling me exactly what you think you're playing at?'

The startled screech she let out was actually quite gratifying. She shot a terrified glance at me, did a quick double take at my unusual get-up and, I have to say, recovered herself remarkably quickly. She started babbling away incoherently in rapid Arabic.

'Now, now, don't give me all that,' I scolded. 'I know perfectly well that you speak English. I saw you at your nephew's lecture the other day, and you were hanging on his every word.'

She was a tiny, wizened creature. Dark eyes observed me from a face creased with the lines of old age and a lifetime spent in a hot, bone-dry climate. Little remained of the great beauty captured in the photographs I'd seen except those eyes. They flashed with a dark brilliance even as she curled herself into a small protective ball on the bed, crouched against the wall in one corner of the room, watching me. She pointed a small bony finger at me. It protruded a bit ET-like from the black folds of her robe. 'You will protect me,' she husked.

I advanced towards her. 'I don't see why I should when your actions have led to one innocent person being shot at, and another drugged up to his eyeballs and almost framed for attempted murder! Not to mention our dahabeeyah now being under siege by dubious members of your extended family.'

'He made threats against me,' she said in heavily accented English.

'This would be Saiyyid? He's your great-nephew – yes? – one of Ashraf's sons. The one who opened your door to Ben and refused to let him in?'

She nodded. 'He threatened to hurt me. He saw the scarab when the girl revealed it in the Winter Palace lobby. I'd sent it to her, you see. He came to my room to terrorize me. He said I must get it back and give it to Ashraf or they would take matters into their own hands. And then, when that young man came to knock on my door, Saiyyid would not let me answer it. When the young man had gone, Saiyyid wrapped his hands around my throat and demanded to know what I had written to Mr Hunter.' She put her own hands up to her throat in a protective gesture, and then sneered, her black eyes flashing again. 'I laughed in his face! "Never!" I said. "Never will I tell you, or give in to your threats!"' She hawked and spat onto the floor, making me jump. 'They are evil men, every one of them. Just like Rosa. Evil! Never will I give in to their demands. No matter how much they terrorize me!'

'So you decided to seek refuge here. But I'd like to know how the hell you smuggled yourself on board.'

She fixed those fine eyes on me. The more I looked into them, the more I saw the beautiful young woman she'd once been. I'd read novels which described someone's eyes as being lit with an inner fire, but I'd never known what it meant; until now, looking into Layla Gadalla's dark eyes and seeing the flame of some deep passion burning in them. 'I wanted only to speak with the young man who is the son of Gregory Hunter, and to my great-niece, Sofia's granddaughter. The young man said he would leave his address at the reception desk. So after Saiyyid left me alone, I waited until nightfall when the night receptionist came on duty. When he was called away momentarily, I collected the envelope from my slot on the shelf and then asked a caleche driver to bring me here. I watched you all from the riverbank. You were eating dinner. I could see you quite plainly. I was hidden, watching and plucking up the courage to approach you when my wicked nephew Ashraf turned up on a moped. I thought at first he had followed me and came to do me harm. But then I saw him creep on board.'

'Yes,' I remarked. 'That will be when he stole the scarab.'

'He stole the scarab?' she parroted in a shrill voice. "This is very bad news. For years he has wanted it. Just for money, you understand.' And she spat again, leaving me in no doubt what she thought about that. I winced and made a mental note to give this room a particularly thorough clean when all this was over. 'He is a wicked man, that one. Wicked! Just like Rosa his mother!'

'Ah yes, the original thief of the scarab,' I muttered.

Her dark eyes gleamed up at me from where she was crouched in the corner on the bed. 'But not for long! I stole it back!'

'So I gather.'

'It was not hers! It belonged to my Freddy. Oh, she was evil, that one. Evil!'

It seemed to me we were going round in ever decreasing circles and straying away from the point. 'So how did you get on board? Adam pulled up the gangplank after your thieving nephew left us that night.'

She eyed my damp and dishevelled state, letting her gaze linger on the sheet I'd wrapped around myself. 'In the same way as you,' she said in somewhat gleeful tones and with a lift of one eyebrow that conveyed something I took to be irony at my need to gain access to my own boat with such difficulty. 'I am not too old to swim. And the dahabeeyah was moored at the bank, so it was not far. I was able to disrobe and toss my niqab onto the little platform at the back and swim across after you were all in bed.' There was a smooth satisfaction in her voice that gave me a glimpse of the adventuresome girl she must once have been.

I remembered my wakefulness that night; how every small sound had unsettled me. And no wonder if this game old bird had been in the act of stowing herself away on board.

'I wanted only to speak with the young man who is the son of Gregory Hunter, and to my great-niece, Sofia's granddaughter,' she repeated.

Reminded of the purpose of my interrogation, I narrowed my gaze on her. 'So, why didn't you? It seems to me you've had plenty of opportunities. Perhaps if you'd let us know you were here right from the moment you arrived, or the following morning at the very least, we could have avoided all this.'

Her dark eyes flashed. 'They make threats against me. And they watch,' she wailed. 'Always, they watch.'

'But –' I started.

'They make threats against me. And they watch,' she wailed again and I realised it might prove more difficult than I'd hoped to interrogate someone who apparently had no wish to be interrogated. But then she surprised me by volunteering: 'Next day, while you were gone, Saiyyid approached the dahabeeyah and attached something to the door. I wanted to go and get it, but he stayed on the riverbank watching for your return. They make threats against me. And they watch. Always they watch.'

I wasn't sure exactly how much of this I was buying. It seemed to me she could have made herself known to us several times over in the time she'd had. She'd certainly wasted no time helping herself to the loaf of bread I'd bought. But perhaps she'd taken it into her head to camp out indefinitely and wait to be sure the coast was truly clear. If so, she'd miscalculated badly. 'Well, your whole family is on board making free with our hospitality at the moment,' I said short temperedly. 'And I want them off. So how do you suggest we go about it?'

A calculating gleam came into her dark eyes. 'Ashraf may have the scarab, but I still have something far more valuable. Perhaps I can use it to lure them away from here.'

'Would this by any chance be the Dead Sea Scroll King Farouk stole from the Jordanian Antiquities Department and spirited out of Egypt when he was deposed?'

Her flashing gaze snapped to my face, full of suspicion. 'What do you know of the scroll?'

'Only that your hidey hole inside the champagne bottles is now an open secret.'

The colour drained from her lined skin. 'But I promised Freddy I would keep it safe!' she keened. 'Where is the scroll? Who has it?'

'It's safe enough for the time being; more through luck than anything else, I admit. But if we want it to stay that way then I suggest you come with me so we can work together on preventing your delightful nephews from getting their hands on it.'

I had to virtually drag her off the bed. I didn't much enjoy this since I've never manhandled a little old lady before.

I imagine we made quite a theatrical impression when we appeared in the doorway of the lounge-bar; Madam Gadalla cringing a bit and swathed in her black robes and hijab, me spurred on by anger and a sense of righteous indignation, decked out in my white Egyptian cotton sheet with my hair curling damply around my face. It was a strange freeze-frame moment for sure as all eyes turned towards us in shock.

It was Nabil Zaal who recovered himself first and leapt up from his chair. 'Aunt Layla! Thank God! You're safe! Maybe you can help me put a stop to this madness!'

I darted a lightning glance around the room to take stock. The *Queen Ahmes* that had once played host to a lavish picnic for the young King Farouk and his entourage was now the setting for a tense standoff between rival factions.

Ben, Freya and Josh were lined up on the divan like the three wise monkeys. With the stolen gun trained on them at close range from the armchair in the hands of one of the younger Egyptian brothers, there was more than enough evil for them to be getting on with. I had no idea whether it was once more loaded with bullets and therefore deadly. But it didn't seem worth taking the chance.

'Who are you?' Ashraf Zaal was on his feet and advancing on me. It was the first time I'd actually seen him in the flesh. He looked much like Nabil, but clearly preferred the native galabeya to his brother's more suave Western dress. He was also taller, and wider in girth. All things considered, he looked decidedly menacing and I took a hasty step backwards.

'I just happen to be part owner of this boat you've commandeered so precipitously. You locked the other one up. And I want you off!' My anger surged again. I hadn't walked away from my old life just to stand by and watch while this lot screwed up my precious new one before it was even out of the starting blocks.

'And just how do you think you're going to achieve that, little lady?' he sneered.

'I have something you want. And the only way you'll get it is by doing exactly what I say.'

In truth, I'd lied to Madam Gadalla when I'd said we needed to work together to prevent her nephews getting their hands on the scroll. I was starting to think if it got them off my beloved dahabeeyah they could have it with my blessing. Although if I could find a way to remove them all whilst leaving Ted in possession of the scroll, that remained my preferred option. If not, I decided I might try my best to ensure Nabil Zaal was the one to get it, since he didn't seem much happier about this situation than I was.

Ashraf went quite still and watchful, and thankfully stopped advancing towards me. Instead he looked me insolently up and down as if checking to see whether there was any way I could be hiding a rolled up parchment scroll under the sheet I was wearing. 'And what might that be?'

'Your brother was on the right track with the champagne bottles,' I said conversationally, clinging to my bravado for all I was worth. 'It was a great hiding place. But, shame for you, we got there first.'

I watched his expression as he registered the full import of what I'd said. 'Oh yes, we heard you, you know. We know you made a search. In fact, we heard everything you said. So we know all about the activities of these two thuggish sons of yours. You see, we were listening at the bedroom door.'

'But how did you – ?'

'Escape?' I finished for him. 'We have a very good friend in the local police force. And he's on his way here with reinforcements right now,' I crossed my fingers behind my back as I said this. 'So if you want to make a bargain for the scroll, I suggest we get started.'

'Where is it? Where's the scroll?'

'All in good time,' I countered. 'First thing's first; I want Adam released from that cabin.'

'For God's sake, do as she says.' This time it was Nabil who spoke. Or begged; rather. He sounded quite desperate. I realised that nothing other than the scroll mattered to him. His life's ambition was within reach and it took precedence over everything else. Perhaps he really would sell his soul for it. 'If you won't let me have the scarab, at least let me have a chance at the scroll!'

'No! Never!' It was Madam Gadalla who screeched this from alongside me. 'Sons of a murderess! You will have to kill me too before I let you get your hands on it! Then she turned on me and lifted claw-like hands towards my face, her dark eyes flashing fury 'You have betrayed me! You are no better than Rosa herself! Everywhere I look – perfidy and wickedness!'

Nabil Zaal was closest so he was the one who caught her hands and pulled her away. 'Please Aunt Layla; this isn't helping.'

'But it is not yours to bargain with! Freddy sent it to *me*!'

To my surprise it was Freya who got up, cast a withering look at the young man with the handgun pointed at her, came across the room and drew Madam Gadalla back with her, settling her on the sofa. 'Why don't you tell us the whole story?' she asked gently, kneeling down on the floor alongside the old lady, looking more Bambi-like than ever.

'I'm going to get Adam,' I announced, and held out my hand. 'Do I need a key?'

Ashraf had watched his son trying to decide whom to keep the gun trained on as Freya got up. Now he turned to me with a return of the sneer. 'You are in no position to issue orders. You forget, young lady, we have the gun.' I couldn't help but notice that it swung in my direction as he said this.

'Oh please…!' Nabil protested, sounding very American. 'Ashraf, see sense; nobody is going to use a gun. The chances are a bullet from that thing would ricochet around the room and kill us all! Just give the girl the key.'

Ashraf sent his brother a truly evil look. But he reached into his pocket and handed me a key with a no less evil look at me to accompany it.

I marched from the room before anyone could change their minds, hoping the younger Zaal with the gun wouldn't decide to get trigger-happy.

Adam's eyes nearly fell out of his head when I unlocked the door and he saw me standing there draped in a bed-sheet.

'Merry! What on earth…?'

Sshhh, there isn't time for explanations now. Just come with me.' I reached for his hand and pulled him after me back out of the cabin. 'If I say anything, just go along with it, ok?'

We entered the lounge-bar to find the young Egyptian with the gun now resting it on the arm of his chair rather than holding it levelled at our guests. This was a distinct improvement and reassured me that Nabil Zaal, as the voice of reason, did have at least a modicum of influence with the less savoury members of his family. Nabil himself had subsided into an armchair opposite the sofa on which his wizened old aunt sat looking incredibly bat-like, but with her dark eyes watchful and alert.

Ashraf was pacing, but somehow he didn't look quite so threatening anymore. Actually, he looked quite nervy. I guess my bold talk of having a friend in the police force must have put the wind up him. But since it didn't seem there was much the police could do with us floating at anchor in the middle of the Nile in the dark, I assumed he'd taken my threats as empty ones and was in no immediate hurry to abandon ship.

I led Adam to the two-seater sofa set under the window and we sat down. 'So, Madam Gadalla,' I said, deciding to go on the offensive since the conversation didn't seem to have moved forward much in my absence. 'Why do you call your sister a murderess? Surely she wasn't there in the Ile de France restaurant with King Farouk on the night he died?'

She sent me a malicious glance. But for those eyes, it really would just take a tall, pointy hat to turn her into the archetypal witch, I decided. 'Rosa? I spit on her memory,' she announced, and looked very much as if she were about to fit the action to the words. Perhaps in deference to the cleaning job I'd have to do later, or maybe because all gazes were upon her, she thought better of it.

'But you loved her once,' Nabil nudged her gently, leaning forward.

Those fine eyes took on a faraway look. 'Ah, yes, in our girlhood together. Those were happier times. It was the 1940's and the world was emerging from the grip of War. Cairo was a city brimming with optimism. My sisters and I were the toast of the town. We were nightclub singers at the famous Omar Khayyam rooftop bar. That is where Freddy discovered us. We called ourselves 'The Tambourines', but before long everyone in town referred to us as 'Farouk's

Fancies'. Ah, the parties and the lavish royal receptions; soon we played exclusively for the king and our lives became a whirlwind of glittering balls and banquets where we entertained the rich and famous from all over the world. We sang and danced for film stars, politicians and royalty. Farouk loved and indulged us all. He showered us with gifts and took us everywhere with him.' A rather malicious glint flashed in her eyes. 'Farida didn't like it, of course. Their marriage was crumbling and she found it easy to blame us. She disapproved of the favour he showed us and of the favours we bestowed upon him in return. We loved him; me, I think, best of all.'

I glanced sideways and met Adam's sidelong gaze. It was the closest I suppose she was likely to come to admitting she and her sisters were high class prostitutes for the king – or, as Adam had described them, *courtesans*. No wonder Farida had objected. I looked back at Madam Gadalla, lost in her reverie. This is what she'd wanted, I mused, this opportunity to tell her story. This is why she'd brought Ben and Freya all the way from England. Her current life as a withered up old lady clinging to a sense of grandeur in her old-fashioned rooms at The Winter Palace must seem a far cry from those heady and flamboyant days of her youth as a royal favourite.

'But of course it couldn't last,' she said bitterly, blinking at the memories. 'It started to go wrong when silly Sofia became pregnant.'

Still sitting at Madam Gadalla's feet, Freya let out a gasp and stared up wide-eyed into the old lady's face.

Madam Gadalla smiled, and then leaned forward and patted her on the head, gazing at her with a new softness in her eyes. 'Dear one, you are wondering I think if King Farouk of Egypt was perhaps your grandfather and whether you have the blood of royalty running in your veins. Alas, no. Freddy was not the father of Sofia's child. Mr Gregory Hunter was the father of Sofia's child.'

This time it was Ben's turn to gasp. He jolted forward, staring at Freya and no doubt working out that this revelation meant they were related since his father was her grandfather. Quite what sort of relatives this made them was beyond me for the moment.

Ah well, I thought, Freya had come to Egypt in search of family; and she'd found it – although quite what she made of the assortment of uncles and cousins sitting around the room I couldn't imagine. But Madam Gadalla had only paused in her narrative, and went on with a faraway look in her eyes.

'Sofia always had a love of the British. I never understood it myself, since they felt their occupation of our country permitted them to lord it over those of us they dismissed as *the natives.*' Again, she spat the words out to show us just what she thought of the way her fellow Egyptians had been patronised under the British colonisation.

'Did Gregory Hunter know my grandmother was pregnant?' Freya whispered.

'Oh no, my child. Sofia loved him too much for that and did not want any whiff of scandal to stain his glittering career. The British were very narrow-minded about that sort of thing back then, and he came from a good family, you know. Not that Freddy would have cared. It was Freddy who made all the arrangements for Sofia to go to England. She was determined her child should grow up British since she had a British father. You see; she had strange, romantic ideas, our Sofia. Freddy knew a family from his time in England as a boy at the Royal Military Academy. He promised to keep the whole thing secret from Gregory and he arranged for Sofia to go to this family so they could care for her during her child's infancy.' Madam Gadalla's eyes came into focus for the first time and she stared down into Freya's upturned face. 'And perhaps Sofia was right to be so insistent about where her baby would be born and brought up. Look at you, her granddaughter – a proper young English girl.' Then her expression closed up again and her eyes hardened. 'You know I'm not sure Gregory Hunter even noticed Sofia was gone. Such is the faithlessness of British men.'

A big, fat tear rolled down Freya's cheek, wobbled on the bottom of her chin for a moment, and then plopped onto the front of her cotton dress.

Josh took this as his cue to turn from something resembling a waxwork dummy back into a living, breathing human being again. He reached forward and squeezed Freya's shoulder, perhaps wanting to show that not all British men were so unfeeling or so faithless.

'This little trip down memory lane is all very well,' Ashraf scorned. 'But it's not getting us any closer to getting our hands on the scroll.'

'Ah, the scroll,' Madam Gadalla murmured, her eyes losing focus again. 'Yes, Freddy was very excited about the scroll. I daresay he should not have stolen it; but he was strangely unable to help himself with things like that.'

'He was unbelievably lucky, to select the one scroll that made the link between Pharaonic history and the Bible,' Adam remarked from alongside me. 'None of those published has been found to have such incredible content.

Nabil Zaal's head snapped up and he sent Adam a long, narrowed glance. But Madam Gadalla went on as if she hadn't been interrupted.

'He loved unusual and beautiful things and he had a good eye for what was valuable. He collected ancient Egyptian artefacts; and he had fine collections of rare coins and stamps.'

I remembered what Shukura had said about his equally fine collection of pornography, and bit my lip.

'But he discovered the scroll too late in his reign to decide what to do with it. His enemies were massing against him. Those cheats the nationalists formed the Association of Free Officers and talked of freedom and the restoration of Egypt's dignity. Pah! What did they know of dignity; leading a revolution to overthrow a divinely anointed monarch? It was only under pressure from the Americans that the revolutionaries agreed to allow Freddy and his family to leave Egypt unharmed and with an honorary ceremony as befitted his status as king.'

She wiped a tear from her eye. 'So I had to watch my beloved pack his treasures and leave. He out-foxed them, you know. Ah yes, he smuggled cratefuls of gold and antiquities, including the scroll, to Europe. They forced him into exile, but they couldn't stop him living like the king that he was.'

Debauching himself, basically, I thought.

'None of which explains why you accuse our mother of being a murderess!' Ashraf barked.

Madam Gadalla's dark eyes blazed with emotion. 'She betrayed him!' she shrieked. 'She betrayed us all!'

'Her crime,' Nabil said gently, 'was to fall in love with one of the head honchos of the Secret Service in Egypt, who supported the new nationalistic regime.'

'Shinouda Yanni.' Madam Gadalla uttered the name as if she were pronouncing some evil incantation. 'She didn't fall in love with him. She *sold* herself to him and became his creature.' She seemed to see nothing in her own relationship with Farouk to compare unfavourably with this remark. 'He recruited her as one of his spies and she followed Freddy to Europe once rumours about Freddy and the scroll started circulating. Shinouda made her steal the scarab from Gregory Hunter to see what she was made of. Sofia was the one who let slip that he had it, you know; and what it was supposed to prove about Joseph of the Bible. But I wasn't having that – so I stole it back when my sister returned to Egypt!' she said with satisfaction.

Slowly she turned her head until her gaze settled on my face and she finally answered the question that had started her on her monologue. 'Rosa may not have been there with Freddy at the Ile de France restaurant that night in Rome. But she was the one who was paid to make the arrangements for him to be there with his latest young fancy-piece. She always claimed it was just so that Shinouda Yanni's man could meet with Freddy to strike a deal to buy back the scroll. But instead Shinouda arranged for one of his Secret Service agents to pose as kitchen staff and poison him.'

She glared around at us all looking like an avenging demon in her black robes and with her dark eyes flashing fire.

'So he wasn't killed by religious fanatics after all,' Adam murmured to me under his breath.

'But why?' Nabil asked quietly. 'Why would the Intelligence Service in Egypt want him dead after all those years of exile?'

'They wanted the scroll,' the old lady said looking wistful. 'When Freddy started to talk about it they realised it was political dynamite in his hands. You see, Freddy wasn't just offering to sell it. He was plotting to come back to Egypt and restore the Mohammed Ali monarchy, for his infant son Fuad II if not for himself. He was coming back to me.'

'Phewee,' Adam whistled beside me. 'I didn't see that one coming. Ted said there was no motive for Farouk to be murdered. A plot to take back his throne sounds like a pretty damn big motive to me.'

'The Saudi Arabian royal family pledged to help him,' Madam Gadalla went on. 'King Faisal of Saudi was a supporter of Freddy's in exile. After his death he even offered to have Freddy interred in his country. But I am getting ahead of myself. Between them, Freddy and Faisal hit on the idea of blowing the whistle on the contents of the scroll on Easter Sunday at the Vatican. They saw it partly as striking a great blow for Islam. You have to remember, religious persecution under Hitler was very recent. The world has changed very much since then. Better still, it would have rocked the foundations of Christianity itself.'

Adam leaned towards me again and whispered, 'So we were right in thinking Farouk was playing with fire as a high-ranking Muslim staying so close to the Vatican in a Catholic country.'

Madam Gadalla didn't appear to hear him. 'Freddy thought he could use the scroll as political leverage to strengthen his position. But that snake Shinouda Yanni, for one, wasn't willing to give up Egypt's nationalistic triumph. Farouk was suddenly too dangerous to be allowed to stay alive. So my sister's lover decided on assassination made to look like a seizure through over-indulgence in rich food. It got Freddy out of the way and served as a warning to the Saudi royal family not to mess with the nationalistic regime in Egypt.'

Nabil's eyes were fixed on his aunt's face. 'But wasn't there an investigation?'

'No,' Madam Gadalla confirmed in a tight voice. 'Those fools in Rome accepted, officially at least, that Freddy had pretty much eaten himself to death.'

'Didn't anyone think to perform an autopsy?'

'Freddy's first wife Farida took control of things in the immediate aftermath of his death. She refused permission for an autopsy saying it was against Islamic religious rituals.'

Adam leaned forward. 'And is that true? Is an autopsy against Islamic religious rituals?'

'Strictly speaking, yes,' Nabil confirmed. 'The body is seen as sacred in Islamic teachings. But where a death occurs in suspicious circumstances I've known of cases where autopsy and post mortem procedures have been permitted.'

Adam remarked, 'It has to make you wonder whether Farida was suspicious and acted to protect herself, her daughters and Farouk's baby son from any further attacks by the Egyptian secret service on surviving members of the royal family. If Farouk really was plotting with the Saudis to take back the throne then it's possible all remaining members of the royal family may have been seen as a threat to the republican regime. I'll bet they turned Rome upside down looking for that scroll.'

'But Farouk had already been clever enough to get the scroll out of Italy,' Nabil commented. 'He wanted to keep his collateral somewhere safe while he entered negotiations.'

The old lady's face took on a smug and self-satisfied expression and her eyes gleamed. 'There was nobody else he could trust. He knew I would keep his precious scroll hidden; and I have done so through all of these long years.' Then her expression changed as she glared at her nephews. 'But now you, evil men, you seek to rob me of it!'

Without warning, she sprang up from the sofa with her hands extended into claws and flew at Ashraf. 'You may have stolen the scarab! But I won't let you steal the scroll! You'll have to kill me first!'

Ashraf looked as if he might like to do just that as her long nails raked down his cheek, drawing blood. He lashed out at her, slapping her away from him as Nabil and the two young Egyptians jumped up. One of them sent a lamp stand crashing to the floor in his haste to drag their great-aunt away.

'Please,' Freya leapt to her feet. 'Please don't hurt her.'

Josh pushed himself up off his chair, attempting to pull Freya back with him, when it looked as if she might try to physically wrestle Madam Gadalla out of the detaining grip of her two young nephews.

Adam and I darted forward to set the lamp stand right again.

I'm not quite sure what Ben was intending, but he too levered himself off his seat and picked up his walking stick, looking as if he'd very much like to do someone some damage with it.

So, what with one thing and another, we were all on our feet when the lounge-bar door suddenly swung open. Ted stood there, looking very dapper in a tailored linen jacket with the light from the corridor glowing on his silvery hair. 'My goodness, what a racket!' he exclaimed. 'I gather this is what you're all so worked up about…?' And he held out the scroll, rolled into a tube between his hands.

Madam Gadalla let out a shriek. Nabil Zaal gasped. And Ashraf Zaal gave a shout and lunged towards Ted.

I didn't see what happened next, for at that moment the lights flickered and went out, plunging the room into darkness.

Chapter 15

My reaction to the sudden blackout was of the automatic type born of much practise. I groped along the windowsill behind me for matches and set about lighting the candles ranged along the surfaces to counteract the power cuts. My efforts were accompanied by the sound of assorted grunts, crashes and bangs.

By the time I'd got the first couple of candles alight and was able to take a quick look around, it was to see things had changed somewhat in the lounge-bar.

Josh had somehow managed to snatch up the stolen handgun from the armrest where it had been so recklessly placed and was sitting; a gleeful look of justice on his young face, with the gruesome thing trained on the two young Egyptians who'd led him such a merry dance. 'Don't make the mistake of thinking I'll be too frightened to use it!' he warned them 'One wrong move from you and you'll have a bullet hole in you!'

Wedged alongside each other on one of the smaller sofas, the Egyptian pair didn't look at all happy, so I can only imagine they knew the gun to be once more full of ammunition – probably because they'd reloaded it themselves. I tried not to think about what might happen if Josh fulfilled his threat.

He deserved this moment of triumph. I could only hope the young Egyptians would take him at his word.

Freya was holding Madam Gadalla down on the divan with one arm looped through the old lady's at the elbow.

Nabil Zaal had his brother in a similar grip, holding him bodily away from Ted who was still grasping the scroll and, indeed, looked to have changed his position the least since the lights went out.

But what made me squeak with astonishment was the sight of Adam with his hands gripping Ben's shirt collar, looking very much as if he had every intention of throttling the life out of him. 'Adam – what in God's name…?'

'Time for the truth, Ben!' Adam growled. 'Or should I call you Martin, since that's the name on all the papers I found in your cabin…? Martin Cody. I always suspected there was more to you than met the eye!'

This surprised me very much, since as all good hoteliers should, I'd taken a photocopy of Ben's passport at check-in, and it had most assuredly been in the name of Benedict Hunter, with a rather nice photograph to accompany his personal details. I spared a glance at Freya who was staring big-eyed like the startled deer she so much resembled, no doubt wondering if she'd just been gifted a blood relative only to have him snatched away again.

'For goodness sake, Adam!' I cried. 'Let him go! You must have made a mistake!'

'So, how do you explain all the documentation he's got –?'

Ben prised Adam's hands away from his throat, slowly and purposefully. 'I am exactly who I say I am,' he said levelly, and then managed a smile with a flash of his more usual debonair courtesy. 'But since you have rumbled me, I suppose I have little choice but to fill in the gaps in the story I told you.'

This surprised me more than I cared to admit even to myself, since I'd taken him trustingly at face value. Adam, I knew, had taken a bit longer to warm to our guest. But I'd had that down as a rather touching indication of his discomfort at having this rugged and urbane Englishman turn up with his mystery with which to tantalise me. It made me wonder if for once Adam was the one whose instincts were on the money.

Nabil pulled his brother away from Ted in the doorway and shoved him into the nearest armchair. 'Don't move!' he barked. 'You're not to lay a finger on that scroll.'

But it was a temporary distraction. The rest of us were all staring at Ben, awaiting his explanation.

He slumped back onto his chair and flexed his wounded leg a couple of times. 'Martin Cody is a member of the British counter-intelligence service. I understand investigations into the suspicious circumstances surrounding Farouk's death have been going on behind the scenes for many years; although after this passage of time I have to say

I'm at a loss about what they'd do if they were ever able to actually prove anything.'

'Farouk's son, Fuad II is still alive,' Ted murmured thoughtfully. 'Perhaps there's still some far-fetched belief they can re-establish the monarchy in Egypt, particularly now Mubarak's regime has been toppled.'

Ben looked as if that idea may not have occurred to him.

'So what happened?' Adam prompted, still sounding deeply suspicious.

'Martin approached my father a number of years ago asking about the time Dad spent with King Farouk in Rome during his exile from Egypt. You see, Martin's father, a wealthy art historian, was in Rome at the same time and was one of the people Farouk made noises to about the scroll. I think Mr Cody senior had some idea of buying it from him. But before matters could proceed, Farouk was dead, apparently as a result of indulging in one of his famous gluttonous feasts, and the scroll vanished – if, indeed, it had ever existed. Cody put out a few feelers to see if it might surface on the antiquities market, but the trail had gone stone cold. Then, when his son Martin was assigned to the Farouk case a few years back, he told him the story and it got all Martin's investigative juices flowing. He did some research and speculated that there was one person Farouk might have trusted enough to look after the scroll for him; and that was my father, Gregory Hunter; who'd been such a staunch friend to Farouk through so many years. So Martin approached my dad to see what he could learn and to perhaps authenticate the tale about a stolen Dead Sea Scroll, which apparently made it clear certain key Biblical figures were in fact ancient Egyptian pharaohs.'

'But I thought your Dad didn't know about the scroll,' I interjected.

'That's right. All he'd ever heard were the vague rumours circulating in Cairo before Farouk was deposed, and then again in Rome shortly before his death. But it made him remember the scarab that was stolen from him at about the time Farouk died; and I think it's fair to say it's this that sparked his own fascination with ancient Egyptian history.' Ben glanced towards the doorway. 'That's why he asked you those questions, Professor, when he attended your lecture at the British Museum.'

Ted nodded, but didn't interrupt the telling of the tale this time; so Ben went on: 'Dad had to send Martin away disappointed. Of course, as we all now know, nothing was heard again about the Dead Sea Scroll because Farouk had managed to spirit it out of Italy inside his annual birthday gift of champagne to his devoted Egyptian fancy-lady, and she kept it well hidden for him.' He nodded in a respectful way to Madam Gadalla as he said this. 'The irony is, my father was the one responsible for organising those annual gifts, which, I guess, most usually contained money. If, as we now know, he

317

was planning to take back his throne then it made sense for Farouk to have a stash of cash available in Egypt. My father saw nothing unusual in the consignment of champagne Farouk entrusted to him shortly before his death and just ensured safe delivery of it to Egypt in the usual way. It was only when Madam Gadalla's letter arrived that my father put two and two together and realised there was someone else, beside himself, whom Farouk had trusted with his deepest secrets. But my father was a very old man, and not able to act on Madam Gadalla's invitation himself.

'So he contacted Martin Cody in MI5, or wherever he hails from,' Adam deduced.

'Exactly. Except, Martin is getting on in years himself now and has suffered ill health recently. He suggested I should come in my father's place. And he gave me some of his papers so that if I should be lucky enough to get my hands on the scroll and should find myself in trouble with the authorities, I could call on his name and hopefully claim some sort of diplomatic immunity to get the scroll back out of Egypt.'

Adam took a step backwards, cleared his throat and held out his right hand. 'It seems I owe you an apology,' he said gruffly.

Ben gave his hand a hearty shake. 'Please; not a word of it. I don't blame you for jumping to conclusions. Let's face it; I've brought you nothing but trouble from the moment I stepped on board. It's me who should apologise.'

And with male harmony thus restored and, in my case at least, a big sigh of relief, Ben turned his head towards the doorway, 'But I hope you think it's been worth it, since, as we can all see, the fabled scroll really did exist.'

All eyes turned back towards Ted. He looked a bit spectral standing there in the shadows beyond the flickering candlelight still clutching the ancient document.

'An unknown Dead Sea Scroll,' Nabil Zaal breathed in a strangely sanctified tone of voice. 'Throughout my whole career I have waited for this moment, dreaming something may exist that would prove my hypothesis to a doubting world. Sir, please; I must beg that you allow me to be the one to take custody of that document. Just name your price.'

'But –' Ben started.

'Damn you!' Ashraf cursed.

'No!' Madam Gadalla shouted and lunged forward, wrestling herself out of Freya's detaining grip. 'Never shall a son of Rosa's lay claim to the scroll! No price is high enough! I have not kept it safe for all these long years only to see it pass into the hands of Freddy's enemies!' Her movement took Ted as much by surprise as it did the rest of us. He had no time to dodge backwards out of her reach. Her claw-like hands grabbed at the scroll, snatching it from his grasp. She clutched it against her wizened bosom for a heartbeat. I expected her to turn and pass it to Freya or Ben, since they were the ones she presumably wished to take custody of it.

Seeing as Josh still held the handgun and had it trained on the descendants of her dear Freddy's enemies I could only think we held the upper hand. But what she did instead made me gasp with shock. With an air of almost calculated deliberation while the rest of us watched in motionless horror, she reached out towards one of the coffee tables and lifted the candle I'd managed to light there in its fancy Victorian holder.

'No! Please! Stop!' Nabil Zaal and his brother sprang forward at the same moment, but it was too late.

Madam Gadalla held the flame to the end of the rolled parchment. It flared brightly and quickly took hold as she emitted a long, keening wail that might have been grief or maybe self-righteousness. 'It is better that it should be destroyed than become a trading token between greedy men! I don't know what I was thinking! The only one who knew how to use it was Freddy. And he is gone. Gone!' The last word left her on a long wail as she watched the scroll burn in her hands.

Adam leapt towards her, but there was nothing he could do.

I was the one who moved then – to run as fast as the sheet would allow me, and grab the fire bucket from underneath the bar so the old witch could drop the burning remains into it and not set our beautiful dahabeeyah alight. She did this with such an air of pain and distress it took my breath away. It was almost as if the loss of her dead king had only just hit her.

The cries of horror from both Nabil and Ashraf Zaal finally drowned out her wailing as she watched the roll of parchment she'd protected all these years go up in flames.

I snapped my head sideways to look at Ted, dreading to see his reaction to the wanton destruction of this priceless relic from antiquity.

To my amazement there was a strange kind of calm in his expression. As the scroll crackled and burned in the metal bucket, his gaze moved with a slow deliberation from Madam Gadalla's agonised visage to the gaping expressions on the faces of her two nephews. His composure gave me the clue for what was coming even before he spoke. It was unnatural somehow.

'Let it burn. It's a horrible fake,' he declared, moving his gaze finally to the bottom of the fire bucket I'd thrust underneath the blazing scroll. He stared unemotionally at the charred embers as they burned themselves out.

I had no time to note the reactions of everyone present. I barely had time even to register my own, beyond the no doubt inelegant gaping of my jaw as my mouth fell open. 'No!' Madam Gadalla screamed. 'It cannot be true! Freddy said it was genuine!'

'I think you'll find someone played a rather dirty trick on your beloved King Farouk,' Ted said with a note of sympathy in his voice.

'But the people at the museum – '

'– May well have been in on the scam for all we know,' he finished for her.

'So all these years –'

'—Yes, you've been protecting a forgery.'

She dropped backwards onto the settee alongside Freya as if the floor had fallen away beneath her. And perhaps, in her world, the feeling of solid ground beneath her feet had indeed been ripped away. I felt a rush of real compassion for her, looking at the bereft expression on her lined face.

'Why have you kept hold of it all these years?' Ted asked her gently.

Her still-lovely dark eyes filled with tears. 'Freddy made me promise to keep it safe. He said he was coming back to me…'

It was Freya who put a gentle arm around the old woman's thin shoulders. 'And after you knew he was dead…?' she asked softly.

'After I knew he'd been murdered!' she said with a return of the old bitterness. Then her eyes took on a distant look as she reflected aloud, 'It occurred to me I could sell it. But I had no need of money. I had the money Freddy sent me from exile. And, once he was gone, I had the money he'd sent for me to keep safe for his return. At first I thought maybe King Faisal would act alone to claim back Freddy's throne for baby Fuad. It occurred to me I could give the scroll to the new king. But of course that did not happen...'

'So you just held on to it...?' Nabil Zaal prompted her. 'And when I wrote my first book, didn't it occur to you I might have had use for it?'

A spark of the old anger flickered in her eyes. 'Yes, now I know it to be a fake, I should have given it to you,' she said bitterly. 'Instead as my time approached I thought only to give it to those who could prevent you from claiming it.'

'Aunt Layla, you hate me that much?'

'I hate your mother,' she said. 'Never can I forgive or forget her betrayal.'

It was an odd little freeze-frame moment as we all contemplated the burnt out scroll and pondered its dubious origins and the manner of hoax that Farouk had apparently fallen foul of. But if I'd thought there could be no more shocks in store this evening, I was wrong. Before I could even begin to work out what part the forged scroll might have played in Farouk's last days, a bright white floodlight illuminated the lounge bar with artificial brightness and a stentorian voice shouting through a loudspeaker announced, 'Police! We have de boat surrounded! Come out wid your hands above your heads and nobody will get hurted!'

My attention wrested back from the charred remains of the scroll and what it might mean, I wondered how long our police buddy had longed to say that. I was glad we'd been able to give him the opportunity of a career highlight. It wasn't hard to imagine his gleeful expression, with the amplifier clamped firmly against his lips.

'Good old Ahmed,' Adam murmured. 'Just in the nick of time, as always.'

'When he said he had a dinghy back at the police station I took him at his word,' I muttered back. 'But it looks as if he's called out the whole river police department.'

It was true; the bright white floodlights poured into the room from all directions, proving the *Queen Ahmes* really was surrounded.

We felt the bump as the leading boat came alongside the dahabeeyah and was tied up, and then the bouncing motion of being boarded. The next moment, Ahmed burst into the room. 'Hands up!' he yelled.

'Ah, that's really what he wanted to say,' I said to myself.

Armed with his police issue machine gun, he stood there looking more impressive than I'd ever seen him. Poor Josh, still pointing the stolen handgun at the two young Egyptians, looked like a school kid playing at being a grown-up in comparison; although I couldn't knock the conviction of his stance.

As another officer followed our police pal into the room and stood in the doorway with his feet apart, Ahmed advanced across the room with a heavy tread. He reached towards Josh and with his rather broken-toothed smile apologetically prised the gun from his grasp, waving it about a bit theatrically. I wondered briefly how many guns he felt he needed to bring the situation under control. But then I realised he'd divested Josh of the handgun with more purpose in mind than simply to prevent him accidentally firing it. 'Dis is de gun I collected from de Western Valley,' he announced, thrusting it in the faces of the Egyptian contingent. Then he held it back out towards Josh, almost as if he were holding out for inspection something Josh had never seen before, as opposed to something he'd been aiming with deadly intent not ten seconds earlier. 'You recognise dis firearm, my son?'

It took Josh a moment to cotton on to what Ahmed required of him. 'I – er – well – that is to say – Yes! I think it might be the same one I used – er – they made me use – to – er – to shoot at Ben.'

'Dese are de two?' Ahmed demanded, waving the barrel of the handgun rather casually at Saiyyid and Hanif, while they glared back at him and tried to look defiant.

'Er – yes.'

Now Ahmed held out the gun towards the two young Egyptians. 'And you? You recognise dis gun?'

325

I'd never quite got it straight in my head which of them was Hanif and which Saiyyid, since I'd always had them down as an Egyptian version of Siamese twins. One of them spoke up, shaking his head in a vehement denial. 'I've never seen it before in my life.'

'You lie!' Ahmed roared. 'You are Hanif Zaal, yes? De same Hanif Zaal who is a member of de Luxor gun club from which dis weapon was stealed two days ago!'

Ashraf suddenly burst to life as if he'd been ignited. 'Fool!' he shouted at his son. 'You said nobody would notice it was missing, at least, not for days!'

Ahmed now rounded on Ashraf with all the zeal of an avenging angel. 'But I have you, not your son, to thank for bringing to my attention dat it was gone! You telled it to your brother when you did not know dat you were being eavesdropped!' He looked very proud to have been able to use such a fine English word. 'Mereditd; she heared everything, and she telled it to me! I went at once to de gun club to get de evidences. And now,' he spun back to face the younger brothers squashed together on the sofa, 'you are under arrest!' He motioned the other officer forward and stood back, watching with evident relish as his colleague clapped handcuffs on the pair of them.

I'd never really seen Ahmed in action before – well, except for the night he came close to arresting me for breaking and entering into the Howard Carter Museum. He was really quite impressive, if not downright entertaining to watch.

But one person decided he'd seen enough, and used the temporary distraction of the handcuffing of his sons to make a bolt for it. Ashraf darted across the room, yanked open the door and disappeared from sight onto the little platform outside where the spiral staircase led up to the upper deck.

Ashraf! No!' Nabil Zaal rushed after his brother, and Ahmed immediately gave chase.

Seeing the younger Zaal brothers were pretty well immobilised in their handcuffs, Adam and I decided as one to follow to where the action was headed up on deck.

It was no easy feat negotiating the spiral staircase in my bed sheet. When Adam turned back to help pull me up the last couple of steps onto the upper deck, it was to find Ahmed squaring up against the two men. 'Ashraf Zaal, you are a robber and a thief. You went to de old lady your aunt's rooms today to steal from her.'

I'll admit to the flush of guilt this brought to warm and redden my cheeks, knowing full well the same accusation could be levelled at me. Ashraf looked as if he might like to make a dive for it into the dark, shifting waters of the Nile. His brother was pleading with him. 'See sense, Ashraf; just look at the number of police boats. They'll scoop you up in seconds, if they don't shoot you first. And you're no good to me dead. For pity's sake; you've got to tell me where the scarab is before you go and do anything rash!'

Considering the stress of the moment, I could only admire his remarkable single-mindedness. But this was Nabil Zaal who'd made a lifetime's mission out of his theory that there was a link between the Bible and Pharaonic history. If I'd learned anything at all about Madam Gadalla and her relations it was that family affiliation didn't count for very much.

'Ah, the scarab...' Ashraf said on a note of enlightenment. 'Yes, in all the excitement I had rather forgotten that.' And he reached into his pocket.

'Freeze!' Ahmed shouted.

'It's alright, mate,' Adam interjected. I don't think he's got a gun. He'd have shown it by now.'

I thought Nabil Zaal's eyes were going to fall out of their sockets as Ashraf withdrew a small object from the pocket of his galabeya. 'It's been in your pocket all this time?' he croaked. 'You had it even while we were in Aunt Layla's rooms? Please, Ashraf,' he begged. 'You've got to let me have it. It's the only thing left now the scroll is gone.' His voice was a wheezing rasp and I took a step forward, in some fear once again for his blood pressure.

Ashraf looked across at me, a calculating expression on his face. Then he glanced with a bit more uncertainty at Ahmed, who was slowly and purposefully advancing towards him by the handrail. 'Come, man;' Ahmed said in authoritative tones. 'You are in trouble up to your eyebrows. Let de man have de scarab.'

I'm not sure he meant to say eyebrows. Eyeballs or maybe even his neck would have been more the thing, but neither Adam nor I made any attempt to correct him.

Ashraf cast one more evil-looking glance our way and then seemed to come to a decision. 'It doesn't seem it's going to do me much good where I'm going,' he said. 'So, here... catch!' And before any of us realised what he was about to do, he swung his arm in a wide arc, a bit like a cricket-player about to bowl the ball, and flung the scarab high up into the air.

I don't know if Ahmed has ever been a fielder in a cricket match but if not, it's a sport he should take up professionally. He launched himself upwards in one great burst of energy and both hands clamped around the flying object. The trouble was, his upward and outward trajectory was so great it took him sailing right across the handrail and plunging down into the river below. The almighty splash as he hit the water sent spray raining across the deck, splattering us all in cold wetness.

We all shot forward to hang over the rail.

There was a wild threshing in the dark water far below and then Ahmed's head erupted above the waves. But it only bobbed above the surface for a moment before it started to sink again.

'OhmyGod, Adam! Quick! You've got to do something! I've just remembered... *Ahmed can't swim!*'

Chapter 16

A little while later it was no longer me who had the distinction of being the member of our party wrapped in a bed sheet. I'd had time to return to our cabin and don a bathrobe. No, it was Ahmed who was the one struggling to hang onto the last vestiges of his manly dignity with his big bare feet protruding out from the bottom of the swathe of fabric he was draped in. The trouble was, no one had any clothes big enough for him to borrow.

I was feeling much happier. Ahmed's colleagues from the Luxor police department had escorted Ashraf and his sons Hanif and Saiyyid from the dahabeeyah onto their own motorised vessel, ready to transport them into police custody. They'd also offered to take Madam Gadalla back to The Winter Palace where she could continue to mourn her long lost king and her own lost youth privately and in peace and luxury. And who could blame her for feathering her own nest with Farouk's cash once the king was dead and it was clear he'd failed in his mission to take back his throne? It felt wonderful to have the *Queen Ahmes* restored to those of us whose rightful place it was to be on board.

Nabil Zaal had asked us with great courtesy if he might be permitted to remain for a while. That he wanted to make the professor's acquaintance properly now all the hoo-ha had died down was evident. I imagine he was looking forward to a nice long scholarly chat.

The scarab was sitting pooled in lamplight in the middle of the coffee table in front of the divan on which Ted was sitting. It was to Ahmed's great credit that throughout his terrifying dunking in the Nile he had managed to hang on to it. Knowing Ahmed, I'm actually quite certain he'd have opted for drowning over the ignominy of being rescued by Adam only to admit he'd let it go.

But with the scarab and the electricity now restored to us, strangely enough the scarab wasn't the artefact uppermost in everyone's minds.

Ben had taken it upon himself to be the one to dispense the brandy, since three of us in the room had all enjoyed the dubious pleasure of a night-time swim in the Nile and he seemed concerned we might take a chill. I was quite happy to have him playing host since it meant I could tuck myself in alongside Adam on the sofa and make myself comfortable. I was incredibly proud of the way he'd hauled Ahmed from the water. The swallow dive he'd performed from the deck railings into the river had been worthy of Olympian Tom Daley at his best.

Glancing across the room, I could see Freya was nursing equally fond feelings for her cousin Josh. Perhaps having had the opportunity to contrast him to the other branch of her extended family, she'd realised how favourably he compared. But I had a suspicion his heroics in snatching up the handgun from Hanif's side when the lights went out might actually be what accounted for her leaning so cosily up against him with her coppery head resting on his shoulder. I daresay she'd seen a different side to him; one she found altogether more attractive than his rather hectoring guardian angel persona. There's a world of difference between being bossed about and bullied by a man who is ostensibly trying to protect you, and having that man take courageous action to keep you from harm. I could only hope Josh realised that, too. Noticing the way his arm crept around her shoulder and the contented expression on his face, I'll admit I fostered some hope.

'What I don't understand,' Ben said handing a glass of brandy to Ted, 'is whether the people in the Cairo Museum who studied the scroll back at the beginning of the 1950s did so knowing it was a fake. I mean, they can hardly have failed to spot it was forged. Professor, you were able to denounce it after only a couple of hours. And yet they apparently led Farouk to believe it was genuine.'

Nabil Zaal nodded, then leaned forward and stared intently at Ted as if he were about to reveal one of the secrets of the universe.

'You think it was planted on him,' Adam exclaimed, sitting forward slightly. I had no choice but to move with him since his arm was around me.

'Well, yes; I think it's the most likely explanation,' Ted admitted. 'You see, Farouk already had a well-known reputation as the "thief of Cairo" when the Jordanian Department of Antiquities brought the Dead Sea Scrolls to Egypt. I just can't imagine they'd have let those scrolls out of their sight for even a moment, certainly not for long enough for the light-fingered king to make off with one of them.'

Adam grunted. 'I always thought it was a remarkable coincidence that he'd stolen the one scroll that supposedly made the links between The Old Testament and the 18th Dynasty. I mean, really! What were the chances? The alternative was always that it was some kind of elaborate hoax.'

'But who would have perpetrated it?' Ben asked. 'Surely not the Jordanians themselves. I mean, I know there wasn't always much love lost between Jordan and Egypt back then, but even so…'

'No, I think there were others with a far bigger vested interest in getting Farouk into trouble,' Ted remarked.

'The nationalists?' Adam queried. 'You think the revolutionary powers in Egypt hit on the idea as part of their plan to overthrow him?'

'I think there's a good chance of it, yes,' Ted said.

'But that still doesn't explain the experts at the museum taking a look and telling Farouk he had a genuine, and potentially explosive, religious document.' I argued.

'I daresay we could get our friend Walid to do some research and, if there's anything to be found after all this time, I think it will be the discovery that a lot of money changed hands, possibly from this Shinouda Yanni of the Secret Service to someone at the top of the museum hierarchy. They were probably hoping Farouk would make a fool of himself with it and cause some sort of international scandal that they could use to remove him. But he obviously decided to hold onto the scroll for a while.'

'Another rare antiquity to add to his collection,' I murmured.

'Well, it would certainly explain why the Jordanian government didn't kick up a stink at the time,' Adam said. 'They had no need to complain about one of their precious scrolls being stolen, because in actual fact, none was.'

'If it wasn't actually planted on Farouk, someone must have made it remarkably easy for him to steal the fake scroll, thinking he was taking one of the genuine articles,' I added. 'I almost feel sorry for him. It sounds like a dirty trick to play.'

'But in the end the nationalists didn't need the scroll to get rid of Farouk,' Ben remarked. 'He proved to be enough of an embarrassment without it. His European gambling spree for his honeymoon during the holy month of Ramadan was the final nail in the coffin.'

'Quite,' Ted agreed. 'You know, Gamal Abdel Nasser notified both the American and the British governments of his intention to lead a coup against the king two days before he put it into action. Both agreed not to aid Farouk. That shows how shockingly low his standing was in the international arena.'

'But, with the Free Officers having led such a successful campaign to topple him from his throne, do you really think the Egyptian Intelligence Service under this Shinouda Yanni would have needed to do away with him altogether, and so many years later?' I asked.

'Perhaps that's where the scroll becomes significant again,' Ted commented. 'Say Farouk really had sold it to Martin Cody's father? As an art historian with contacts in all the major museums, he'd have blown the whistle on it being a fake in no time. Farouk must surely then realise that he'd been the victim of some sort of foul play. Since it turns out he was in league with the Saudi royal family to get his throne back, I imagine he could have made much of being the victim of a conspiracy.'

Ben sipped his brandy thoughtfully and then put the glass down. 'So you think they decided to silence him and do everything possible to get the scroll back.'

'I won't state it as fact, but I'd certainly be prepared to run with it as a theory.'

I glanced across the room at Freya and Josh, both silently following the conversation; and at Ahmed who was sipping a cup of coffee and doing his best to look invisible in his sheet. But his eyes were alert and lively, shifting from face to face as he looked at whoever was speaking.

'But didn't Madam Gadalla say that Rosa arranged for Farouk to go to the restaurant believing he was there to strike a deal with an agent to sell the scroll?' I objected.

'If Farouk really was scheming to return to Egypt, it made sense to get him out of the way,' Adam responded.

'The scroll certainly gave them a handy excuse,' Ted added.

Nabil Zaal sat forward and joined in the conversation for the first time. 'My mother was the one they sent to search for it, you know,' he remarked. 'She became an agent for Yanni's Intelligence Service; Aunt Layla was right about that. Yanni may have been the one she took up with, but I think President Nasser was the one she idolised. She always said his actions in ridding Egypt of its hedonistic and debauched king were those of a hero. And, you know, I'd have to agree with her. Farouk was a disaster as king, but Egyptians everywhere hailed Nasser as a hero and a symbol of dignity and freedom. All in all, I'd say my mother was the one with the good taste in men; not Aunt Layla.'

Ted leaned back. 'Your mother never told you about the scroll?'

Nabil looked a bit dejected. 'No. At least, only as a type of fairytale.' Then he brightened. 'Although, thinking about it, it sounds as if she might always have known it was a fake. So she wouldn't have wanted to send me down a blind alley.'

'It doesn't sound as if it ever occurred to your mother that Farouk might have sent it to her sister for safe keeping.'

'No, and that's probably just as well; there was bad enough blood between them as it was. You've seen the bitterness my aunt still harbours. If Aunt Layla cottons on that my mother may have known it was a fake, it will fuel her hatred even further.'

'But Rosa didn't marry Shinouda Yanni?.'

'No, but she did marry one of Nasser's most trusted aides, Kairy Zaal. Sadly my father was killed in the Six Day War in '67.'

'And the fake scroll has languished rolled up inside a champagne bottle for all these years,' I murmured.

Nabil Zaal grinned suddenly. 'Yes, while revisionist historians like me started concocting all sorts of wild theories about how the Bible might be explained through a study of ancient Egypt. It probably helped that it took so many years for the genuine Dead Sea Scrolls to be published. It enabled me to get quite a foothold in the popular history market.'

I sat back as a sudden idea struck me. 'Perhaps the reason it took almost fifty years for the content of the scrolls to be made available was because certain people in-the-know were aware there was a fake scroll knocking about somewhere that might suddenly come to light and blow up in their faces. I'll bet that would have taken some explaining!'

Ben smiled at me. 'No chance of that now since that old witch Madam Gadalla has seen fit to set a match to it!'

'Shame, really;' Adam added. 'I'd have quite enjoyed seeing how the Egyptologists of the world reacted to the news that King David was actually Thutmosis III and King Solomon was none other than Amenhotep III in disguise.'

'Turncoat!' I accused. 'You, for one, were never prepared to believe it!'

'Why not?' Nabil addressed Adam in an utterly reasonable tone of voice. 'It seems to me, if we can use the scarab to prove that Yuya was the Biblical Joseph, there's still every chance some evidence will one day turn up to prove I'm not so wide of the mark with my other theories about the Hebrew Patriarchs of the Bible and Egyptian history.'

Still sitting on the coffee table, the ancient scarab started to glow. Or perhaps it was just my imagination that made it seem so. We all stared at it and Ted leaned forward and picked it up, turning it over in his hands.

'I don't suppose there's any risk that thing's not really a genuine 18th Dynasty artefact?' Ben asked, sounding a bit doubtful.

'It's the real thing alright.' Ted said reverently. 'How did you describe it, Adam? As an ancient form of Twitter? Well, it's certainly got a message carved onto the base.'

Nabil Zaal leaned so far forward he looked in danger of tipping off his chair altogether and onto his knees. 'Are you able to read it?'

Ted pushed his glasses up onto the bridge of his nose, holding them there with his forefinger and squinting through the lenses. 'Yes, I think so.'

It seemed to my suddenly thrumming senses that the *Queen Ahmes* herself was holding her breath. I couldn't even hear the usual creaking of the old timbers. The silence was absolute.

'It starts with the usual list of the pharaoh's royal titles,' Ted said, and proceeded to read them aloud, *'"Strong bull who appears in the glory of Ma'at; he who establishes the laws and who pacifies the two lands; Horus of Gold, great of strength, who defeats the Asiatics; The King of Upper and Lower Egypt; Son of Ra, Amenhotep, which means Amun is pleased; the ruler of Waset, given everlasting life."'*

I shivered. I've found listening to these ancient inscriptions always has that effect on me, especially when Ted intones them in such a sonorous voice. It's like hearing a faint voice echoing out of antiquity.

I was aware of Nabil Zaal sucking in a deep breath.

Ted cleared his throat and went on, *'"His southern boundary extends toward Kary."'* Ted looked up. 'I think that's somewhere in modern Sudan. *'"His northern boundary toward*

Naharyna." That's somewhere on the Euphrates river in north-eastern Syria, I believe'.

'So far that's no different in wording from any of the other marriage scarabs that have been found,' Nabil said, sounding a bit crushed.

'But there's more,' Ted smiled. 'Listen to this...' And frowning with concentration he translated, *'"The great royal woman is Tiye, may she live forever. Her father's name is Yuya, great of praises; he who is Overseer of the Granaries and protected Egypt from mighty Set's displeasure during the great famine that afflicted the two lands. Her mother's name is Thuya, mistress of music. Tiye is the woman of a strong king and will reign in glory.'*

Nabil jumped up out of his seat and I thought for a moment he was going to snatch the scarab out of Ted's hand. But he stopped himself. 'That's it! Read it again! The bit about the famine ...!'

'We all heard it the first time,' Adam said mildly, smiling at him. 'I'm not sure it's as conclusive as perhaps I was hoping. But ok Nabil, I'm willing to run with it. Congratulations! You've got your proof!'

Two days later Adam and I stood on the gangplank of our dahabeeyah waving Ben, Freya and Josh off in a taxi for the short trip to the airport to catch their flight home. We'd spent the last couple of days giving them a whirlwind tour of all the historical sites of Luxor. Ted went along in the taxi with them since he was also flying back to Cairo this afternoon ready to keep his appointment with Walid and Shukura at the museum this evening.

Nabil Zaal had departed for America yesterday. He'd been persuaded to leave the scarab in Ted's custody only because he accepted that having it displayed in the Egyptian Museum of Antiquities for the whole world to see was the best way to silence his doubters. I wished him well with his next book. I had no doubt it would be a runaway best-seller. Although the shame of it was it might put his theories about the true owners of the pyramids on the backburner for a while. I'd been rather hoping to learn a little more about that.

As the dust settled behind the taxi, Adam smiled at me and drew me into his arms. 'D'you know what, Merry?' he murmured against my hair. 'I'm quite sure you're itching to get cracking on updating our website with all your newfound knowledge. But do you think you could put it off for just another couple of hours? Never have the words *just the two of us* sounded quite so appealing.'

THE END

Author's Note

Many writers have tried to associate the Hebrew Joseph of the Bible with known viziers who served at the Pharaonic court of ancient Egypt. Probably the most famous among them is Ahmed Osman who published his book *Stranger in the Valley of the Kings* in 1987 setting out the case for the nobleman Yuya who served at the mid-18th Dynasty courts of Thutmosis IV and his son Amenhotep III. Osman's book sold well, capturing the public imagination, but attracted strong criticism from traditional Egyptologists who found his claims extreme and pointed out a number of scholarly errors in his work. But many followers of Osman found his hypothesis compelling enough that even now, a generation later, the argument still rages and neither his proponents nor his critics have been able to prove the case for or against once and for all.

Both sides in the debate will accept that the Biblical stories cannot be taken as literal accounts due to the fact that they were originally handed down generation to generation in the oral story-telling tradition. However those for and against will also rely on literal interpretation of the Bible when it suits their argument. To my way of looking at it, all the time it remains impossible to make absolute claims there must be some room for conjecture. And while we cannot make an unequivocal identification, I think there are enough circumstantial or perhaps coincidental similarities between the historical Yuya and the Biblical Joseph to whet the appetite.

Writers of pseudo-scientific history continue to peddle their latest theories with some success, and who can blame them when the overlaps between history and the legends of the Bible are so suggestive? For example, when Amenhotep III published his scarabs engraved with pronouncements about his marriage to the commoner Tiye, not only did he mention Tiye and her parents Yuya and Thuya but the scarabs also defined the boundaries of his empire as stretching from (modern) central Sudan to (modern) northern Iraq. In the Book of Genesis the Promised Land to be given to Abraham's descendants is said to stretch from "the river of Egypt" (the Nile) to the Euphrates. This describes the same territory as the scarab and provides fertile ground for those seeking to make a connection between the Old Testament Patriarchs and Egypt's 18th Dynasty.

It is impossible to make any absolute claims, so into this wonderful void a fiction writer can step with alacrity.

King Farouk's unsuitability for kingship was as described. Farouk was widely condemned for his corrupt and ineffectual governance, the continued British occupation, and the Egyptian army's failure to prevent the loss of 78% of Palestine to the newly formed State of Israel in the 1948 Arab-Israeli War. On 23 July 1952, the nationalistic and revolutionary Free Officers Movement, led by Muhammad Naguib and Gamal Abdel Nasser, and supported by the American CIA, staged a military coup that launched the Egyptian Revolution of '52. Farouk was forced to abdicate, and went into exile to Europe, where he continued his decadent lifestyle unabated until his death. It is true that King Faisal of Saudi Arabia offered for Farouk's body to be interred in his country. But despite some wild rumours circulating on the Internet, I've seen no evidence to suggest the Saudi royal family ever plotted with Farouk to take back his throne.

Nasser, as president, became one of the towering political figures of modern Middle Eastern history and politics in the 20th Century. When he died of a heart attack in 1970, his funeral in Cairo drew five million mourners and an outpouring of grief across the Arab world.

The Dead Sea Scrolls have captivated the world since they were found in the remote desert landscape south of Jericho in 1947-56. It took decades for scholars to decipher them while the public waited in the dark, wondering what the secrecy was all about. This long delay in publication allowed all sorts of wild conspiracy theories to emerge, with some claiming the Vatican was suppressing publication as the scrolls contained information to challenge the teachings of Christianity. Since publication, these theories have been largely debunked. The scrolls are a mixture of biblical and quasi-biblical texts, plus some previously unknown writings produced by a dissident Jewish community called the Essenes just before and during the time of Jesus Christ. But those who love a conspiracy theory are reluctant to let go of their suspicions and some still claim there are scrolls that have mysteriously disappeared or been excluded from publication.

I hope you've enjoyed this latest book following Meredith Pink's Adventures in Egypt. If so, please do leave me a review on Amazon. It's always a thrill to see a new review. I also read and respond to all comments on my website https://www.fionadeal.com

Fiona Deal
December 2013.

If you enjoyed Farouk's Fancies, you may also enjoy Akhenaten's Alibi – Book 5 of Meredith Pink's Adventures in Egypt, available from Amazon.

Here is Chapter One …

Akhenaten's Alibi

Chapter 1

Summertime 2013

Our good friend Walid Massri told us he was being blackmailed on the same day President Mohamed Morsi announced he was appointing a former Islamist terror leader as the new governor in Luxor.

'We may as well pack up and go home, Merry,' Adam said in disgust. He looked up from his iPad screen, where he was reading the BBC News online. 'Morsi has just appointed Adel el-Khayat, a former jihadi, as our new governor. He's the same man whose fundamentalist group committed the massacre at Hatshepsut's temple in 1997.'

I stared back at him in horror, and moved to stand behind him so I could read the news article over his shoulder. I whispered the words aloud as I read, *"Adel el-Khayat was a founding member of the fundamentalist group Al-Gamaa Al-Islamiya. During the 1990s Al-Gamaa Al-Islamiya carried out a wave of terrorist atrocities targeting civilians and Western tourists. Scores were murdered, leading many analysts to speculate that Egypt was succumbing to an 'Islamic revolution on the Nile'."*

Adam took over and voiced the next paragraph, "*In 1997 the group committed its most high profile operation. Over the course of 45 minutes, six gunmen systematically murdered 58 tourists and four Egyptians inside the Temple of Hatshepsut in Luxor.*"

I felt my stomach shift as a wave of nausea hit me. Hatshepsut's temple is one of my favourite places on earth. I knew about the tragedy, of course. But hearing it described like that made me feel physically sick.

'If Morsi is trying to kill the tourist industry in Egypt stone dead, he's going the right way about it!' Adam bit out. 'I don't see how we can possibly hope to survive this. Tourism's already on its knees thanks to the 2011 uprising that removed Hosni Mubarak from office. This feels like the last nail in the coffin!'

His gloriously mixed metaphors told me much about his agitated state of mind. 'But, look!' I interjected, desperate to close my ears to the resounding death knell to all our hopes and dreams I could hear ringing from the wooden beams of our dahabeeyah. 'It says here that Al-Gamaa Al-Islamiya renounced violence ages ago.'

'Try telling that to holidaymakers weighing up the relative merits of a week on the Nile versus a week sunning themselves on a beach in the Canaries,' Adam said with a defeated air. 'It's no use, Merry. The writing's on the wall and we have no choice but to read it. Thinking we could set up in business offering luxury Nile cruises to discerning travellers in the aftermath of the Egyptian Revolution, and with an Islamist like President Morsi running the show was naïve at best, and sheer lunacy at its – probably more accurate – worst! Any traveller worthy of being described as 'discerning' will be giving Egypt a wide berth as a holiday destination for a good long while to come. Let's face it; we haven't had a sniff of a booking since Ben Hunter was here in April. We can't go on like this.'

'But, surely we shouldn't just give up and go home with our tail between our legs,' I argued. 'There's bound to be protest at this appointment. I don't believe the hoteliers and tour operators in Luxor will sit idly by while this Adel el-Khayat takes up his new office. And we know there's already a lot of bad feeling against President Morsi. All the talk on the street is of plans to hold nationwide anti-government rallies at the end of this month to mark the one-year anniversary of his election as president. If you ask me, we should just sit it out and wait to see what happens.'

'The Muslim Brotherhood will never allow Morsi to be ousted,' Adam said, shaking his head. 'They say the calls for his resignation are an illegitimate attempt to undermine democracy in Egypt.'

'But things can't go on as they are!' I protested. 'Every day we suffer power blackouts and read in the News about foreign investors pulling out. And we know how scarce fuel is. Just look how long we had to queue for bottled gas yesterday!'

'You're describing a nation in turmoil, Merry,' Adam said sadly, reaching out to take my hand and drawing me down to crouch alongside him so he could look into my eyes. 'And my feeling is it's going to get worse before it gets better. No, lovely; I think we have to face facts. Egypt's not the place for us right now, no matter how much we love it. And, let's face it; it's damnably hot here in June, July and August. Maybe we should head back to England for the summer and sit things out there, out of harm's way.'

And that's when we heard the shout from the causeway outside where our dahabeeyah is docked, announcing the arrival of our good friend from the Egyptian Antiquities Museum in Cairo, Walid Massri.

He'd called us last night to say he had business in Luxor and asked if we could put him up on board the *Queen Ahmes* for a couple of days. Of course we were delighted to have him come to stay.

But it was obvious something was badly wrong from the moment we clapped eyes on him as we leapt up to greet him and he stepped onto the gangplank to come aboard.

Walid wears a perpetually world-weary air. This may have something to do with being slight of stature, with sloping shoulders and a just discernible stoop; probably the result of years spent bending over the antiquities it's his duty to conserve. He also looks to be permanently coated in dust; with dry, flaky brown skin and wispy hair that he combs carefully forward but sadly fails to disguise his seriously receding hairline. Yet when he speaks he has an aura of quiet authority about him, which subdues many who might take it into their heads to debate any particular point. And he has a fearsome intellect; regarded as one of the foremost Egyptologists his nation has produced - whilst never actually having courted fame or the Discovery Channel cameras in quite the same way as his more famous ex-colleague and erstwhile director of the Cairo Museum, a certain Mr Zahi Hawass.

Looking at Walid now, I was struck by how particularly dejected he looked. I'd call it more defeated than world-weary. It was enough to have me worriedly reaching out to him as he stepped off the gangplank into our little wood-panelled reception area. 'Walid! You look exhausted! What's the matter? Are you ill?'

He attempted a smile and patted my hand where I'd reached out and grasped his. 'No, no; I am quite well, thank you Merry.'

'But you look as if you're carrying the weight of the world on your shoulders!'

Adam reached for Walid's overnight bag. 'Let the poor man get his feet over the threshold, Merry!' he chided. But I could see he shared my concern from the narrowed glance he quickly masked behind a broad smile of welcome. 'Let's deposit your bag in your cabin, Walid; then you can take a shower and join us up on deck in the shade for a nice refreshing drink.'

Walid seemed only too happy to put this plan into action and wash away the travel-fatigue of his flight down from Cairo, if not whatever was so clearly bothering him.

'He looks positively done in,' I murmured to Adam as we prepared a fruit cordial in our gleaming stainless steel kitchen, adding quantities of ice made from our specially purified water to the pitcher to counteract the aggressive Egyptian heat.

'Give him a chance to catch his breath before you pounce on him,' Adam admonished with a small smile to show his tolerance of my habitual impatience. 'I'm sure he'll tell us what's worrying him without you needing to wrest it from him in one great heave.'

I took his advice and sat fiddling with the braiding on my chair cushion when Walid joined us up on deck. I turned my attention to the felucca being hauled up the Nile by a motorised water taxi, against the flow of the water, and in the non-existent breeze. It was preferable to fixing my gaze on the hollowed cheeks and harried expression of our friend and waiting for him to speak.

'So, what business is it that brings you to Luxor?' Adam asked in jovial tones after a long pause during which Walid intermittently sipped his cordial and shredded the paper napkin he'd draped across his knees in readiness for the small finger sandwiches I'd prepared.

Walid sent him what I can only describe as a hunted look. Then his shoulders slumped. 'There's no point in putting it off any longer,' he said in his softly Arabic-accented English. 'I have come to share something with you both and to ask your advice. I thought about confiding in Shukura...' he gave a small shake of his head, '...but she is too volatile in her nature. And Ted ... well, Ted draws on in his years, and I have no wish to worry him if it should prove unnecessary...'

It's fair to say the towed-up-the-Nile felucca immediately ceased to hold my attention. My gaze snapped to Walid's face the moment he started speaking.

'Of course, Ahmed is probably the one whose help I should seek. I daresay this is a matter for the police. But ...' He let the sentence trail off.

To say I was impatient for him to get to the point would be putting it more than mildly. It felt as if someone had replaced the blood in my veins with Tabasco sauce. 'But...?' I prompted.

He looked at me squarely and I watched him draw a deep breath, steadying himself. 'But the find was yours, Merry; yours and Adam's. So it's only fair I should speak to both of you first.'

The breath left my body in a great collapse of air at the mention of the word 'find' as if someone had whacked me in the solar plexus with a cricket bat. There was only one thing he could be referring to.

'I was foolish to think we could keep it a secret … such an overwhelming discovery …'

'One of us has broken ranks?' I cried, jumping up from my recliner and sending the cushion spinning across the deck. 'I don't believe it! We promised never to breathe a word! Who…?'

'No, Merry; it's not what you think,' Walid entreated, sending a look of naked appeal across at Adam. I was clearly proving myself every bit as volatile as Shukura.

Frowning, Adam stood up, reached out for me and drew me back. I slumped onto my seat; aware I was gaping inelegantly at our guest.

'I received a … *communication*,' Walid said, choosing the word with care. 'Enclosed with it was a photocopy of a letter; a letter I had every reason to recognise … and curse … Because of course it was my idea to write it, and to make sure it was replicated several times over so each of us had a copy…'

My racing brain was starting to grasp his meaning. But Adam beat me to it.

'You mean, the letters you asked each of us to copy and sign the morning after you first rescued Merry and me from the …' He trailed off.

'…from the tomb…' I whispered. 'My God, Walid! Someone's got hold of one of the letters? But I thought we'd all agreed to keep them locked up in bank vaults or safe deposit boxes?'

'Well, yes…' he said, looking uncomfortable. 'But we were counting without one of our number meeting an untimely end and leaving behind his personal effects to be sorted through and cleared after his death.'

'Mustafa Mushhawrar,' Adam breathed.

I felt a chill go through me and shivered despite the blazing heat.

'Quite,' Walid said in grim tones.

I remembered the fastidious former official of the ministry for the preservation of ancient monuments here in Luxor with a shudder of distaste. His untimely end had been of his own doing. Realising he'd been caught in the act of robbing the tomb we'd made a solemn pact to keep secret and protect, he'd deliberately set off a rock fall, burying himself and his shady companion beneath tonnes of rubble.

I found it impossible to regret his passing, since that same rock fall had imprisoned Adam, together with our best-buddy-cum-police-chum Ahmed - and not forgetting me - within the dead-aired sepulchre. But it was clear Mustafa's death had left a dangerously loose end hanging.

'So, one of Mustafa's bereaved relatives has come into possession of Mustafa's copy of the letter,' Adam said, his brain slotting the pieces together. 'And ...what...?'

'And he knows about the tomb!' I cried on a rising note of panic. 'It's obvious, isn't it?'

'...And he's seeking to blackmail me.' Walid said rather more slowly, even though he started speaking at the same time as me. His tone was so heavy it seemed to have lead weights attached.

'*What?*' Adam and I spoke the single word in unison. It managed to convey our shock, outrage and alarm as eloquently as a good many more words might have done. I was still grappling with the revelation that some stranger was now party to our closely guarded secret. That he'd hit on the idea of using his newfound knowledge so callously was a body blow that left me reeling.

Walid ran a rather shaky hand over his forehead, brushing away beads of perspiration. Then he reached into the breast pocket of his shirt and drew out a folded sheet of paper. I could see as he smoothed it out that it had rows of words cut from Arabic newspapers pasted onto it.

'Hmm, that old chestnut,' I muttered. 'Not very original, is it?'

356

Adam's Arabic is less than fluent and mine, apart from a few spoken words, remains - to my shame - largely non-existent. So Walid cleared his throat and translated aloud for our benefit.

"*I know your secret. Here is the proof. You will pay me, or I will talk. If you value your job at the museum and your reputation, you will be quick to pay. I want LE 10,000,000. You have one month. Await my further instructions.*" Walid folded the paper and sat slumped in his chair, a picture of misery and fear.

Adam and I stared at him with bulging eyes, assimilating the stark contents of the letter.

'Ten million Egyptian pounds is around a million pounds sterling, give or take,' Adam calculated.

Walid dropped his head forward into his hands and sat holding it, 'Where am I supposed to get hold of that sort of money?'

'When was the letter dated?' I asked, my brain working frantically. 'How much time do we have?'

Walid looked up and rubbed his eyes. 'It was sent to me at the museum last week.' It didn't look as if he'd slept a wink since. 'We have until early July.'

'And he enclosed Mustafa's letter along with the blackmail note?' I frowned.

'A photocopy of it,' Walid nodded. 'I don't imagine he's going to let the original out of his grasp for love nor money.'

He clearly realised what he'd said and was quick to rectify the error and rephrase it. 'That is to say, we can only hope ten million Egyptian pounds will be enough to prise it from his sticky fingers. The alternative doesn't bear thinking about.'

I didn't need to see the photocopied letter to remember its explosive contents. In simple terms it told the story of perhaps the most earth-shattering archaeological discovery of all time.

I don't suppose there can be many discoveries that would make Howard Carter's of Tutankhamun's tomb seem little more than a warm-up act. But I think I can say without fear of contradiction that ours - once the world came to learn of it - would easily claim that distinction.

Astonishing, incredible, unbelievable as it may be ... and, take my word for it, I could go on with the superlatives all day ... we had the dubious honour of being the finders of a hidden tomb that remained unknown to the rest of the world. Our tomb – for that's how I thought of it - contained the mummified remains and spectacular treasures of two of the most iconic names to come down to us from the depths of antiquity. These were none other than the heretic pharaoh Akhenaten and the world-renowned beauty, his queen and great royal wife, Nefertiti.

It was almost too much to take in, even now; and I'd had quite a long time to come to terms with it. Adam and I made the discovery almost exactly a year ago.

You may well ask how two ordinary people such as Adam and me – who may share a love of Egypt's ancient history – but have no Egyptological or archaeological qualifications or credentials between us (apart from Adam's unfinished degree and more recent online studies) should come to make such a remarkable find. The briefest answer I can give is that it started when, on a tourist holiday in the spring of last year, I found myself locked inside the Howard Carter museum. Trying to escape, I smashed a framed picture of an original Howard Carter watercolour. Inside I found a cryptic message from the great excavator himself. Suffice it to say the message led us to discover an ancient papyrus originally from Tutankhamun's tomb. And decipherment of the papyrus led us to discover the tomb.[1]

Your next question might be to ask why we failed to announce our discovery. Particularly pertinent this, since it quite clearly left us frighteningly exposed to the blackmail scenario it seemed we were unhappily embroiled in now.

It was no great comfort to recall the vow of secrecy had been Walid's idea. He'd been determined the world should learn of the tomb, but deemed the timing all wrong. Egypt was a country in crisis, he'd said. To be fair, it was starting to feel as if it had been so for a long time, certainly since the Revolution of the Arab Spring in 2011. And it was looking

---

[1] *Carter's Conundrums* and *Tutankhamun's Triumph* – Books 1 and 2 of Meredith Pink's Adventures in Egypt

increasingly and distressingly as if this may remain the case for some considerable time to come.

In the immediate aftermath of our discovery a year ago, Walid decided we should wait for a cooling off period of six months. The presidential elections were in full swing. Egypt was taking its first tentative steps towards real democracy. Walid decreed we should say nothing before December to allow time for things to settle down and then take a view on the merits of coming clean.

But by the time December arrived the decision to maintain our vow of silence was coloured by a couple of weighty considerations.

Firstly, the new democratically elected president Mohamed Morsi had ceded himself what some described as 'almost Pharaonic powers' enabling him to legislate without judicial oversight or review of his actions. Whilst he rescinded the extremities of this position under pressure, his new constitution stirred up huge political unrest. Fully-fledged street battles broke out in Cairo between his opponents and supporters.

Secondly, one of the small band of conspirators bound by our solemnly sworn oath of silence broke ranks in quite spectacular fashion. Unlike the rest of us, Mustafa Mushhawrar was forced by the nature of his job as a member of Luxor's ministry for the preservation of ancient monuments to report for duty every day at Hatshepsut's mortuary temple on the west bank.

I don't recall if I've mentioned that our tomb lies hidden behind the walls of the Hathor Chapel on the first elevation of Hatshepsut's magnificent temple. This is where Tutankhamun and his chief vizier Ay decided to bring their 'precious jewels' Akhenaten and Nefertiti for reburial from Amarna (ancient Akhet-Aten). They reckoned nobody would think to look there since Hatshepsut's temple was dedicated to the god Amun, whom Akhenaten sought to destroy when he elevated the Aten for sole worship.

They were right. They reburied Akhenaten, Nefertiti and a glittering selection of their treasures in something like 1333BC. We discovered them in June AD2012. In all the millennia in between, nobody thought to look for any trace of an Amarnan royal burial in the Deir el Bahri cliffs. The controversial pharaoh and his glorious queen lay undisturbed all the while, just as Tutankhamun and Ay intended.

Undisturbed, that is, until Adam and I sleuthed our way inside. Our plan was to lock up and leave their tomb as we found it until Walid deemed the time was right to announce the discovery. Sadly we counted without Mustafa and his surrender to temptation.

It turned his head to report for work every day, draw his meagre salary, and know he was within a stone's throw of riches beyond his wildest dreams. Over the course of a few months he single-handedly dug his way through the rock of the cliff face behind the temple. His calculations proved unswervingly accurate, and he broke through into the burial chamber, shoring up the crumbling walls of his tunnel as he went. Who knows what riches he might have spirited away had we not caught him in the act.[2]

Caught red-handed, perhaps he felt he had no choice but to set off the avalanche of rock that trapped Adam, Ahmed and me inside the tomb. It sent clouds of dust and loose chippings billowing into the tomb, smothering everything in a thick coating of filth, and successfully cutting off our escape route. I flatter myself I'd been making pretty impressive progress towards setting us free after Ahmed managed to impale himself on a stake. But my efforts proved unnecessary when our stalwart friends arrived in the nick of time to rescue us.

Perhaps you'll think I'm stretching credulity to the limit when I tell you there were nine of us who'd signed up to Walid's vow of silence before Mustafa went to the bad.

There was Ted, of course; Adam's old university lecturer, an Egyptologist specialising in philology. He retired out to Cairo a few years ago. He'd helped us decipher the hieroglyphic message I found inside Howard Carter's smashed picture frame. He also painstakingly translated the

---

[2] *Hatsheput's Hideaway* – Book 3 of Meredith Pink's Adventures in Egypt

papyrus that led us to discover the secret location of the tomb. So it's fair to say he was in it with us up to his neck. Then there was Ted's daughter Jessica. She'd entered into a disastrous marriage with a smooth-tongued Egyptian who turned out to be a double-dyed criminal guilty of breaking into the Cairo museum during the 2011 Revolution. He and his villainous brothers made off with priceless artefacts, which they were gleefully selling onto the black market before we intervened and put a stop to their shenanigans. This proved a happy outcome for Jessica as it not only released her from the bonds of her ill-judged marriage, but also introduced her to a certain ex-boyfriend of mine, Dan, with whom she was now happily co-habiting in the suburbs of south London.

It also provided a once-in-a-lifetime opportunity for Shukura al-Busir, a colleague of Walid's from the Egyptian Antiquities Museum in Cairo, to hog the limelight, featuring prominently in Egyptian newspapers as the local heroine credited with foiling the villainous brothers' thievery.

Then there was Walid himself. He was involved up to his eyeballs for permitting the "loan" of genuine Tutankhamun treasures, needed to free us from entrapment within the tomb.

Which left just Adam, myself, our police buddy Ahmed; and of course the dearly departed Mustafa Mushhawrar to make up the numbers. Nine people was quite a large cohort to swear to secrecy. But we'd each taken the oath with all due solemnity, never thinking this could happen.

I stared wild-eyed at Walid. 'We've got to find this blackmailer and we've got to stop him!'

Walid met my gaze, 'Yes, or else he'll pick us off one by one or simply blow the whistle and destroy us all. I was mad to think we should wait.'

'But with the political situation as it is, and with the tomb needing a few solid days' worth of effort with a dustpan and brush, honestly what choice did you have?' Adam asked. 'You couldn't possibly have foreseen this!'

'So, what are our options?' I demanded, thinking frantically. 'Surely the only way to call his bluff is to announce the discovery of the tomb now.'

'But how do we account for the delay?' Walid moaned, shaking his head. 'No, the authorities would lock us – or at least me – up and throw away the key. I'd lose my job for sure. And you two would be flung out of Egypt and have your visas rescinded. You'd lose this beautiful dahabeeyah and never be allowed back into the country. I can't have that on my conscience.'

I agreed these outcomes were too horrific to contemplate, but my brain was still whirring madly. 'Ok, so maybe we need to somehow 'stage' the discovery, so it looks as if we've only just stumbled across the tomb now. You've still got the papyrus safely locked away in a vault at the museum, haven't you?'

'Well yes,' Walid said slowly, looking doubtful. 'But all the reasons for keeping the tomb secret are still valid... perhaps even more so considering the planned protests against President Morsi.'

'Which will only get worse now he's appointed an ex-terrorist as the new Governor of Luxor,' Adam added darkly.

'Law and order broke down during the 2011 Revolution,' Walid reminded us. 'Even now, security at our archaeological sites is woefully lapse. Stories of unauthorised digging are reported to me at the museum almost daily. The tanks on our streets and the armed militia seem ill-equipped to protect our precious heritage. If there is a full-scale military coup to remove President Morsi from office as some predict, things will only get worse. Our country is breaking apart. I repeat what I said last year. I cannot even contemplate revealing the tomb at a time like this. I would hold no jurisdiction over what might happen to it. I cannot and I will not allow that magnificent tomb to become a pawn in a political or nationalistic power struggle.' He broke off and mopped at his perspiring brow with the remains of his shredded napkin. 'No, my friends, our tomb must remain protected. Staging its discovery is not the right thing to do.'

'And besides, it would still leave our friendly blackmailer in possession of Mustafa's copy of the letter,' Adam pointed out. 'Staging the discovery now wouldn't necessarily stop him blowing the whistle on us and making it clear we've known about the tomb for a year.'

'But there must be something we can do!' I cried, raging at the sweeping sense of impotence.

Walid slumped back in his chair and swung his despairing gaze from me to Adam and back again. 'I have only two choices. I fear I must become either a thief or a murderer.'

About the Author

Fiona Deal fell in love with Egypt as a teenager, and has travelled extensively up and down the Nile, spending time in both Cairo and Luxor in particular. She lives in Kent, England with her two Burmese cats. Her professional life has been spent in human resources and organisational development for various companies. Writing his her passion and an absorbing hobby. Other books in the series following Meredith Pink's adventures in Egypt are available, with more planned. You can find out more about Fiona, the books and her love of Egypt by checking out her website and following her blog at www.fionadeal.com.

Other books by this author

Please visit Amazon to discover other books by Fiona Deal.

Meredith Pink's Adventures in Egypt

Carter's Conundrums – Book 1
Tutankhamun's Triumph – Book 2
Hatshepsut's Hideaway – Book 3
Farouk's Fancies – Book 4
Akhenaten's Alibi – Book 5
Seti's Secret – Book 6
Belzoni's Bequest – Book 7
Nefertari's Narrative – Book 8
Ramses' Riches – Book 9

More in the series planned.

Also available: Shades of Gray, a romantic family saga, written under the name Fiona Wilson.

Connect with me

Thank you for reading my book. Here are my social media coordinates:

Visit my website: http://www.fionadeal.com
Like my author page: http://facebook.com/fionadealauthor
Friend me on Facebook: http://facebook.com/fjdeal
Follow me on Twitter: http://twitter.com/dealfiona
Subscribe to my blog: http://www.fionadeal.com

Printed in Great Britain
by Amazon